BURN (BAYONET SCARS, NO. 5)
Copyright © 2015 by JC Em~~~ & Loft Brook Press

CH01506525

Find JC Emery on the web!
JC Emery Twitter Facebook Goodreads
Cover Design by Brenda Gonet at Gonet Design
Timeline created by The Illustrated Author
Formatting by JC Emery
Editing by Michele Milburn

Mature Content Warning: The Bayonet Scars novels are a
dark romance series which features graphic sexual content,
violence, and foul language that is intended for a mature
audience. Each novel features a different couple, though it's
not recommended that they be read out of order due to the
series story arc.

A BAYONET SCARS NOVEL
BURN

JC EMERY

Vicky,

I am "burns"
for you.
Get it? Burns!
LoL.

Vicky!

Ian "buns".

for you.

Get it? Buns!

Lol.

SERIES & TITLES BY JC EMERY

Bayonet Scars
Ride (No. 1)
Thrash (No. 2)
Rev (No. 3)
Crush (No. 4)
Vow (No. 4.5)
Burn (No. 5)

Ladder Company
Fall for Me

Men with Badges
Marital Bitch
The Switch

A BAYONET SCARS NOVEL
BURN
JC EMERY

TRAGEDY CUTS DEEP. REVENGE BURNS DEEPER.

The blood of their enemies coats the leather of their cuts and a trail of bodies lie in their wake, but the Forsaken Motorcycle Club isn't done yet. Carlo Mancuso still needs to pay for his sins. Nobody knows that more than Ian Buckley, the Treasurer for Forsaken.

Ian prefers his pleasure mixed with pain and he's only ever at peace when he's doling out justice. Convinced that he's too unstable and sadistic to take an old lady, he keeps his trysts, like all of his relationships, brief and anonymous. But with his club at war, and the stakes being so personal, Ian's feeling the events around him more deeply than he expects.

Mindy Mercer is the sweet daughter of Fort Bragg's most respectable cop. At least that's how the town sees her. Very few people know the Mindy who hides her tracks and battles her cravings by lying to everyone around her. She thinks she has control of her addiction until she suffers an attack that leaves her searching for a way out of her own personal hell.

Mindy has never been more desperately in need of a savior and Ian has never seen a more beautifully destroyed creature in his life. Their attraction is intense, but their damage is extreme. Some scars never heal, and some people never get better.

Love is never more painful than when it can kill you.

FEBRUARY

14 months to Mancuso's downfall

Mindy

Prologue

THE CERAMIC MUG warms from the inside out as I fill it up with freshly brewed coffee. It's my new addiction-- caffeine. The French roast smells divine-- sweet and spicy-- and even better when I add a splash of creamer and a teaspoon of sugar. It's not quite sweet enough for me and he's going to object, but I know him better than he thinks.

Left to his own devices, Ian Buckley drinks his coffee black even though he doesn't like it. I know this because when he makes it himself or orders a black coffee, he never drinks but half. But when there's cream and sugar, he can't drink it fast enough. I don't get it-- his resistance to admit that he likes things a little sweet. It's just one of the many things about him that I don't get.

That's okay. I have time to learn about him.

I cross the kitchen, mug in hand, and try to wipe the smile from my face at the sight of his big body at my kitchen table. His back is to me and his shoulders are hunched forward with his arms outstretched on the wooden table. I round the table and place the mug in front of him. He leans back and gives me a small head nod. He's not much of a talker which can drive me a little crazy since I like to talk. He never tells me to shut up though.

Taking my seat beside him, I drag my half empty coffee mug toward me. The mug is sweating from the ice I dumped in it in an attempt to cool myself down. I should be grateful that my parents have been so good to me, but I can't help the irritation that creeps in every time Mom turns the thermostat up another degree. It's sweltering in here.

The dampened ceramic is uncomfortable to the touch, stirring up thoughts I'd rather not have. The wooden desk, damp from my tears. The pain. The sick way they speak to one another. The hate.

My skin crawls with the memory as I try to focus on something else-- anything else-- and wipe my hands on my yoga pants to dry them off. With my eyes cast downward, I take a deep breath and notice that my fingers are shaking.

"You're in your kitchen with Ian," his deep voice says so quietly and so calmly that I barely hear it. I know where I am. I haven't forgotten this time, but helping me seems so important to him that I can't bear to take that away.

When I raise my eyes, I take a deep breath and offer him a small smile. He doesn't relax. His brows stay pushed together and that scowl is still on his face. The raised skin of the scar that runs from his ear to his eye has caught a drop of sweat that has yet to slide down his cheek. He's beautiful in a way I can't make sense of and don't want to.

Without taking his eyes off mine, he brings his mug to his lips, tilts his head back, and gulps the contents then sets the mug down and reaches across the table. He grabs two napkins from the stack that I have yet to put away. I should have gotten to it already. He drops one napkin on the table and uses the other to wipe my mug free of the condensation. He wraps the other around my mug to keep my hands dry.

"Thank you." The words feel so empty in comparison to what he does for me but they're all I have. No nod, or smile, or even a flicker of his eyes tells me he's heard me. Just because I didn't slip into the rabbit hole this time doesn't mean I won't and it doesn't mean I don't need him.

I need Ian Buckley more than I need the breath in my lungs, more than the blood in my veins, and more than a shot of whiskey.

He's everything.

"You're getting better," he says. It's an observation, not a question, but I nod my head anyway. When my hands have stopped shaking, I bring my mug to my lips and take a sip. It's watered-down now, but a sense of comfort washes over me instantly in a way that I'm sure isn't healthy.

"I won't," he says and his voice trails off at the end. There could be a million things he won't do, and he hasn't even finished his sentence yet, but my stomach sinks and fear seeps in. I force deep breath after deep breath in order to stop the shaking.

I'm losing him.

"Fuck, are you okay?" He shoves the empty coffee mug out of his way and leans across the table, taking my hands in his in the process.

"I'm fine." It's a lie. I'm anything but fine, but lying has become my new normal. The way his eyebrows crease together and his brown eyes implore mine, I know he knows I'm lying.

"I won't be around tomorrow," he says steadily. He leans in just a tiny bit closer and takes a deep breath as he says, "The club needs me."

"I get it," I say quietly. And I do get it. It just sucks and I feel absolutely defeated by the news that he won't be here tomorrow. What does that mean for the next day and the day after that then?

I'm not losing him. I've lost him. I guess it's time. I mean, he's been hanging out with me for months now. Every day he's here. Every day he's been here. He leaves after coffee in the morning, but he's here and if I'm being honest with myself, his presence is the only thing I look forward to every day.

"Hey." His voice gets quieter, somehow. Softer somehow. "I'm right here. I just got to take care of some club bullshit that I've been avoiding."

"That's where you should be, not babysitting my lame butt." I try to sound strong and confident, but I don't think I succeed. "I'm fine here. Really."

"Tell me anything but that you're fine because we both know what fine actually means."

I guess we do, but that doesn't mean I'm up for telling him how I really feel. I spent every waking minute and most of my sleeping ones as well trying to avoid feeling anything, and being sober, that's fucking hard. I could make it better.

I could.

I want to.

"Nic's about to have her baby," I say. Counting down the days to Nic's due date has been excruciating. Aside from Ian's daily visits, I don't have a lot to look forward to. But this baby is something special and I like Nic a lot. I have to be there when she gives birth. I just can't miss it.

"I'll still take you to the hospital once Duke gives the all-clear for visitors. I'm not disappearing, babe."

I lower my head and take a deep breath to force the blush from my cheeks. I hate how he affects me like this. It's just a word, but it makes me do crazy stupid things.

Babe.

"We good?" he asks and pulls away before I'm ready. My hands clutch his for a brief moment before I realize what I'm doing and I release him. No need to seem as pathetic and needy as I really am. When I raise my head and catch his eye, I nod and try to smile. His jaw ticks just once before he gets it under control and steps away from the kitchen table. He takes two steps back, still watching me, before he turns and strides toward the front door. Ian meets Dad's eye in the living room and nods toward the door. Dad responds quickly and follows him out, closing the door behind himself.

I hate it when he leaves. It's like one moment everything's fine and normal as it should be and the next the entire world is falling apart again.

I walk to the front door and press my ear up against the wood. Their voices are faint, but as I move around and find a better position, they get louder.

"For the best. Tired of havin' the boys at the station wonder why I got Forsaken at my house every morning," Dad says in his best attempt at casual conversation with Ian. They don't really like each other, but Ian hasn't really given Dad much space seemingly able to deal with his dislike of Dad much better than Dad's dealing with his dislike of Ian.

"Any of your *boys* get to wondering what I'm doing, you tell them to ask me," Ian says. "None of their fuckin' business what I do regardless of where I'm doing it."

Dad grunts.

"It's their business when they think one of their own is compromised," Dad says after a long pause. Thankfully, he's checking his temper, I can tell from his clipped words. It makes me nervous having Dad and Ian in the same space so often. Dad won't hesitate to arrest Ian if he gave Dad even half a reason to; but even Dad knows the hellfire that Forsaken rain down on him if he does—legitimate cause or not.

"Are you… *compromised*… sergeant?" Ian says. He has this way of making his voice sound so cold and calculating that the words practically slither from his mouth. It's the little things like this that remind me that the man who sits at my table in the morning, the man who wakes up to take panicked phone calls from Holly, the man who helps teenage girls out of a jam, is also as disturbed as they come. I see it in his eyes often enough. The light in his eyes dims to almost nothing and his expressions smooth leaving a blankness about him that always saddens me. He knows my damage, some of it at least, and I'd like to know his damage as well. Maybe that's part of what I like about him. With Ian, it's entirely possible that I'm not the most fucked up person in the room.

"You already know the answer to that, Mr. Buckley," Dad says in reference to Ian's officer position in the club. As the treasurer, he's the numbers guy. He once told me that his job is boring, like being an accountant. We both know he's lying, at least in part.

"Hmm." Ian's voice is followed by the hard clack of his boots sound against the pavement. I close my eyes and take one deep breath after another in an attempt to keep the panic at bay. I hate this part.

Ten.

He's ten steps away from the house now.

Fourteen steps away.

My hands shake.

Nineteen.

In six more he'll be at the curb and fifteen seconds later I'll hear his bike start up.

My mouth fills with saliva. I'd swallow, but my throat feels so tight like it would be physically painful to try to do so.

Twenty-one.

My veins feel like they're on fire, so hot and itchy. Like the only thing that will make his leaving any better is to shoot up. The thought sickens me.

Twenty-four.

Oh God.

Oh God.

Twenty-five.

I slink down to the linoleum, still pressed up against the wooden door. Outside, I hear the guttural sound of Ian's Harley starting up. When I'm waiting on him in the morning, it sounds like a purr. But when he leaves it's the most awful sound I've ever heard. Every. Single. Time.

Ian pulls away from the curb and within seconds the sound of his bike disappears. My veins still burn and my lungs now ache from the restricting lump in my throat that makes it challenging to breathe. Everything around me sounds like white noise, a subtle but constant buzzing around me that drowns out everything but the blinding panic that's set in.

Vaguely, in the back of my head I know the front door is opening, pushing me along the linoleum. It's only a foot or two and it stops. My cheek is damp from being here so long. The low-level buzzing dissipates as the voices get louder.

Holly's sobbing through her shaky words.

The men snarl and laugh with every touch, every stroke,

and every horrible push and pull against my unwilling flesh. The contents of my stomach rise into my aching throat. My face is pressed against Eileen's wooden desk.

Watch, you fucking slut!

His voice is so loud as he screams at Holly. Loud, raspy, and full of such hate that my stomach rolls. A fresh wave of nausea overtakes me. Somewhere, somehow, I know I'm no longer pressed against the wood. Somehow, I know I'm curling into a ball on the floor of my parents' entry way. Somewhere in my brain, the rational, logical part of me knows this is all just a horrific memory. A horrific memory of an event that I'll never move past, never forget, and never get over. And yet, when I smell my dad's cologne and feel his arms around me all the logical and rationality in the world doesn't seem to matter.

Hands touching me, clawing at my skin.

I'm here, Minds.

I love you and I'm here.

It's Holly. She's trying to reach out to me—to offer what little comfort she can. It makes no difference, but I don't tell her that. Halfway through, her words take on a deep baritone and she doesn't sound like herself, but rather more masculine. She sounds like my dad and I know, despite the fear and sickness, that it's my dad who's trying to hold me and provide me with some semblance of comfort.

"It's just Dad, baby girl," he says. I used to find comfort in his words, but not now. Not in this moment. I can't get my mouth to work. Every time I try to speak, a fresh wave of nausea rises in my throat that I try to force away. It doesn't work and once I start dry heaving Dad lets me go. Every place he touched me feels slimy and disgusting like it wasn't him at all, but rather it was *them*.

On hands and knees, I crawl hurriedly down the hall and into my bathroom where I kick the door shut behind me. The tile in here bruises my knees but I don't slow down to avoid the injury. It's nothing really, more bruises. Maybe with enough battering they'll look as they did *that* day, not just in my mind but in reality as well. I shove the toilet bowl lid up and out of the way as I expel the contents of my stomach into the water.

It's not always this bad, not anymore at least. I was getting better, stronger, and less dependent on Ian. I was finally in a place where I could watch him leave and instead of the sickening panic, I'd just cry until my eyes hurt. I don't even try to hide the tears anymore.

"Want me to call him?" Dad asks from the other side of the closed door. Dad knows how I feel about Ian. He sees how Ian helps me work through the breakdowns which is the only reason, in my estimation, that he even allows a member of Forsaken into his house every morning.

"No," I say as loud as I can. Ian said he wouldn't be by tomorrow morning. That he won't disappear but that he's got club business. I know what that means—he's tired of babysitting me and taking care of me like I'm an infant.

I push off from the toilet as quickly as I can and clamber to my room in search of a pair of shoes. Any shoes will do. I just have to get out of here. I grab the first pair I can find—a new set of runners that I haven't touched since last summer when I thought I might take up running one day. I shove my socked feet into the runners, and lace them up as quickly and as tightly as I can before sprinting from my room and rushing down the hall to the front door. I don't see Mom or Dad as I fling the front door open and rush onto the front lawn. The cool spring breeze feels wonderful on my heated skin. I don't spend enough time outside. Somewhere in the house Mom is asking where I am and instead of telling her a truth I can't explain, I head for the street on hurried feet and don't slow at the curb, instead opting to take off in the direction Ian's left. Soon, my lungs are burning and the coastal breeze is doing nothing to keep me cool. My body is heated and my feet ache in the unfamiliar set of runners.

Watch, you fucking slut!

The voice propels me forward at a speed I didn't know I was capable of. My strawberry blonde hair flies around my face, blocking my view in parts as I race toward the edge of town. I strain to get oxygen into my lungs and the muscles of my little used legs ache under the punishment I'm delivering them. It hurts, the exertion of pushing myself to a limit I'm unfamiliar with. Everything in me hurts, both physically and emotionally and it never gets better—except when Ian is around. Only then do I feel less dirty, and broken, and hopeless. But Ian's not an option anymore, so I keep running. I run past the library, and further away from town, and into the outlying neighborhoods with larger homes and better manicured lawns, and better concealed secrets. The faux perfection churns my stomach so I keep going despite the painful ache that's set in. I just want out of this—out of here—and to keep running until I find a place where I can feel some semblance of normal. Maybe it doesn't exist.

Only, it does with Ian. I have to try to get better on my own though, without him. I don't want to, but it looks like I don't have a choice so I keep running until I literally fall into a tree on the side of Sherwood Road and scream and cry and kick at the goddamn thing until I'm exhausted and I head back for the house.

APRIL

12 months to Mancuso's downfall

Chapter 1

FIFTY-NINE DAYS AND counting since Ian's stopped coming by every day. Fifty-nine mornings I've been left to wonder where he is, what he's doing, and if he's drinking his disgusting black coffee. I don't know why he punishes himself with black coffee, nor do I know why he's punishing me by staying away from me. All I really know is that it's painful for him to be so distant.

My only relief is my daily run. I make it as painful as possible, pushing myself to my limit every time. I haven't reached my limit until I'm close to pitching myself in front of the next vehicle that passes to stop the ache in my muscles. It used to be a few miles before the punishment got to be too much to bear and I'd be doubled over on the side of the road flipping out because I'd maxed out my ability to torture myself. It was always so much easier to hit that high with a needle in my arm or a bottle to my lips. Now, though, I can make it around Ruby and Jim's property, which is an eight-mile loop from start to finish. It's the only thing I have now since Ian's left me.

I want to ask Holly about him, but I don't dare. She's got a big mouth and is likely to tell Grady I've asked about Ian, and the next thing I know, Ian will be showing up out of obligation rather than because he wants to. As it is, he had promised to take me to the hospital when Nic gave birth, and he didn't. He probably got busy, but still.

But he *doesn't* want to show up, or he would be showing up a hell of a lot more often.

I let out a heavy sigh and try to push away my disappointment. This morning when he arrived, it marked the eleventh time he's shown up since he stopped coming every day. Unlike before, now he's short-tempered and grouchy. He's still silent, as always, but it's different. There's a frustrating aloofness to his presence that makes him more unreachable than ever.

He rode up on his bike, same time, same path he always takes, but he left in one of the club's vans. He and Dad had a few words on the front lawn before he climbed in and the van sped off. When the van returned this evening, he walked straight to his bike, started her up, and disappeared down the road without a single look at the house. It's for the best, I guess. Otherwise he'd have seen me peeled to the window in the living room, staring out at him hopelessly like a lost puppy just begging for love. God, I'm pathetic.

"Eat, please," my mother says in her most stern voice. Even trying to be firm, she's still soft.

My mother, Claire Mercer, tries her hardest to be relatable to me but fails miserably at almost every turn. I'm her only child, and she's insistent on reforming our relationship. She's even stopped going to church every Sunday to spend more time with me. She's trying to be kind, really she is, but I used to look forward to that time alone. Now I'm forced into awkward family brunches with Uncle Edgar and Aunt Naomi, who try their best to act like everything is fine. Not that I make it easy on them. I mean, anyone would be off their game if their niece had a breakdown every time she heard a loud noise or touched the wrong surface. God forbid they look at me wrong when I start dry heaving and sobbing in the corner of the room. That only makes it worse.

"Melinda." Mom's voice is harder this time, and I know she means business.

I shake my head of my thoughts and take the plate she's offering. Pulling my legs up on the couch, I reposition to get comfortable as I stare at the sandwich and chips she's assembled for me. Mom made soup for her and Dad earlier, but the steam of the bowl had me straining to breathe through the violent shaking of my body. The white bread hasn't been toasted, and the meat is from a cold deli package. Nothing hot—good. Maybe I'll be able to keep this down. She's even cut the sandwich into quarters to make it easier for me to eat.

"Thank you," I say and meet her eyes.

"You shouldn't run right after you eat," she says with a soft smile. She's trying, I know she is, but damn it if she isn't annoying the hell out of me. She's worried that eating and pushing myself so soon after will make me sick. I bet it will. In fact, I'm counting on it.

"I'll be fine." If she knew I actually enjoy the sickening discomfort that settles in a few miles into my run, she'd be horrified. Claire Mercer isn't doing so well with knowing how fucked-up her daughter is. Nervously, she eyes my sandwich on my plate. To appease her, I scarf it down as quickly as I can without looking like a maniac.

Fifty-nine days since Ian's left me, and it's time that I start acting like a normal person. Funny that I know how long it's been since he's disengaged himself from me, and yet I don't have much of a clue how long it's been since *that* day. I stifle the humorless laugh that creeps up at the thought. I never imagined my nightmares would be eclipsed by the absence of my dreams.

"I'm proud of you for taking up running. Maybe tomorrow I can go with you?"

No, you can't.

You absolutely can't.

"Yeah, maybe." I finish the sandwich and start in on the chips and try my best to ignore my mother's curious stare.

"Mindy, I'd like to talk about therapy again," she says carefully. Her voice trails off at the end, and she's speaking slowly as to not offend me. The topic itself is as offensive as they come. What am I supposed to talk to a therapist about? *That* day, or Ian, or the tracks on my feet? What damage am I

15

supposed to work on exactly?

"I'd rather not."

"Running is great, but you're not working through your trauma. You have to speak to someone about it. You have to get past this so you can have a normal life again."

"Normal? What precisely is normal?"

She's hit a nerve with me, and she knows it. "Working, having friends, even dating. You haven't dated since Heath."

"I'm not discussing Heath with you."

"Why not? You never even talked about it. One day he was here and the next he was gone. You can't just keep everything bottled up forever."

"Sure I can," I say and hand her the now empty plate. I grab the glass of water at my right and down half of it before setting the glass back down and standing from the couch.

"Mindy, talk to me. Please."

"We talked." I open the front door and close it behind me with a hard thud. Of course she thinks this is about Heath. I don't even really know what *this* is—I'm just dealing in the only way I know how. I take off from the front stoop and run toward town. The sun has already set, and it's later than I would normally be running, but I placated my mother this morning by promising to spend the day with her. I can only handle so much pampering and sly begging before I give in. Maybe it's not a total loss. The evening air is cooler than it is earlier in the day when the sun is out. The chill feels wonderful on my skin. It seems I can never get cool enough these days, regardless of the temperature around me.

The downside with running through town is that there's a lot more traffic, so a lot more stop and go. I can't just take off and run at full hilt through town like I can on the outskirts along the country roads. The days it hurts less, I run in town, and even though I'm feeling it something awful today, I can't bring myself to run along the woods at this time of night. I might enjoy the self-inflicted pain, but that doesn't mean I'm a total masochist.

So instead, I opt for the lesser evil and manage my run through town all the while ignoring the occasional wave and verbal greeting. I used to just be a local, and now I'm something else—something I never wanted to be. I'm somebody people want to protect and to care for, and it makes me so fucking angry that my skin crawls with their pity.

I'm a few miles into my run when Mr. Hill, of the hardware store, gives me a sad smile and a kind wave. He is—or was—a lonely old widower who never quite got over his wife's death—that is until he started spending time with Lisa Grady. According to Holly, Old Man Hill is caught up in a torrid affair with Forsaken's sergeant-at-arm's mother, and the old goat couldn't be happier. I try to summon up some happiness for him, but I don't even have any for myself, let alone some to share. The forced wave and smile is enough to make my sandwich want to come up.

I hate feeling this way—bitter and angry—but I can't help it. The hate of *that* day has seeped into my soul, and I can't seem to get it out. The insidious hatred spreads through my veins, bringing on a craving that I don't want. I try to block it out, but before I realize what I'm doing, my feet have taken me in the direction of the house I used to buy from. It's a run-down old thing.

I don't want this, but I'm here. Only a couple hundred feet away and I'll be on the front porch. I don't have any cash with me, but that's never been a problem before. They know I'm good for it.

But I can't. I've worked too hard for my sobriety. I've done too much, been through too much, and come too far to throw it all away on a high that can't and won't last.

And where has that gotten me? I'm a bitter as fuck recluse who wants nothing to do with the real world and only finds refuge in a man who has abandoned her for God only knows what. A new project, maybe. Or a woman who won't throw up at the idea of being touched sexually. Maybe there's more than one—several most likely. He's Forsaken. They must throw themselves at him shamelessly, and I'll bet he doesn't turn them down. I'm never going to be for Ian what he is for me. I can't be, not with how goddamn broken and fearful I am.

I take a few steps toward the house and pause before continuing. If I'm too fucked-up for Ian, then what's the fucking point in even trying to stay sober?

There is no point.

Unless . . .

No. If I had a chance with him, I could find the strength to deny myself the bliss I know will come once I get my fix. But I don't have enough strength on my own.

I walk up to the front door like I have a hundred times before, ring the bell, and wait. My brain remembers this, hasn't forgotten how to score. So when the voice comes through the intercom, all slimy and up to no good, I'm not startled.

"What?" the disgusting voice says. I can't remember his name. It's something stupid, like Smirk or something, that he calls himself.

"I'm looking for some H," I say.

There's silence on the other end, which is normal. Except that it stretches out longer than I expect. Nobody comes to the door, and nobody says anything through the speaker. And still I wait and try to be patient. Every instinct I have tells me to make a run for it and to back out now. The moment I have it in hand, there won't be any turning back. I'm not strong enough. Bouncing from foot to foot, I wait impatiently. Two minutes pass, and then five, and I'm about to chicken out and give up. This part always made me nervous and disgusted with myself. Now it's too difficult to even think about who I was back then, when I was scoring on the regular.

"Nothing here for you," the voice on the other end of the intercom says.

"Well, what do you have?" I ask instinctively. He knows it's me. It wasn't *that* long ago that he was trying to bargain my body for a baggie. The knee to his groin was memorable, I'm sure.

"Nothing for you."

The rejection is a welcome relief, like it gives me permission to back out. I don't want this, I really don't. I'm just on autopilot. I don't let myself wonder why he's turning down a customer, and instead I take the steps two at a time and run toward the street. I push myself to run at a speed I can't maintain and ignore the blaring car horns that sound as I haphazardly fly in front of evening traffic—well, what little traffic we get here in Fort Bragg.

Somewhere in the distance, a motorcycle revs its engine and closes in on me. Like the crazy-obsessed bitch that I am, I'm convinced it's Ian and he's going to pass me any minute. It's unrealistic to think he'd be in this neighborhood at exactly this time. Even more unrealistic to think he'd stop and offer me a ride home. I don't need it, but I'd take it because it's him and I'll do anything to get him to touch me. Even if it means swallowing the panic and ache that sets in when another person tries to offer me comfort. I wouldn't know if I'd freak out if he were to touch me, though, since he never has, which is actually more painful than the running and the trying to score combined.

The guttural sound of the Harley closes in on me, pushing me to run faster. I round the block, and soon I've run so far that I'm back in the lush neighborhood that looks too perfect to be real. It is. I recognize two of the houses I pass. One belongs to a local teacher I've seen at my NA meetings in Willits, and the other belongs to one of Smirk's best customers. Nothing's perfect, I guess.

A landscaping truck pulls out in front of me suddenly, knocking me out of my reverie and sending me onto a lawn so pristine that it must cost a mint to maintain. The driver waves his hand apologetically but keeps going and zips away. I fight back the urge to yell at him about residential speed limits and instead stand from the grass and dust myself off.

Once the truck is around the bend in the road and has disappeared, I refocus my attention on picking up where I left off. Without the landscaper distracting me, I realize how loud the motorcycle is behind me. It's practically deafening, sucking me in and swallowing me whole at the same time. I used to think Nic was nuts when she would know who was passing by on their bikes. Somehow, she could always tell the difference in the sounds of their engines. I thought she was nuts or it was one of those things you have to grow up with to understand, but I think I'm getting it now. I can't explain why Ian's bike sounds different, but it does somehow. The engine sounds darker, more menacing and, in a way, inviting than the others' bikes. It doesn't make any sense, and I might just be insane, but I swear I know the sound of his bike. It's unique, just like the man himself.

Just to confirm my suspicions, I cast a glance over my shoulder at the approaching Harley. I expect to find Forsaken, of course, but someone I'm not very familiar with. I'm feeling all kinds of guilty and hopeful that it's not actually Ian after all. He'd stop if he saw me in passing, wouldn't he? He said he would always be here for me, didn't he? Of course, he also said he wouldn't disappear. Even if he did see me on the side of the road, would he even bother to slow down enough to wave?

None of my stupid worries or fantasies matter, though, because when I see the rider come into view, I gasp and turn around and take off running. Just barely, through the glare of the bike's headlight, I see his light brown hair flowing freely from underneath his half helmet. It *is* Ian, and he looks pissed. Not that he doesn't always look like something crawled up his ass, but there's something in the hard set of his features that worries me. Most likely, it's the guilt from almost fucking up my sobriety that's got me so paranoid. I mean, he's too far away to *really* be able to tell if he's pissed or not. On further thought, yeah, I'm insane.

"Mindy!" Ian's deep voice screams over the sound of his ridiculously loud engine. I've heard the man yell before, both when he's pissed and when he's not, and now I know I'm not crazy. He is pissed.

I don't know what I did to anger him. Running at night, maybe? I might be bothered by how much of a hermit I've become, but Ian doesn't seem to think it's a problem. At least when I've rambled about being worried about it, he's just shaken his head and said, *"Don't push yourself, babe."* The idea that he's worried about my safely sends a glorious fluttering to my belly. I grin through strained breaths and keep going. I've been wanting Ian's attention for months now, and in this moment I have it, so why the hell am I running? I'm being a bit silly, but my gut tells me that I'm not going to like his mood if I stop, so I don't.

Chapter 2

"MELINDA CLAIRE MERCER!"

Crap-a-doodle! The bend up ahead is getting closer, and maybe, just maybe, if I run fast enough, I can make it past the last house before the bend and into the park where Ian's Harley can't follow. I'm only a few miles from home, but I'm not stupid enough to think I can outrun a Harley. But I don't have to outrun it—I just have to outsmart the man on the Harley.

Easier said than done.

The bike creeps up beside me and slows down. Ian turns his attention toward me and shakes his head in disapproval.

"Stop now and I'll make it easy on you," he shouts. I raise my eyebrows and shrug my shoulders, trying to keep up my frantic pace all the while, and turn back to the road. I'm almost at the bend. If I can just get to the par . . .

"Five. Do *not* make me get to one." His voice is clipped but still smooth and comforting like always. It's occurred to me that this is, perhaps, the most I've heard him speak in such a short time frame. I'm so distracted by the sound of his voice that I don't focus in on what he's saying. What *did* he say?

"Four," he shouts.

A countdown. He's given me a countdown. Oh, this isn't good. I'm in trouble over something, and I'd probably feel a bit better about this whole situation if I had any clue what's made him so angry.

But I already know, don't I?

Maybe it's not paranoia. Maybe he knows what I was just

doing.

No, that can't be it, can it?

The road bends, and instead of following it around the curve, I take a sharp right into the park and head for the playground. I slow myself down just slightly with an ignorant confidence that I'll likely regret.

"Fuck!" Ian screams from behind me. I stop for a moment, my lungs burning and chest heaving, legs aching and mind spinning, to turn around and eye him stopped on the road. With a shake of his head and a disapproving scowl on his face, he backs his bike up and pivots it to face me.

"Oh no," I find myself whispering with a hand clamped over my chapped lips. With a quick peek behind me, I find that the park is deserted. He wouldn't, would he? His engine revs, and he comes barreling toward me with a speed and ferocity that I'm sure is going to get me flattened by a couple hundred pounds of steel and muscle. I've nowhere to run now, so I do the only thing I can to put some distance between myself and the crazy angry outlaw—I run into the playground's sandy circle and climb up to the top of the play structure. It's not like I think I'm hiding up here, but the distance will give me a moment to figure out what's crawled into his jeans and died.

Don't be stupid, I think to myself. I already know. It's not paranoia. Smirk said he had nothing for me, not that he was out. He kept me waiting for well over five minutes before telling me I wasn't getting anything. I was barely at the curb when I heard the Harley behind me, and it's not left me since.

Oh God. What have I done? What has he done? Even more important—what's he going to do?

Ian pulls the bike up to the edge of the sand-laden circle and cuts her off. With jerky movements, he shoves the kickstand down and climbs off the bike. I've seen a lot of things in life, courtesy of my poor choices, but this is—without a measure of doubt—the most terrifying thing I've ever seen.

"Two," he says as he approaches the metal slide that leads up to the top of the structure and to the landing I'm perched on. With a thud, he places one black boot atop the bottom of the slide and leans forward. Good job, Mindy. Not only have I gotten myself into being chased by an angry biker, but I've also got him giving me a countdown to God only knows what. As far as poor choices go, I'm doing fabulously today.

"You forgot three!" I shout and white-knuckle it to the durable plastic of the play structure. Go big or go home, I guess. If I've already dug myself a hole, I might as well make it a deep one.

"No, babe. You just didn't hear me." His lips curl up in the corner, and he purses his lips. "Now, do I have to get to one, or are you going to go easy on yourself?"

"Why are you following me anyway?" I ask and crouch down behind the thick plastic, raising up just enough to peek over the top and bracing myself for whatever Ian has in mind.

"Not your time to ask questions."

I scrunch my eyes shut and curl into a fetal position as tightly as I can as I wait for his deep voice to bellow out the number one. I don't know him well enough to assume what move he's going to make. One deep breath, and then a second, and a third, and I'm halfway to resigning myself to my situation. He won't hurt me, I already know that. It's the disgust that I'm sure to find in his eyes that I want to avoid. People try to pretend that they understand or that they're nonjudgmental, but it's all a lie. The first time they look at me and try to figure out how high I am or what I've taken is always the beginning of the end. It doesn't take much to figure out how little they think of me. And sometimes they have the courtesy of just outright saying it—I'm a pathetic junkie.

"Come down, Mindy." Ian's voice is gentle, soft even. He's closer now than before. The metal slide creaks in front of me, the only piece of the playground that hasn't been replaced since my childhood. The whole thing used to be metal and wood. Holly and I would burn our legs in the height of summer under the hot sun, and when we were really tired, we'd forget about the worn wooden beams that held the whole thing up and would get dozens of splinters in a single afternoon. Now everything but the slide is made of a hard hazard-free plastic. Why they kept the old metal slide, I don't even know.

I can feel him approach even though I can't see him. My eyes are still clamped shut, and I'm preparing myself for the worst. Is he going to hate me, judge me, or—even worse—abandon me? I can take the hate and judgment. It wouldn't be the first time someone I've loved has looked at me with such disgust and contempt that I've hated myself all that much more for it. It wouldn't be the first and certainly won't be the last, but it will be the most painful. Ian's only ever known me as the broken mess that I've become. He never got the chance to meet the perky girl who couldn't imagine saying a curse word in public or who was afraid of body modification. Even getting a second hole in my ears was once a bit too taboo for me, even though I loved the look of it. No, the only thing Ian has known or ever will know me as is this pathetic, broken, scarred mess that I've let myself become.

"What happens when you get to one?" I ask, keeping my voice small. The night's breeze disappears and is replaced by the emanating heat of his body. The slide continues to groan, and the plastic I'm clutching onto shakes as he gets to the top of the slide and grabs ahold of it.

"I will never hurt you," he says. His hot breath washes over my face. Slowly, I open my eyes and blink rapidly. He's closer than I expect, but for the first time since *that* day, such a close presence doesn't scare me. It comforts me instead. I should be pulling away, at least that's my MO as of late. But instead of pulling back, I'm leaning toward him.

"I know," I whisper.

Ian's deep brown eyes probe mine, asking a question I don't understand and looking for an answer I can't fathom. I just don't know or understand anything anymore, and I'm tired of trying. He very slowly, cautiously even, brings the palm of his hand up to hover over my cheek. He looks ridiculous, his big body forcing its way through the hole in the plastic molding to reach me. I lean into his touch, welcoming it, surprising myself, so desperate for something to tether myself to.

My grandma used to tell me that everybody needs to have something that matters in life. We all need to be tethered to something, or someone, who grounds us so that we never lose ourselves. So that we can always find our souls. I thought Heath was my tether, but I lost myself anyway. I lost my soul. I used to think that losing my soul was the worst thing that could happen, but being here with Ian, his rough, calloused skin barely brushing my cheek, I finally know the truth—my soul is nothing without this man to keep me from losing myself.

"But what happens when you get to one?" I ask, still determined to find out his answer. Holly once told me that Ian doesn't make empty threats, and I believe her. He must have had something in mind when he started counting down, and I want to know what it is. I want to know everything that goes on inside his brain. Every dirty, sadistic thing he thinks and says and does just adds to who he is, and I'm already addicted to him. Every bit I get, even this first touch isn't enough.

"I own you at one." His words feel like they're meant to be menacing, shrill even. But instead they come out like a warm blanket intended to comfort me. I doubt he feels it, the heat radiating from us. But I do. It's so warm and comfortable and everything I want and need in life. *He* is by far the best addiction I've ever had. I want to tell him that he already owns me. I could convince myself that this will work out. I can pretend it doesn't hurt anymore or that I'm not too damaged for this. I can fake it with the best of them.

"I'm here." I rub my cheek against his rough skin and let my eyes fall closed in delight. This doesn't scare me. For once, my heart isn't beating out of my chest and I'm not retreating back into *that* place where everything's so disgusting and hollow that I'd rather die on that dingy carpeted office floor than to breathe for another second.

But that was just before Ian strode into the room and stood guard to protect me, shield me, from the others. He spoke with such care in an effort to not cause me any more pain. And months later, he's still being careful with me.

"Good girl. You don't want me to own you." When he says the word *want*, his voice pitches slightly as he sucks in a deep breath.

"Why not?" Do I really want to know? Yes, I think I do.

"Because you need gentle. Safe."

"I feel safe with you." I need to just shut my damn chatty mouth already.

"You're not."

Chapter 3

"BEEN AWHILE SINCE you've been around," the old man says with a flat expression and absolutely zero amusement at my presence. Harry Mercer isn't a fan of Forsaken, and he's definitely not a fan of me. Not that I give a fuck. Mindy's gotten under my skin, and his constant, thinly-veiled threats of jail do nothing to deter me.

"Missed me?" I ask, letting my mouth lift into a rare smile. From the way his expressionless face slides into a frown, I'm betting it's more sinister than intended. I don't actually want to fight or argue with the old bastard. I will if he insists, but I have more important shit to deal with. Like his daughter's little outing the other night. She must have known from the moment she saw me that I wasn't fucking around, because she ran like her life depended on it. Once I was able to calm down a bit, I realized I'd scared her, and that's the last thing I want. Mindy should never fear me. What we have is built on something deeper than that, but if I have to scare her to force her to submit to what's best for her, then that's what I'll do. I'm just glad my boys got my back with this shit.

Harry and I stand, staring at one another wordlessly for a few minutes before he blows out a frustrated breath and steps aside to let me in. He tries, but he never has been able to outwait me. He's a patient man, but I've been at this game longer than he has. I reach up and brush the scar on my face as I stride into the house and down the hall to Mindy's bedroom thinking about the man I've been waiting almost twenty-one years for.

Soon, Carlo.

Soon.

Her bedroom door is closed, but there's no lock on it, so nothing stops me as I twist the knob and swing the door open. I keep my eyes on the carpeted floor beneath my black boots and ignore the surprised scream that comes from the corner of the room. I've never seen in Mindy's bedroom before, and as much as I want to look around, I fight the urge. I couldn't barge in here and see her in a compromised position and not hate myself for it. She's been violated in so many ways already. She deserves nothing but respect and love and to be cherished by a kind and gentle man.

Too bad for her she's got me instead.

"Ian?" Her voice is confused, but I hear the excitement beneath her curiosity. Her sock-covered feet come into view as she crawls off her bed and comes to stand before me. My eyes trail up her covered legs, past her tank top, and finally settle on her light green eyes. The last time I saw her, she looked so different. I wanted to touch her on that playground so fucking bad that my veins burned with the desire for it. I wanted to cover her with myself, wrap her around me, and possess her in every way possible. She doesn't want that, though, so I settled for almost touching her. She surprised me when she tilted her cheek into my cupped hand. Before that moment, I thought her wanting me to touch her was just a fantasy my sick brain had conjured up. But now there's this disgusting hope settling in my stomach and worming its way into my soul.

"Get dressed and meet me outside." I don't spend another second in the doorway. The moment the words are out of my mouth, I'm back down the hall and then out the front door. I find my phone in my front pocket of my jeans and pull it out to give Trigger the go-ahead. The sick asshole responds immediately with OK and adds a fucking smiley face emoticon at the end of it. Only arson or torture could get my brother this happy in a text message.

After sending the message to Ryan, I stand and wait on

Mindy's lawn. I can feel Harry and Claire watching me from inside the house, but I pay them as little mind as possible. I've tried to be kind to Claire. She's a soft-spoken woman without a single edge to her. She needs kind, but my kind just makes her recoil.

"Where are we going, and where's your bike?" Mindy asks, startling me as she comes to stand beside me. I'm so off my fucking game here it's not even funny. I don't startle easy but this shit has me on edge.

"Thought you'd prefer the Suburban," I say and hitch my thumb to Ma's red SUV. Mindy nods her head and gives me a small, grateful smile. The other night at the park she wouldn't get on the back of my bike. I was desperate to have her there, behind me, but she was already so fucked-up over being caught trying to score that I didn't want to push her. Instead, she walked alongside me as I pushed my bike from the park to her house. I wasn't going to just leave her there. If she were mine and she had defied an order like that, I would have had a lot of fun with her ass when we got home.

But she's not mine, and judging from the way she freaks out over every little thing, she never will be. Fuck. The very thought of never owning the woman beside me sends me into an angry haze. Somebody might die today after all.

I point at the SUV and walk to the passenger door and open it up for her. Mindy takes a moment to get moving, but when she does, I can't take my eyes off of her. She's wearing a pair of worn black jeans, faded and torn at the knees, tucked into black Doc Martens. Her wavy strawberry blonde hair is up in a ponytail and hanging as low as the small of her back. It's gotten so long in the last year.

My body tenses as she gets closer, and by the time she swings her body into the passenger seat, I have to look down at my boots. Her ass is fucking perfect and curvy. She's lost weight, which irritates me to no end because she doesn't eat enough, but she's still fucking perfect. It doesn't escape me that we're wearing nearly identical outfits, save for her pale-pink long-sleeve button-up and my cut atop my white tee. She didn't used to dress like this. It was always something more feminine, softer, and more librarian than biker chick. I never could imagine sweet, cutesy Mindy in my world.

Until now.

I force myself to close the SUV's door and walk around without thinking about how well she could fit in my world if only she would let me show her what it's like. If only she would let me touch her.

With a turn of the key, the Suburban starts right up, and we pull away from the curb. Mindy's got her hands on her lap, and she's nervously picking at nonexistent dirt under her nails. She's so quiet and worried—I can tell by the frown line that's appeared on her smooth face—that she didn't even put her seatbelt on. Instinctively, I reach over and grab ahold of the belt. The outside of my arm brushes against her stomach, and she sucks in a breath reflexively. She tenses under my featherlight touch, but her eyes shoot to mine. I balance my time between watching the road and her face as I pull on the seatbelt. She doesn't flip out or panic like I expect her to. Instead, she lifts her hands, giving me room to bring the belt over her lap and secure it into its safety lock.. Confidently, I give the locked belt a tug to tighten it.

"You're not wearing your seat belt," she says softly. Her voice seems to pick up confidence toward the end of the sentence, like she's working up to arguing with me. A hopeful smile creeps to my lips at the thought. I wish she would try to fight me. There's nothing better than getting the gift of an unbroken mare and teaching her how to behave.

"No, I'm not." I clear the smile from my face. She's going to hate me in a few minutes, and I don't want this time between us to have her thinking that just because I like her and I'm being nice, that I won't stay true to my word. I always keep my word, even if I have to make her hate me to do it.

"If I have to wear my seat belt, you have to wear yours." She folds her arms over her chest and raises an eyebrow at me.

"That's not how this works." I blow out a deep breath and decide how to phrase what I want to say. She has to understand me, us, this so we don't have to fight it out later. Especially if I can't touch her and truly punish her for misbehaving.

"Explain it to me, then." Her eyes haven't left mine since I grabbed the seat belt to snap her in, and thank fuck for it, too. She hasn't even looked to see where we're headed. I should have put her in the back with the child locks to keep her from trying to jump out, but distracting her seems to be working well enough. For now.

"I gave you my word that I would never hurt you. That includes not putting you in danger."

"But you—" She clamps her mouth shut and shakes her head in dismissal of her thought. I was gearing up for a fight, but she just backed down. How disappointing.

"I have something to take care of real quick, and I need you to stay in the car," I say. Mindy's head snaps around from side to side. Realization dawns on her face as her eyes scan her surroundings. She stares at Trigger's and Duke's bikes as they roll down the street and block the driveway of the fucking crack den she tried to buy from the other day. They climb off their Harleys in unison and remove their helmets.

"What are you doing?" she asks on a desperate plea.

I bring the SUV up to the curb and park in front of the fire hydrant in the red zone. With the Suburban in park and the keys in hand, I open my door and shake my head as she reaches for her door handle.

"Business meeting. Stay in the car, Melinda."

She says nothing, but her eyes practically bug out of her head as I exit the car and lock it up behind me and set the alarm. She can still get out, but at least I'll hear her if she does.

"Ready for s'mores?" Trigger asks as he shakes the bottle of lighter fluid at me with a leather-gloved hand and a huge grin on his face. He walks down the driveway and eyes the house\.

Duke heads past me with a simple nod as he tosses his

lighter in the air and focuses on the other side of the house. He catches sight of Mindy in the SUV and gives her a friendly nod. I take my eyes off the house long enough to see her smile and give him a big wave. I know she was staying with Duke and Nic for a few weeks before her attack, but how fucking close did they get? I fight back the urge to shoot her a dirty look. She doesn't smile enough these days, and if this asshole is her friend and he can make her smile, then fuck it. It's fine. Besides, Nic would cut his balls off and feed them to him afterward if he fucked around on her.

The creaking of the front door draws my attention away from Mindy and Duke and toward the house where Clarence, who prefers to be called Smirk, stands with his hands in his pockets. He's expecting me, but two of my brothers flanking the sides of his house is probably a surprise. With quick strides, I walk up the cement pathway and take the stairs of the porch two at a time until Clarence and I are face to face.

He lifts his arms beside his head and takes a step back saying, "I didn't give her nothing and I called you right away, just like I told you I would."

"I know." I eye his skinny as fuck frame and the scabs that have formed on his chin and the inside of his arms. He's got tracks up and down the inner curve of his elbow, and his teeth are various shades of yellow with tinges of brown at the gums.

"We square?"

"You're selling shit drugs in my town after you were so politely asked to stop."

"Man, you said that shit was cool. Said I'd catch a break if I keep you clued in about your girl."

"And I'm keeping my word. Is there anybody else home right now?"

"Why?"

My eyes narrow and I make a *tsk* sound with my tongue as I shake my head. Duke, who's in earshot, leaves his post and walks to the SUV. I unlock the car with the remote from my pocket.

"Because I'm here to teach a lesson, not deliver a message. Now, it would be wise of you to answer the question."

"Nah, man. It's just me." Smirk shifts awkwardly on his feet, hopping around uncomfortably.

From behind me, Duke clears his throat. He and Mindy are standing at the foot of the steps. She's close to him but not touching. She has her hands shoved in his jean pockets, her eyes volleying between mine and her former dealer's uneasily.

"Mindy, Clarence here is under strict orders not to sell to you." I keep my face firm, refusing to soften under her wide, fearful eyes. She tears up and her chin wobbles, but she doesn't break eye contact. This has to be fucking humiliating and painful for her. As much as I hate to cause her any pain, she needs to know that I won't let anything hurt her— including herself.

"He didn't sell me anything." Her eyes close slowly, and she scrubs at her face with shaky hands. When she returns her attention to me, she slumps her shoulders like she's all out of fight.

"I know," I say. She seems to relax a little. I can't look at her as I say this, so I turn back toward Clarence. "Or he'd already be dead."

Trigger swings himself up on the porch using the railing and tosses Clarence the bottle of lighter fluid. My brother hasn't looked this happy since the last time he and Grady got into it. "Instead, he's just going to burn down his own house. Aren't you, Clarence?"

The pathetic fuck fumbles with the bottle of lighter fluid and nearly drops it on his own damn foot. "I ain't burning down nothin'."

"You don't have to do this," Mindy says in exasperation. My breath catches at how vulnerable she sounds. I hate doing this to her, even if I am doing it for her. Catching Trigger's eye, I nod and jump off the porch, landing in the dirt, and trade places with Duke who, along with Ryan, closes in on Clarence. I position myself between Mindy and the street so I can stop her if she tries to run. I was going easy on her, letting her figure her own shit out, but the moment she tried to score, all that changed. It's clear to me now that she can't do this on her own. She may not know it, but she needs me.

"Yes, we do. I've made contact with every dealer I know from as far north as Eureka down to Santa Rosa and as far east as Reno. Nobody is going to sell to you. The ones I don't know are being put on notice. Any motherfucker stupid enough to sell to you will have a price on his head worth ten grand." I wait for that to sink in. She turns to me with tears in her eyes. She's not angry, but I can't quite make out what's going on in her head. She seems at war with herself. I open and close my fists at my side to stop myself from grabbing hold of her and never letting go. "Let this be a teachable moment for you, Mindy. You hold the lives of countless people in your hands. The next person you try to score from dies. The next person who hurts you dies. The next person who stands too close to you, looks at you wrong, or just bugs me fucking dies."

She whips around and places her hands on my cut above my pecs and leans in. I suck in a sharp breath at the weight of her hands on me. She doesn't seem to realize she's touching me. Good. That means she's fucking listening to what I'm telling her. I don't like repeating myself.

"Why?" Her voice is strangled with untold emotion. She pushes on my chest and then grabs ahold of my cut, fisting it in her hands. Tears fall down her cheeks as she lets her head fall forward. "I don't want anybody else to get hurt."

Very slowly, I raise my hand to her chin and stop before I touch her. She doesn't jump or take a step back, so I give in to the want and let myself feel her soft skin as I tip her face up so she has to look at me. Her chest rises and falls with shaky breaths, and she locks her jaw in an attempt to stop its unwanted movement. Fuck. I'm affecting her, not in the way I'd like, but I'll take it. Everything in me wants to consume, own, protect, and punish this woman. She's strong and defiant and so goddamn broken. It's like she was made for me.

"Nothing and no one will stop me from protecting you."

"It's not Smirk's fault—it's mine." Her chin sags in shame as she lowers her eyes. She speaks with a slowness that's tinged with such guilt and defeat that it's almost gratifying. "I almost messed up everything I've worked so hard for. Don't punish him because I fucked up."

"I'm not. He gets to live."

Her head shoots up in confusion. I'm not sure where I lost her. Feeling brave, I place my hand at the small of her back. She jumps slightly before settling and letting me lead her away from the house. She's back in the SUV as I turn to see Clarence shouting at Trigger and Duke about fairness and customer service and some other nonsense about running his business out of his car. I think I even hear the sad fuck crying. He was warned about selling his shit in town. We can't keep the town totally clean, but at least we can have a policy about quality. What Clarence sells is shit, so fucking far from pure that it's anybody's guess how many of his customers have almost died from it. Aside from the danger, the lack of concern over quality just pisses me off. If you're going to do something, fucking do it right.

Duke tosses Clarence a cheap disposable lighter as he and Trigger hop down off the porch. I walk around the SUV and climb into the driver's seat. I follow Mindy's line of sight to the house as Clarence runs off the porch, followed by a bright, furious flame that's spreading across the front of the house. When he reaches the lawn, he crouches down, clutching his head and rocking back and forth. Duke and Trigger head for their bikes and ride off. I start up the SUV, and we trail behind them but part ways as they head for Ma and Pop's place and I take Mindy home. It kills me to leave her, but she's not mine.

Chapter 4

JIM LEADS MICHAEL from my bedroom and into the living room where he sits down on the coffee table and points at the couch. Michael walks in front of me and Duke with a relaxed gait that I don't expect. Duke and I flank Pop's sides and remain standing. I know Michael and Jim have gotten closer and have almost come to an understanding in the last few weeks as far as his captivity is concerned. As it stands, we're still at odds as for how to handle Michael. I don't even know what we're going to do with Scavo now, too.

"You trust this guy?" Jim says with his gaze firmly on Michael. His brows are drawn together, and he's doing his best to keep a blank look on his face, but it's not really working. As Michael takes a moment before he responds, Ryan is in the other room bitching at Grady for something or other. Probably for not shooting Scavo on sight. Trigger's always had a temper, but his willingness to cap dudes is getting to historic levels. I don't approve simply because a dead motherfucker is a silent motherfucker, and we need some goddamn answers already.

"Yeah, I do. He's good people." Michael leans forward a little bit and clasps his hands together in front of him. "You know you can trust me."

I sit and wait for Jim to agree. Months ago there's no way in fucking hell I'd say Jim and Michael would be getting along. Not because Michael hurt his twin sister. No, for Jim it's because Michael hurt what belongs to him. The way Jim sees it is that if Alex belongs to Ryan, then she belongs to the club. Aside from the fact that she's supposed to be under our protection, she's one of us now because of my brother.

I'm still not at a place where I'm cool with calling her my sister, even if that's who she is. It's hard to go down that road with her being Trigger's woman. Sometimes I think I can't let myself accept her for who she is because of him and not because of our history. Regardless, she's Forsaken, and that means she belongs to us. That much I've come to accept.

Michael's eyes slide over to mine, and he holds them there for a long minute. The kid has already been given the lowdown on his family history. I can't remember when Jim told him since I found out after the fact, but ever since then, Michael looks at me differently. His eyes fall on my scar, and he turns away quickly but not enough for me to avoid seeing the difficult pity in his eyes. I fucking hate pity. It doesn't do me any good. We're all fucked up and scarred—it's just that mine are visible to the entire fucking world thanks to Carlo Mancuso. I wonder what it's like to know your father is such an epic cocksucker. Can't say I can empathize with him since I don't even know who my father is. My dad, though, that's Jim. He couldn't be more my dad if he were my own blood.

"Listen, we just got to make sure this guy is gold before we listen to a fucking thing he has to say," I say. I redirect my eyes from Michael to Jim to avoid having to face the younger brother I still don't really know. Michael and Alex just bring me back to a place I'd rather not be. At least I see some of Ruby in Alex. The only thing I see of Ma in Michael is his eyes. Otherwise, he looks exactly like the bastard he was named after.

"I fucked up and hurt our sister. I won't let that happen again," Michael says and stops there. He's not much for trying to convince me of anything anymore, but this is different. He's bringing up shit he never has before, and damn if it doesn't make my veins run ice cold.

Our sister.

"You're not exactly someone I put much faith in." I can

feel Pop's eyes carefully roaming my face to see if Michael's statement is going to set me off. Part of me wishes it would so I can beat the shit out of the stupid fuck and act like I couldn't help myself. Ma would be pissed if I pulled something like that, though. She's got enough on her plate, and the last thing she needs is infighting between us.

"Your call, son." Pop leans back, letting me take my time deciding.

We don't have much of a choice but to give Scavo a chance to save his own life. He might have intel the club could use, and with the way shit keeps going sideways, we need all the intel we can get. There's so much up in the air right now, especially with Rig's fucking betrayal and subsequent disappearance. I'd have suggested we give priority to finding the pathetic fuck, but he's too much of a pussy to stay around here. He's got to be long gone by now.

I slide my eyes to Duke, who's been silent so far. He gives a curt nod, solidifying my decision.

"Five minutes. If Scavo has anything useful, then you have a new roommate. Otherwise, I'm going to enjoy ending him myself."

Michael nods his head in acceptance and looks down at his lap as he takes a deep breath and waits. I walk away from the impromptu pow-wow and fight the urge to knock Trigger's teeth out when he starts bitching the moment he sees me. Days like today I have no clue how I've put up with this asshole for as long as I have without shooting him. Ma won't like me beating the crap out of Michael, and even though she'd be more understanding of me shooting Trigger—I think—I know better than to push that theory, even if I'd only shoot him a little. Flesh wound, if that.

"Tell me that crazy old fuck isn't thinking about listening to a fucking thing that little parasite has to say." Ryan spits the words out like they're sour to the taste.

"Give it a fucking rest," I say. Christ, it's like he's a fucking ten year-old all over again, pitching a fit when he doesn't get his way.

"What, you spend a few weeks with Junior and suddenly he's your fucking family? You trust him over me because he's blood?"

My eyes narrow at Ryan's words. One of these days I really am going to shoot him, and I'm convinced nobody would really blame me. Ma might, but she's never gotten riled up by Ryan's bullshit the way the rest of us do.

"Feeling insecure?" The words have flown off my tongue before I can stop them. He needs to shut the fuck up, and I need to not instigate this bullshit fight, but I can't help it. "Worried that mommy doesn't like you best anymore?"

I wouldn't see it if I didn't know my brother as well as I do, but his Adam's apple bobs—an indication that he's upset. Otherwise, he gives no sign that my taunts bother him. I don't regret much, but I do regret this. Ryan is particularly sensitive about Michael because of how he hurt Alex. As if meeting my sister for the first time since she was born and her not knowing who I am wasn't enough, having to contend with Ryan falling in love with her has pushed me over the edge. He's protective and as thoughtful as Ryan gets when he's with her.

"We're dealing with this later, brother," he says and shoves his pointer finger in my face. Ryan's cool gray eyes and jet-black hair flood my view as he snarls at me. I'll let him kick my ass later for my comment. I fucking deserve it. I know all too fucking well that he's always been uncomfortable with the fact that he's not really Ma's son. Like since he's not blood he's missing out on something. He's just a dense asshole who can't see how she looks at him. If anyone has a right to feel inferior, it's me. I'm the reason Ma lost so much, including Michael and Alex. I'm the reason all this shit went down. If she'd just aborted me when she had the chance, her life could have been so much better.

"Meantime, get Scavo out of the fucking closet and bring him into the living room," I say firmly. In the corner of my bedroom, Grady is huddled with his daughter, Cheyenne, and her boyfriend and our newest prospect, Jeremy. He grits his teeth but gives me a chin nod and directs a couple of Forsaken from other charters to escort Cheyenne back to Ma and Pop's house on the other side of the property. Jeremy says a few words to Grady and disappears out of the room with Cheyenne. Asshole can play doting boyfriend later. Once she's dropped off, he better be getting his bitch ass back here to help with all the fucking bodies.

"You want answers, just like we all do, Ry," I say, much quieter now. As a way of making amends, I use a name I haven't called him since elementary school. He waits a beat before nodding his head and retrieving Scavo from the walk-in. We have Forsaken here from three different charters. Most of them know each other, some of them don't. Like the good little soldiers they are, they all move automatically to their positions. The men who want to know what the fuck is going on head into the living room, and those who don't want the drama head outside to keep an eye out for any more bullshit.

The entire Fort Bragg charter is crammed into my tiny living room, with Scavo seated on the couch beside Michael. The mood is tense as fuck, but I sense an air of excitement around me. We've been in a fucking black hole of ignorance for almost a year now, and it's wearing on me. I'm supposed to be our tech guy who can figure out puzzles and solve club problems, and it's pretty much impossible to do my job when I don't have a clue where to start and I can't stay upright long enough to figure it out. As the club's treasurer, I'm also the numbers guy. We're not in the red, but if we keep spending the way we have, we will be. Everything's happened in such quick succession this last year that we can't catch our breath, and solving problems takes time and money we don't really have. It's fucking time we got answers and stopped bleeding ourselves dry.

"Talk, asshole," Grady says on a sneer. I can't blame him for refusing to let go of the chip on his shoulder. Scavo scared both Grady's woman and his kid. We're supposed to protect our women and our kids, and we keep failing. It doesn't sit well with any of us.

"Mr. Stone, the last time we spoke, we were not on even ground. It seems I was sent to retrieve the *principe* and *principessa* under false pretenses. Had I been aware of that fact, I believe our last meeting would have gone much more smoothly."

"You talked to Aunt Gloria?" Michael says. He turns his attention to Scavo, who nods.

"So you get it now?" Pop asks. I remember back when he was a total hothead, just like Ryan, mouthing off and smarting off every chance he got. I was only a kid, but it intimidated me to the point where I wasn't sure I wanted to get to know him. The old man's mellowed with age, and he lets shit go that he never would have even a few years ago. Like this meeting. He's way too relaxed for what we're doing here, but that's Pop. He's wearing down, tired, and somewhere in the back of my head I worry that he's ready to hang up his gavel. I'm not ready for that.

"I wish no harm upon Alexandra. She was promised to me once." The moment Scavo says the words, Pop's head shoots up and his eyes narrow in on Ryan. My brother's got his mouth open, ready to fucking snap at the idea of Alex with another man, but somehow Pop's glare wills him into obedience, something that doesn't usually work. This meeting is important, though. We have to get through it without more bloodshed if we intend to take Mancuso out for once and for all.

"I understand she belongs to Forsaken now."

"She belongs to herself," I catch myself saying loudly. My voice booms through the room, surprising me. I didn't expect to speak, didn't want to. Alex does belong to us, but the reality that she's never had the opportunity to figure herself out, independent from anyone else, just pisses me off. Maybe I can empathize with her situation more than I'd like.

"I would very much like to clear the air about recent events that your club may be investigating, but before I provide you with too much information, I need a few reassurances."

"Like?" Wyatt says. He's standing directly behind Pop with his bulging arms folded over his broad chest. The man is a fucking monster, and his deep voice radiates his size throughout the crowded space.

"I am not an ignorant street thug who chases his own ass because he can't lead himself down a one-way street, but that's exactly the kind of leadership the Mancuso family is dealing with right now. Carlo is still in Rikers, and as far as I know, he's not calling the shots. The plays are too messy, the crews have no direction, and even the capos are starting to consider dissent. It's the worst fucking nightmare for a man like me who joined an organization because he believed in what he was doing. I want my organization back, and in light of recent discoveries and events, I no longer believe that can happen with Carlo Mancuso as the head of the family."

"And who the fuck do you think should be running Brooklyn? You?" Michael snaps with a furrowed brow. For the first time since Scavo sat down, Michael appears to distrust him.

"No, *principe*," Scavo says evenly and with a firm belief in his words. "We've talked about this. *You* should be head of the family." Michael sucks in a deep breath and stares at Scavo with a mixture of confusion, fear, and understanding. Something passes between them, an understanding maybe, before Michael nods his head. He scrubs his face with his hands and groans.

Heavy is the crown, I guess. The mention of a massive reorganization surprises me. It's bold for Scavo to say that shit, especially in mixed company. Forsaken isn't a friend to Mancuso, and Scavo mentioning dissent is a capital offense. It's just ballsy and stupid enough to tell me that he's serious. He's earning our trust by refusing to align himself with the old regime even though his position could get him killed.

"It's the right thing," Scavo says on a low tone.

"Something you want to share?" Pop asks.

"We talked about it, but I thought he was full of shit," Michael confesses. "Nobody's really happy with the way things have been going the last few years—some of us haven't been happy since Grandpa died and Dad took over—but I never took Leo seriously."

"Well, you better start," Scavo says, and the room falls silent. If Scavo is planning an upset in power, then maybe we can use this to our advantage.

"Still haven't named your price," Wyatt reminds Scavo.

"I'm not your prisoner. I'm your ally. I want the *principe* free to return to New York when this is settled, and I want Forsaken to agree upon a mutually favorable arrangement that allows you to run your club and us to run our family."

Nobody speaks in an effort to absorb the information being thrown at us. It's a compelling arrangement, that's for sure, but whether or not we'd be fucked over in the process is another question. It's probably better than remaining here like sitting ducks as we have been.

"In an effort to earn your trust . . ." Scavo says and trails off. He raises his arms slowly in the air and reaches inside his suit jacket. I hear the men around me respond in kind, but I'm so focused on what I'm doing that it barely registers. Within three seconds, I have my gun out and pointed at Scavo's head with the safety off. The man moves slowly and pinches something inside his jacket. Only Michael and Pop don't have weapons drawn on Scavo. Is Pop really that fucking confident that the asshole isn't going to blow him away? He's sitting directly in front of him, a few feet away, and is the easiest target.

Scavo pulls out a few folded pieces of paper and hands them to Pop. From over his shoulder, I peer down at the pages as they unfold, and I tuck my gun back into the waistband of my jeans. The first page is a grainy but still readable amateur photograph of an unremarkable sedan that looks like it's leaving the 101 Club. I check the plates on the sedan to ensure the characters are legible so I can investigate this later. Pop flips to the next page, and it appears I don't have to do the leg work. Scavo's already done it for me. The white eight-and-a-half-by-eleven page has two photocopied documents on it. The first is a vehicle registration card that lists the owner as some fuck in San Francisco. The second is the man's driver's license.

"Shit," Pop says as we seem to come to the same conclusion.

"I'll take it that you recognize him. As you should since he's responsible for the botched hit on Forsaken at the 101 Club."

"It was him," I say, barely able to form the words as I stare at the DMV photo of the last man I killed. He hurt *her*. This . . . bastard took something from Mindy she won't ever get back. He tortured her, humiliated her, and destroyed her. For that, I killed him. My only regret is that I did it swiftly as I moved down the hall and into the office at Universal Grounds. I should have made him suffer the way she did. I should have kept him alive and let him beg for death. I should have let myself indulge a little before it ended.

I still hear his voice, breaking up my rest, on the nights I fall into a deep enough sleep to actually dream. The nightmares used to be commonplace, but now they've evolved into something akin to night terrors, with violent thrashing and a suffocating need to make somebody suffer. My pain is enough to piss me off and make me edgy. Holly's pain, her tears, and her panic attacks send me to a place where I think that maybe I should rip off all my flesh, and it still wouldn't distract me from my anger.

But it's when I think of Mindy and how she's suffered that I go looking for something to do. *Somebody* to torture. Even when I'm done and I should be sated, I'm not. Pain makes everything go away—except for this.

I couldn't save Mindy from that horror, and for that, I'll never forgive myself. The only thing worse than what she suffered at *his* hands is what she could suffer at mine if she were stupid enough to ever want me in all the ways I want her.

Thankfully for her, she's not that stupid.

Thankfully for me, I relish the pain that comes with the bitter loneliness of not being able to touch her, love her, consume her the way she consumes me.

Mindy

Chapter 5

"I'M PROUD OF you for doing this." Holly keeps her voice cheerful and steady. I don't respond because I don't know how. What am I to say to that? Yeah, I'm a badass for agreeing to eat hot soup. She seems to catch on to my lack of enthusiasm over our little attempt at home-based therapy. "This is a big deal for you, so stop acting like it's not."

"I feel like a goober," I admit.

"Easier to be terrified of heat and moisture than to work yourself through it." Her head bobs in agreement, but it's her tone and eyes that give her away. She's mocking me.

"Judge not lest ye shall be judged," I snap and wipe my damp hands on my jean-clad thighs. Holly's eyes bug out of her pretty little skull, and she shakes her head disapprovingly. Pre-Heath Mindy cursed occasionally, but post-Heath Mindy never did. She wanted to distance herself from the disaster she had become. But neither Mindy quotes scripture.

"Fuck. I sound like my mother." I cover my face with my hands and suck in calming breaths. Well, they're supposed to be calming, but they're not doing their job.

"The only way that could have been scarier is if your head had spun around and you'd been spitting green stuff everywhere."

I narrow my eyes on my cousin, who also happens to be my best friend, and I shake my head. I huff my irritation for a few moments before the ridiculousness of the situation overtakes me. Holly starts it with a light snort, and before I know it, we've dissolved into a fit of giggles. My belly aches, my chest tightens, and my lungs strain under the weight of my laughter. It's lovely to be laughing again.

When Holly and I calm ourselves down, she clears her throat and shoves the stupid bowl of now-warm soup at me. At least it's what used to be my favorite—broccoli cheddar. The creamy, cheesy substance is laden with bits of bright green broccoli pieces. Taking a deep breath, I focus in on what we've talked about and do my best to follow through. Remind myself how I used to feel about it, focus in on the smell, then the touch, and finally the taste, paying equal measure to each one so I can absorb the entirety of the experience. The first part proves easy enough. I can always remember what I once liked about something, whether it be a food, piece of clothing, song, or even a person. My memories are strong and fierce and sometimes—mostly, actually—fucking crippling.

The smell of the soup isn't altogether unpleasant. Foods carry a slightly different scent when they're warm than they do when they're cold—a point Holly refuses to acquiesce on—and despite the fact that the smell isn't unpleasant, I still find myself desperately trying to will away the disgust. It's just soup. It's just warm soup, is all. Holly's brown eyes are patient, but her fingers are tapping on the kitchen table absently. I told her when she suggested this that we'd end up here. She was bound to become annoyed with me at some point, and it seems some point is now.

This is ridiculous.

Before I lose my nerve, I seize the spoon from the bowl's edge and take a heaping spoonful. I pause for but a moment to meet Holly's wide eyes and then unceremoniously shove the contents of the spoon into my mouth.

Shit. It's hotter than I thought. My tongue burns and the roof of my mouth aches from the awful surprise. My face screws up from the assault, and I slap at the table maniacally. Holly shoves a glass of ice water at me. Its sides are wet with condensation. I think twice before wrapping my hand around it, but somehow I'm drawn to it. As beads of moisture slide down to the table, my brain is assaulted with all the feelings I try so hard to push down all the time.

I hate the memories of my tears wetting my face as *that* man shoves my face into the wooden desk. The room is so warm, and my skin is hot to the touch. Every violent push, every sadistic word, and every single sound from that night floods my mind. My memories start to slip back further in time to when I was in another dark place. Only back then I welcomed the heat in my veins that numbed the aching loneliness of losing Heath. Now, the very thought of the entire process—from scoring to finding a workable vein and all the way to the swollen, red-hot rush that would sweep over me makes me sick.

And to think I almost succumbed to that the other night.

Slowly, the burning in my mouth cools. I force the mouthful of soup down my throat and remind myself that the chunks I'm swallowing are broccoli and not my own vomit. Not a stranger's fluids.

Instinctively, I grab at the damp glass and gulp as much of the water as I can before my poor stomach feels too full to consume another drop. The uncomfortable wetness makes my body tense up, but I don't bother to release it like I'm prone to do. No, I'm here to make progress, and I can't do that if I don't confront what's bothering me.

Across the table, Holly sits perfectly still and watches me with a nervous gaze. I vow to myself to keep my hand on the glass and eyes firmly fixed on my best friend for as long as it takes the irrational discomfort to subside. I'm going to get better. I have to. It takes probably five minutes, at least, for me to feel comfortable enough to set the glass down. My chin wobbles as I fight the losing battle of trying to convince myself that I don't actually *have* to dry my hand. I hate how wet it is and after a minute decide I've made strides in other areas and that it's not such a big failure to give in to the nagging need to dry my hand.

"This is major progress." I let Holly give me the

compliment and try to accept it as gracefully as I can. It's not really that easy, so instead of verbalizing anything, I just nod my head. I took a bite of soup, haven't thrown it up yet, and even held a damp glass without losing myself to the demons and forgetting where I am.

Yeah, I'm such a badass.

"Do you want to try working on touch now?"

No, I don't. My issues with touching and being touched are worse than my temperature and moisture issues. Touch makes my other triggers look like silly quirks.

"Yes."

Because I can't go on in the world in an invisible, self-created bubble of fear. Holly is both my cousin and my best friend. She knows me better than anyone else. This girl has seen me at my worst and has never intentionally made me feel poorly about it. There's nobody safer for me to work through my issues with. Well, there is, but I can't allow myself to go down that road, and I certainly can't tell Holly that in what few fantasies I have left, Ian is helping me through touch. Holly likes Ian, as well she should since she's woken him up in the middle of the night enough times to work her out of her own head, but that doesn't mean she likes Ian *for me*. I wasn't particularly easy on her when she first hooked up with Grady, either. I've pretty much made an uncomfortable bed, and I'd rather not lie in it if I don't have to.

Holly gives me a brief reminder of our touch therapy remedy and how it works. She's not a doctor, and I think she got all this stuff off the Internet, but it's been helping little by little, so I don't much care how legitimate a form of therapy it really is. We're to start out with her hand gently reaching out for mine. She'll place her fingertips on the top of my hand for a very short amount of time and then remove them long enough for me to regain my bearings. We're to repeat the process several times per session until I can reasonably stand her touch for longer periods of time without the sickness creeping up on me.

I liked being able to touch Ian—being *happy* to touch him— and I want more of it. I want human contact once more. I want to feel connected to someone by more than just familial obligation. I want to be loved and protected and *touched*.

So when it's time for Holly to touch me, I don't pull back my hand even though, instinctively, I want to. It's just Holly, and the rational part of me knows that. It's not that I fear she's going to hurt me. It's just that human touch brings back the sordid memories of those men and how I felt before they violated me—the nauseating dread when they put their hands on me, the horrifying anticipation of what kind of hell they intended to unleash. I had no idea. And every time another person tries to make contact with me, I feel the same terror I felt even before they forced themselves on me.

I manage through three rounds of hand touches, even initiating two touches on Holly's wrist because I'm feeling brave. Holly suggests we give in after that, because although I'm making consistent progress, she doesn't want to push me too much. While we're on our last touch of Holly's fingertips to my hand, the house alarm beeps, signaling that the front door is being opened.

Loud voices fill the Grady residence immediately. Holly slowly pulls away and grabs the soup bowl to take into the kitchen to clean off. I'd offer to do it myself, but I've never done well with food floating in water. Even before *that* night, I've not been a fan of cleaning up soup bowls. First in view is Grady, Holly's man, and then comes Duke, whom I'm rather fond of. Before my life was flushed down the loo—again—I stayed with Duke and his woman, Nic, for a few weeks. That was back when she was pregnant with their daughter, Robin, who is now pushing two weeks old.

Ian had promised he would take me to the hospital to meet the baby, but I guess he forgot. I didn't call or text him once Holly called to tell me that Nic had gone into labor. I just sat and waited by my phone, stupidly expecting him to remember a promise he'd made two months prior. I felt like such a sad sap, because it would have meant the world to me for Ian to take me to meet baby Robin. My disappointment at his absence was so profound that when Holly asked if she could take me, I selfishly turned her down and have so far denied myself baby time.

"Hey, Minds," Grady says with the softest smile I think he's capable of. By my estimation, Grady is the second-largest member of Forsaken. He's a hulking man with a gruff attitude and one of the scariest glares I've ever seen. Holly used to share my opinion on this matter, but now she insists that he's really just a big teddy bear. She's clearly biased, but I'm also starting to suspect she might have some form of brain damage. Just looking at him reminds me of how defenseless I am by comparison. Not that he'd hurt me. None of the members of Forsaken would hurt me. I know that. Still, their muscled frames are intimidating.

"Hi, Grady." I offer him a kind smile but can't help the nervousness that sets in around him. I give Duke a wave and my best smile, which he returns in his own badass biker way. He opens his mouth and pauses, hanging there mid-motion for a long moment before the most exhausted yawn escapes his mouth. His heavy boots thump against the floor, and he throws himself into the kitchen chair nearest to me.

With drained piercing blue eyes, Duke fixes his eyes on mine. "I'd give my left testicle for a full night's sleep."

I fight off the snicker as best I can.

"Quit freaking crying," Nic says, her voice nearing with every syllable. I perk up at her arrival and hope against hope that she brought Robin with her. I just want to look at her, that's all. As Nic comes into view, my heart leaps as my eyes land on the baby carrier. She offers me a happy but tired smile—something I don't remember seeing before Duke came along—and gently sets the carrier down on the floor in front of me.

"Hey," she says. "It's about time you met the baby."

Wrapped up in a pale yellow blanket and a white and

yellow onesie with ducks all over it is the tiniest, cutest little person I've ever seen. It's crazy to think that humans go from living inside one another to being this small to eventually growing into what we are in adulthood. There's so much damage that can happen along the way. So much that can go wrong given half a chance. And this little baby is just starting out. God, the very idea of something hurting her, anything hurting her, makes my stomach roll. I was a tiny baby once. So was Nic. As hard as it may be to believe, so were Grady and Duke and even Ian. We all started out this tiny, innocent, and vulnerable.

I spy Grady and Holly wandering over to the carrier and peeking in on the star of the show. I don't miss Holly's hand reaching for Grady's as she stares down at the perfect little creature, and I definitely don't miss the way Grady grabs hold of her and squeezes tightly. I let the significance of their connection seep in to my heart, past the jealousy and irritation. They want a baby together. That much is obvious. I wasn't sure about Grady before, but now I know him better and I know how much he loves my best friend.

"You're lucky, Holls. Grady makes cute kids," I say without thinking.

Nic and Duke shoot each other knowing glances that signal for the other to keep their mouth shut. It's cute how in sync they are. Holly freezes and seems uncomfortable with my comment, but it's Grady who surprises me. He lets go of Holly's hand and bends down, crowding his big body beside mine. I brace myself for the verbal lashing I surely deserve. It's none of my business if they want to have kids, and a man like Sterling Grady is probably displeased with me pushing my nosy way into his personal business.

"This mean you're over your shit?" he asks as he levels his gaze with mine. I should be slinking away from him, tears welling in my eyes, and on my way to a heart attack by now. But I'm not. This is so fucked-up. I hate how the only people I feel safe and normal around are a bunch of felonious outlaw murderers. It doesn't make sense. My parents, my God-fearing, gentle, kind parents make my stomach sink and my skin crawl. It's not fair to them. I should welcome their presence, but I just don't. It doesn't feel normal or right, and if I'm going to be honest with myself, they haven't felt safe since before Heath.

"Your shit with me, Minds. Not the rest of it. Some shit you don't get past." Grady's words shock me back into the moment. He heard Holly call me Minds once, and he's been using it exclusively ever since.

"You're good for her. That's all that matters," I say quietly. I force myself to keep eye contact with this intimidating man. Holly once told me that he'd die protecting me. Not because he feels the same for me that he does Holly, but because that's who he is. I matter to her and therefore I matter to him. If I weren't in such shock over the entire conversation, I could probably hug the man.

Or maybe not.

He grunts and lifts an eyebrow in the air, accenting the handsome wrinkles that are slowly setting in with age. He's teasing me, I think. Feeling brave, I roll my eyes and smile at him.

"Holly belongs with you." I was worried Grady and the club would be a bad influence on her. She followed me to hell and back and is still by my side. Her loyalty knows no bounds, and I was terrified at what it would mean for her if she hooked up with a man who has zero disregard for the rest of the entire world. But I was wrong. He's good for her. He's given her a home, a teenager she couldn't be crazier about, and something to fight for—him. "She's Forsaken."

"So are you," Grady says. His eyes pull from mine. He lifts the yellow blanket away from Robin and unsnaps her from her seat. Very carefully he lifts her out of the carrier. She stirs in his arms just slightly, her eyes opening and then closing just as quickly. She blows out a little breath and settles in his arms.

"You're one of us now. Sorry how it went down, but you're

one tough bitch."

The scuffling of shoes sounds on the floor behind Grady. I tense up immediately, having not previously known someone else was in the room. I can't see anyone, but I know they're there. My nerves are on edge, and my hands are shaking. I shove them under my legs to try to control my stupid response. I don't want to be like this forever, unnerved so easily and quick to panic. Grady seems to notice. Before he can say anything, I excitedly blurt out, "I ate soup!"

He smirks, and a few muted laughs echo in the room. He's taken up so much of my line of sight that I forgot Holly, Nic, and Duke are in the room with us. I want to crawl into a hole to hide my embarrassment.

"One tough bitch," Grady reaffirms with a nod. "Only gonna say this once because I'm no pussy, but I'm high as fuck off new-baby smell."

"Does Sterling Grady have baby rabies?" I hear Nic chide and then laugh through a covered mouth. She used to fear him, but I guess seeing him hold her daughter gives her a comfort she didn't previously feel.

"Well, he better, because now *I* have baby rabies," Holly says without shame. Jeez. She used to be pretty closed-off about these things, but a few months in this man's bed and she's as bad as me with blurting shit out left and right.

"Can't get far if you're waddling," Duke says. I lift my head and catch the wink he sends Nic. "More babies you pop out, less chance you have of going anywhere."

"Fuck you," Nic says. "Our kid is a week old. You want a fucking baby factory, you better look at someone else. Don't know how you'd manage it, though, without your dick attached to your body." Nic's angry rant exhausts her. She rounds the table and plops down in Duke's lap despite her chastising of him.

"No spinning, babe," he whispers into her ear, and she settles against his chest. Fuck. These people are so happy together and there's a baby here and she's perfect, and despite how goddamn ruined I am, I don't feel totally out of place. I know for a fact that three of the people in the room have taken a life, committed multiple felonies, and regret none of it. And then there's Nic. I don't know too much about what she went through, but I know she understands me. The fact that these are now my people should have me blacking out with panic, but it doesn't. I've spent too long wanting to be a part of Ian's world to try to run once I'm finally being welcomed into it.

I try to keep my eyes on Grady's, but it's too hard. I lift my gaze over his shoulder to the wall behind him and gasp. It's like Ian knew I was thinking about him. He's leaning against the wall, his tense eyes fixed on the back of Grady's head and his lips set in a flat line. He's practically boring a hole into his sergeant-at-arm's skull, so focused on the man in front of me that it's almost like I'm not even here. I don't know what I want from him, not really, but it would be nice if he would look at me. I miss his eyes. Not the ones I see now, but the ones that stare at me in silence while I blabber on about one thing or another. I even miss the sorrow in his eyes when I'm panicking.

"What happened is a result of a Forsaken fuckup. We failed to protect our women, and because of that, those bastards went after Nic. I can't make this better for you, and it's not fucking right—not at all—but it happened. If Nic had been there . . ."

Grady stops talking, and I shift my attention back to him. I know what he's trying to say, but he can't seem to bring himself to say it—if I hadn't been covering for Nic that night, it would have been her they hurt. And Robin wouldn't be with us now. This poor, innocent, sweet little baby with her entire life before her wouldn't have survived their vile hatred.

"Not a gift you meant to give, but her life is because of you." Holly tries to shush him, afraid he's upsetting me. He's not. Not in the way she thinks. I spare a glance at Ian to find a scowl on his face that I can't really identify. Maybe he's remembering that night like I am. Maybe he's not as unaffected by it as I think. Having to listen to everything Holly was telling him must have been difficult. I know it was difficult for her to say it. A regretful weight settles in my belly at the thought. Ian's a human being just as much as the rest of us. Of course it hurt him as well.

God, this is all so fucked-up. I get hurt because those sick bastards think I'm someone else and I can't even bring myself to be angry with Nic for asking me to cover for her that night. She would have lost her baby. It's a high price to pay for someone else's kid, but I know what Grady's saying. It's not okay, but in a sense it is. I can feel it in every fiber of my being as I stare at Robin's sleeping face. I know what her mother went through. I know how miserable she was. Duke gave her Robin, and Robin gave her something to fight for. I don't know that she would have gotten over losing Robin, and I bet her guilt over the entire situation weighs on her. I know it would weigh on me worse than it does now. I would hate to be in her shoes.

"Better me than you," I whisper to Robin. And I mean it. For the first time since it happened, I feel a sense of acceptance wash over me.

Chapter 6

IT DIDN'T TAKE long for Robin to wake up once she was in Grady's arms, and when she did, she woke up screaming bloody murder. Grady just shook his head and passed Robin off to Holly while Nic pulled out a bottle and handed it over. There was a minute there where Holly struggled with how to tip the bottle just right to get Robin to eat, but when Grady wrapped his arms around Holly and showed her how to do it, Robin calmed down immediately. It was cute and kept my even mood going, something that's not easy these days. I'm relaxed—at least as relaxed as I can get—for what feels like the first time in months. It probably *is* the first time in months.

Halfway through her bottle, Robin stops eating and starts wailing again. On tired feet, Nic stumbles over to Holly and takes the baby in her arms, walking off without a word. I stare in confusion at the abandoned bottle in Holly's hands.

"Kid prefers the tit," Duke says through a yawn and then stands. He fixes his eyes on Grady and then over Grady's shoulder to Ian. "We ready?"

Grady gives a grunt and grabs ahold of Holly's butt. With lustful eyes, he says, "Hope Minds doesn't mind, but when I get home I'm going to fuck you so hard you're going to wake the neighbors with your screaming."

My jaw hits the floor, and I cover my face. I so didn't expect this when Holly invited me to stay the night. I bet if I look at her, she's going to be bright red and quietly chastising his crudeness. "I mind, I mind," I chant.

Her voice is breathy but demanding as she says, "Don't be

late, or I'm starting without you."

Oh dear God. I retract everything I just thought about Grady being good for her. I'm not a prude, but holy cow, that's the last visual I need. Ever.

I search the room for something else to focus on—anything else to focus on—and my eyes land uncomfortably on Ian. His deep, thoughtful, maybe even angry expression has been redirected to me. His gaze feels weighty, important. I can't look away even though I want to. His head is tipped slightly forward with his chin down and his wavy light brown hair falling in his face. He's gorgeous and dark and just everything I want to be in a position to want. I'm not, though—in any position to want him, I mean—and that frustrates me. It makes me want to try harder to get better, to push myself to be better now. Fake it 'til you make it, I guess.

Eventually, though, the staring becomes too much. I clear my throat, tear my eyes away from Ian's, and head in the direction Nic went. I don't miss the searing kiss Grady gives Holly or the low hum of his voice as he says, "Lose your pills, baby. I'm ready."

My heart flutters right out of my chest as I turn the corner and head into the guest bedroom I tossed my stuff in earlier. Apparently Grady can be as romantic as Holly swears he is. And here I thought she had totally lowered her standards to be with him. Not that I'm one to pass judgment. If only she knew how I feel about Ian . . .

The door to the guest room is mostly closed now, though I left it fully open earlier. I slow my gait and notice Nic's feeding Robin in the armed chair in the corner of the room. Her eyes lift to mine, and she gives me a soft smile.

"Should I leave?"

"No. You still haven't had a chance to properly meet her." Robin seems to have filled herself up, and Nic adjusts herself back in place. "I swear, for someone so small, she's always freaking hungry."

I offer a polite smile. I don't know anything about how

much babies eat, let alone how to keep one alive. I think I've figured the basic principles, like how they need air and food and a clean diaper, but the mechanics of all that are beyond me. Nic, my crazy, grouchy, troubled coworker, has her man now, and he's strong and bossy as all get-out. He gives her what she needs and even what she wants sometimes. Now she has Robin, and she's all settled down. Holly started staying with Grady back when I was forced to stay with Duke and Nic. Holly never left, and now they're all about having a baby and Grady's teenage daughter is half a step from calling Holly "mom." They're all growing up and moving on with their lives, and here I am, stagnant and even regressing in some ways. My biggest accomplishment is avoiding a panic attack. Yay me.

Nic stands from the chair and nods her head to the bed. "You look nervous. Sit down." Huh?

"Why?"

"No bullshit?" she asks. Oh no. Nic's always been pretty forward when she finally decides to address something. She may let it eat at her for a while, but eventually she just goes all in with it.

"No bullshit," I say. My voice is faint. *Be brave*, I tell myself. Face this head-on.

"Those men would have killed me. They would have killed my baby."

"It's fine," I say. It's not, but that's not on her. It's on the people who tried to hurt her.

"You said no bullshit."

"I don't know what to say," I admit.

"I know what you went through. I know they hurt you. There's no way we can compare the shit we've been through, but I think you know how well I understand your pain. I know what it's like to be hurt like that."

My throat closes up and my eyes well with tears. I'm fucking tired of crying and getting emotional about every little thing. But this is Nic, and this talk is long overdue. She wanted to talk to me when I was still in the hospital recovering, but I didn't want to see anyone at that point. Ian stood guard outside my door, and he was the only one I wanted in there with me. I haven't stopped wanting him. I don't think I ever will.

"You don't want anyone to touch you, hate the feel of your own skin. You ask yourself why it happened. In my case, I asked myself why it kept happening and why I couldn't just leave the guy who was doing it. In your case, you know why, and I can't imagine knowing makes it any better."

"Makes it worse," I confess. I've talked more about *that* night in the last hour than I have since it happened. It's easy with Ian. He never talks about it, never asks me to relive the brutality like my dad does. Ian doesn't suffocate me with worry like my mom does. I thought it would be too painful to talk about this with Nic or anyone in the club. I thought acknowledging it would be more painful than living day in and day out skirting around it.

"How can I be angry with you? You didn't do anything wrong, and neither of us knew what I was walking into. I can't be angry, because if it was you instead of me, then Robin wouldn't be here. How can I be angry with the club? They did exactly what I would have wanted to do for that jerk hurting you? How can I hate anyone when the men who hurt me are dead? I can't, and it leaves me with this ridiculous self-pity about not getting better that I just can't get rid of."

Except now. Right now I don't feel like I'm not getting better. Even saying the words means I am better, and I know it. And now that I've had a little taste of being better, I feel a surge of impatience. I want everything right this second, which is so predictable. I don't know the meaning of *slow down*.

"Well, it's not a cure, but I know of a little something that always helps me," Nic says. She blows a piece of her stringy bleached-blonde hair out of her face and puffs out her cheeks. She's not as thin as a rail anymore, but even with the added baby weight, she just looks healthy now. I didn't even realize how tiny she was before she got pregnant. She must have been so unhealthy.

"I know of a few things that help, but I'm kind of avoiding them," I say and pull my black chip out of my pocket. I wouldn't normally share this part of myself, but this is Nic. She's the last person to judge. "Busted my ass for this thing."

"How long?" She eyes the chip thoughtfully.

"Four years, two months, and fifteen days."

"Grady was right. One tough bitch."

"I don't feel tough." I shove the chip back in my pocket. It feels at home there, comfortable.

"Even superheroes have their moments," she says and nods her head to the bed again. This time I don't argue and sit down, expecting her to join me. Instead of sitting down, she gives me a firm nod and, with outstretched arms, offers Robin to me. I fight back the lump in my throat. I've been wanting to see her for months, but not once did I really think about holding her. I can barely hold a glass without having a freak-out over condensation. How in the hell am I supposed to hold a tiny little human?

"I can't."

"Yes, you can. You just have to be brave. I trust you."

"You probably shouldn't." What if she's hot to the touch and I tense up and squeeze her too hard? What if she sneezes and the moisture freaks me out? What if she hates me? Too many what-ifs flying around my head for me to hold her. No, I think I'll just sit here with my hands to myself and watch her as she slips back into sleep.

"I'd die protecting her, so trust me when I tell you that I feel safe with you holding her. I wouldn't say that if I didn't have faith in you."

"I might hold her wrong."

"I'll show you."

Balancing her baby in her arms, she shows me how to properly hold Robin's neck and everything. I will myself to be okay with this, to fight off the panic before it begins, and to— for once—refuse to let my damage get the best of me. Nic tries to avoid touching me as she places Robin in my waiting arms, but it proves too difficult. My eyes slam closed as my heart rate picks up, and I find it hard to breathe. My lungs fight to keep the flow of oxygen going as the heaviness in my arms stretches her tiny little legs and yawns.

The reminder of her presence brings me back to the here and now. If I selfishly let myself fall into the blackness, I'll never get to hold her again, and that would break my heart. I always wanted to be a mom. I was *that* girl who fantasized about growing up and becoming a wife and mother. There's so much I wanted in life, and it's all gone now. I'll always envy Nic this—her beautiful daughter.

"See?" she says reassuringly. "Not so bad."

"What do you know about Ian?" I instantly regret the question. Nic's face screws up, and she shakes her head. Unable to look at her, I redirect my attention to Robin, who is sound asleep in my arms. I should have asked Holly, but I don't need the lecture or concern that's sure to follow by asking her anything about Ian. Not that she doesn't already know.

"Be careful with him. Lost girls talk and, well, I don't think this is a road you want to go down. What about Wyatt? He's not tied down. There's always Diesel."

"It's not like I'm looking for a man," I defend. "I'm too messed up to try to hitch my wagon to someone else's."

"But you like Ian?"

"I was just curious if you know anything about him," I say a little harsher than intended. Nic's tough. She doesn't quibble about it.

"Oh no you don't. You have the same look you did back when that Italian fuck would come into Universal Grounds. You'd get this goofy smile on your face. Christ, I can't believe I didn't realize it sooner."

"Is it so terrible for me to like Ian?"

"Yes." The sound in the room echoes with not just Nic's voice but Holly's as well. Well, shish kebobs. I didn't realize

Holly had made her way in here, but apparently she has and just in time to scrutinize my affections. I watch carefully as Holly and Nic make eye contact. Neither seems comfortable with the topic at hand, and neither will elaborate. Instead I'm left with burning questions and no answers from either of them.

It looks like I'll just have to get them from Ian.

"Here you go," I say and nod to Nic. She lets out what I think is a disappointed sigh and takes Robin from my arms. I give her and Holly both a reassuring smile and stand. I hitch my thumb to the open doorway and say, "Bathroom."

I exit the room quickly and get into the hall bath before anyone catches up with me. I'll have to come out eventually, but for the next few minutes, I can be alone and avoid the judgmental questions regarding Ian. How dare any of them judge him. He's no more screwed up than the rest of us.

It takes a few minutes, but when I eventually realize that I can't very well spend the entire night pretending to be occupied in the bathroom, I splash water on my face and open the door. I take one step into the hall before my eyes land on the leather vest crowding the space in front of me. My hands fly up in front of me and land on his hard chest. His chin is tilted downward, and his deep brown eyes are almost kind now, a slight difference from earlier at the kitchen table. His blank expression gives way to a regretful one. He lifts his hand and pushes his hair away from his beautifully scarred face and gives me what I think is supposed to be a smile.

"You ate soup." His words are so soft and comforting. It's lovely. I want more of this softer side, but honestly, I'll take any side he wants to show me. Even the angry, maniacal side I know lingers just below the calm exterior he always displays around me.

"I did."

His chest rises and falls a little quicker now, and ever so slowly he lifts his hand to cup my cheek but stops just before touching me. Just like the other night. I give him a gentle, discontented smile. My head tilts into the palm of his hand. I relish the feel of his touch. He won't hurt me. He'll never hurt me. I don't even have to will away the panic. It never creeps in. For a split second, my eyes fall closed. I let my body settle into this feeling of security, something I don't think I've ever had quite like this. When I open my eyes again, I find that his are closed. I want to let this moment drag out forever, but I know it will end eventually. Everything good must end.

"Did good, babe." Cautiously, he slips his hand away from my cheek and opens his eyes. I lift my head and give him a gentle nod. I don't want him to leave. God, I don't want him to leave so much it hurts.

"Where are you going?" I ask. It's none of my business. Damn it. I hate that it's none of my business.

"Clubhouse. Party."

"Oh." I want to come but don't want to ask. My lingering comment hangs in the air awkwardly. Somehow he understands that I want to go. I know he does. I can see him working out the options in his head. Leave me here, take me with him. Stay here with me. He kind of has to go. The club would probably rag on him for ditching out. That is, assuming, he doesn't even want to be there. What do I know, anyway? Nothing, that's what.

"We're on my bike." His words come out tense and uneven. He's not happy with what he's saying, but he does anyway. I try to hold back the squeal that builds in my throat. My cheeks heat from the effort. "You remember what I told you? Anyone caught dealing to you answers to me?"

"Yes, sir. I haven't forgotten," I say casually with a huge smile on my face. I can't help it. It's like a date, only it's not a date. But it's with Ian, and I'll take whatever I can get. Something in my reply catches him off guard. His eyes darken and he smiles, a look so sinister I think Satan himself would run for cover. But I don't run. Instead I take a step closer to him and slowly reach out for him to take my hand. He wraps his large hand around mine gently and pulls me down the hallway. It feels amazing. My stomach does flips and my heart speeds up.

I've always been addicted to something. As a kid, it was Barbies. As a teen, it was nail polish. Then I met Heath and it was all about him, and then the drinking and the drugs, and then the no swearing. And now it's Ian and getting better.

He's my favorite addiction to date.

Chapter 7

WE WALK OUT of the house hand in hand just in time to see Grady and Duke take off down the driveway and speed off down the road. The deafening growl of their bikes quiets as they disappear in the distance. And it's just us. Beside me, Ian lets out a heavy breath. He's not relaxed, exactly, but he seems to be settling into something. I like him like this, when he seems so settled and just here in the moment. Just us. We won't be alone for long, but I like the little bit I get.

"You ride?"

I shake my head. He turns his face toward mine and waits as though I haven't answered him. Maybe he thinks I haven't. I guess I've been silent too long, because he squeezes my hand and continues to stare at me with searching eyes. I shake my head again, and this time he sees it and nods his head in return. He drops my hand and climbs on his bike. He nudges the kickstand up and holds the bike upright, offering me a helmet with an outstretched hand.

"Wear this, then climb on like I did and place your feet here," he says and points to a cylindrical black peg that juts out of the bike. "Don't drop your feet and let your body lean into the turns."

He's patient with me as I stand here and psych myself up. I've had maybe a fantasy or two about a sexy man on a motorcycle, but until Ian it was just that—a passing fantasy that went as quickly as it came.

With his pointer finger, he summons me forward and sets the helmet on the tank between his legs. His eyes aren't kind, exactly, and they're not dark and sexy. They're something else that I'm desperate to place but can't. I close the distance between us and stand before him. Slowly, he reaches out and brushes a lock of hair from my face and tucks it behind my ear.

"Tell me where you're at," he says quietly. He tucks my hair behind my other ear as well. I let out a soft, unintentional sigh. I barely hear the question—or order rather—and instead have all my attention focused on his touch. Being able, and even wanting, to be touched is such a wonder. "Tell me I help."

There's such a vulnerability about him in this moment as his fingers lightly weave through my messy hair and he asks for reassurance. My breath halts in my lungs. I both loathe and love the sound of his plea. I didn't even know he was capable of this. Ian is always so strong for me that I think I sometimes forget he's human.

"I need you." The words come out on a whisper. I should be mortified, but I'm not. It's the realest thing I've ever said.

He's silent. Too silent. I don't like it. His eyes tell me he's a million miles away, and with every moment that passes, he seems to get further and further away.

I lift my hand to touch his cheek but stop, thinking better of it. I just . . . want to touch him. I want to initiate touch. I just don't know if he's going to be okay with it. More than worrying about upsetting him, I fear I may never heal past this point if I don't act now. So I let the tips of my fingers touch his jaw.

He sucks in a sharp breath and instantly, he's back with me. Focused deep-brown eyes practically dive into my soul. I want to look into his eyes, I want to drink him in, but it's too much. My eyes are back on my fingertips as they ghost across his cheek up to the side of his nose. They travel over his nasal bridge so slowly, lovingly, and across the ridge of his brow. I can barely contain the excitement at the prospect of what I'm about to do, what I've wanted to do for months. At the outer edge of his brow, I watch my fingers slide down to the corner of his eye. The raised, damaged skin is rough to the touch. Uncomfortable even. My fingers have traveled halfway across the scar to his ear before his hand shoots up and he pulls away from my touch.

"You don't like people touching your scars." I get it. I don't like people touching my scars either. I just couldn't help myself.

"I don't like the pity that comes with that scar." Despite the rushed, almost angry way the words come out, his voice is still soft. Even when he's uncomfortable, he's gentle with me. Maybe too gentle.

"It's not pity," I say. I always thought he got the scar that runs from the corner of his eye to his ear from some kind of club-related run-in. I might have pitied him when I first found out the truth—that his mother's ex, his siblings' father, sliced his little six-year-old face up—but that was before I knew him. I like him just the way he is—scars and all. "It's acceptance. You are who you are because of your scars."

He nods his head after what feels like a long time but is probably just a moment or two. I've done everything but write *Mindy loves Ian* on my freaking forehead, and all the man does is nod. I'm such an idiot. While I'm beating myself up for falling for a guy whose primary means of communication is a head nod, Ian goes about placing the helmet on my head, securing the strap beneath my chin, and making sure it fits properly. To my surprise, it fits almost perfectly.

"What about your helmet?" I ask, looking around for another helmet. There isn't another one, though.

"Don't need one." Ah, it's another one of his double standards. I want to ask about those but decide I've pushed his communication capabilities enough for one day. I want Ian to feel comfortable opening up to me, and that won't happen if I try to force it.

Placing my hands on Ian's shoulders, I swing an unsteady leg over the bike. I settle on the small, raised passenger seat and make sure my feet are on the pegs as they're supposed to be. I don't know how I'm going to be able to hang on when this thing gets moving, but I can't back out now.

Be brave.

There's several inches of space between my legs and Ian's back, so I wiggle forward until the insides of my knees comfortably meet the leather of his cut. My hands drag down his shoulders to the curved patch that says FORSAKEN. I don't give too much time to it and continue on my path. I pause at the rough, worn feel of the beautifully stitched patch at the center of the leather. I've done a little research on the club but haven't found much. I've even managed to get a bit out of my dad, who grouched that, unlike some clubs, Forsaken doesn't have much of an online presence, making it more difficult to find out what they're up to. The little bit I did find out is mostly stuff I don't want to know.

"She gets loud. You'll feel her when I start her up."

"I'll be okay."

Because I have you.

Ian's shoulders jerk and he leans forward. I hear a click and then the bike roars beneath us. The bike feels alive with its warmth and vibrations. It's intoxicating. The noise and the motion should all be sending me into a panic, but they're not. Somehow, they center me. Being on such a strong, powerful machine gives me a sense of perspective. I could freak out over the noise or the vibrations. But then, we could also crash and die on the side of the road. Thinking of it that way kind of mellows me out. The worst that could happen is that I could die, and then none of it matters anymore.

"You have to hold on tight," he says over his shoulder. His voice is just loud enough for me to hear him.

I smile softly to myself and wrap my arms around his torso. The cool, worn leather of his vest feels wonderful against my body. Ian's chest expands as he sucks in a deep breath and revs the engine. The bike jolts forward, and we roll down the driveway and accelerating when we're on the street. He blows out a breath when our speed evens. My hands grip his torso, and I pull my chest into his back and place my cheek against the leather. I can't really describe how it feels to be here, on his bike, with my arms wrapped around him.

I love this. I really love how freeing and altogether exciting this is. With anyone else, I would be terrified and hating the rush of wind that presses in on us. I can't imagine I would be able to handle the way our bodies lean into the pavement when we turn, or that I would be okay pressing myself into another person in such an intimate way. But this is Ian, and it seems he's the exception to every rule.

We make it across town without hitting a single red light and only have to slow down twice on our journey. Even when I've been running late to work or for an important meeting, I've not been this happy to speed through town. The rush, even at slow speeds, is just too incredible to be forced to break at a light. I can't even believe he gets to do this every day—be this free, in the wind, and so exposed to the world around him. It's all too much and yet not enough at the same time.

"What's the big deal about motorcycles anyway?" I ask Nic. She looks at me blankly for a long moment before nodding her head. Nic's dad brought her up on the back of his bike, so of course this question would catch her off guard. She seems to get it, though. I don't know anything about the lifestyle she's so accustomed to.

"It's not something you can explain. It's something you have to feel." She doesn't elaborate. She doesn't have to—her smile says it all.

I remember being jealous of Nic at one point—being jealous that she understood this unexplainable thing. This urge to ride and be free and feel like you're living your life to the fullest. Even if you're not doing anything but getting from point A to point B, the ride itself is exciting enough to make you feel like you're living on the edge.

Excited shouts take me out of the moment. My eyes dart ahead of us, finding that we're pulling into the parking lot of Forsaken Custom Cycle. Up ahead is the tall chain-link fence that surrounds the clubhouse. Black privacy slats keep Forsaken's home base private. Two prospects, Jeremy and Rob—nicknamed Baby Boy and Squat, respectively—stand at either end of the open gate. It's rare these days that the clubhouse gates are left open, really only at times like now when there's a party going on and somebody is standing guard. There's too much danger in our small town.

Ian pulls us through the open gates and gives both Jeremy and Rob a head nod. I turn my attention toward Rob and give him a sad smile as we pass. He raises a hand, his expression much like mine. Apologetic, sorrowful. Angry. I don't really know him, but Aaron talked about him a lot. They were best friends. They decided to prospect together, lived together. Rob and Aaron were as close as brothers. Now that Aaron's gone, I can't help but worry that Rob's all alone. Nobody should have to lose their best friend. Especially not a friend like Aaron.

The bike slows as we near the line of Harleys backed up against the fence near the clubhouse's entrance. Ian places his heavy feet on the ground and backs us into a wide opening in the middle of the lineup. He cuts the bike off and waits while I slowly realize it's time for me to get off. I don't want to, but I can't very well just sit here all night. If I thought he'd even remotely let me get away with that, I'd huddle in closer to him and never let go. But I'm not that brave and don't know his limits well enough yet to be that obstinate.

Ian's abs flex under my touch as I slide my arms from around his middle and up to his shoulders. I steady myself with his solid, masculine frame as I climb off the bike. The ride was only a few minutes, but it was so addictive. My inner thighs feel a little strained by the position, but in a good way. In a way that tells the story of a woman who did something new. I like this Mindy a hell of a lot better than the Mindy I was even a week ago.

On the pavement, I back up a few feet to allow Ian room to put the kickstand in place and swing off the bike. He's behind me now as I walk toward the door to the clubhouse. There are random people hanging around on the worn wooden picnic benches, some smoking and all drinking. The parking lot is full of cars and bikes and men standing around in leather vests appraising the Harleys and the women. I like the scene before me. Nothing is particularly scary or awful, despite what my parents would say about the lifestyle the club perpetuates. Ian's eyes catch my attention, and they're focused on something to my right. I follow his gaze to find a black Mercedes sitting at the end of the lot, hogging up two spaces. If he's surprised by the presence of such a pretentious car in the lot, he doesn't verbalize it. We look away and our eyes meet. I see something in his expression that I dislike immensely. His deep-brown eyes watch me closely, and even though he's not speaking, he doesn't really need to. He wants to say something, but he doesn't know how.

"Whose car is that?" There. I took the weight off his shoulders by asking.

"The Italian's," he says. His words feel like a betrayal with how little emotion he shows. Now I get it. The Italian is the guy who kept coming to the coffee shop I used to work at. He's the one I thought was going to ask me out before he kidnapped me and Holly. He was polite about it, but that doesn't mean I enjoyed the experience any more. It was awful. Aside from being handsome, any man who kidnaps a woman—regardless of the reasons—is an asshole.

I focus on the man before me and try to decide if that's necessarily true. I don't consider Ian to be an asshole, but that doesn't mean he isn't one. He's been good to me. Kind even. Still, from the way Nic and Holly talk about him, I know he's done far more for the club than just politely kidnap a couple of women. Ian Buckley has blood on his hands. I just don't know how much.

"You good?" Ian asks. I nod my head and let him lead me inside the clubhouse.

I can't get into the whole kidnapping-forced relocation-attack drama right now. I've been doing good today, and I refuse to ruin it with my memories. I ate soup today and I rode on a Harley and Ian is good to me, and that's what really matters. What he does apart from me is none of my business.

Inside, the clubhouse is filled with people hanging off furniture and one another haphazardly. They're drinking and smoking—more than just cigarettes—and eating baked goods that I bet have a little kick in the recipe. I make a mental note to avoid baked goods at the clubhouse before asking Ian about them first. There's more men than women here, but the women who are here are all either totally naked or mostly naked. It feels weird being here and not being one of their girls. Not that I want to be one of their girls. I just . . . I've heard how these parties go. I know the old ladies don't hang around the clubhouse unless it's either family time or their old man is with them. I'm not Ian's old lady, so would I be welcome here without him?

Probably not.

As the crowd thickens, Ian reaches back and takes my hand in his. He keeps me close to him. This is all so overwhelming and even though nobody is really paying attention to us, being in an enclosed space with so many people I don't know is starting to prickle my fear. I give his hand a squeeze. For reassurance or appreciation—I don't know which.

He stops, spinning around quickly and leveling a furious gaze at everybody around us. I blink back my surprise and do the only thing I can to make the situation less intense. I rub my thumb along the back of his hand in what I hope is a soothing manner. Something he sees settles him, and we go back to trudging through the crowd. Ian's head swings to the left and the right with precision as he mean-mugs everyone we pass. A few of the members of the Fort Bragg charter shoot him confused looks until their eyes land on me, like I'm a missing puzzle piece, and they give me one of those man nods.

Wyatt, the club's vice president, stands at the bar up ahead. A young brunette, whom I think I recognize as one of Cheyenne's friends, hangs off one of his arms. In his other arm, he's holding a beer that he finishes off and slaps on the bar top, not paying the girl any mind. His eyes lift as he spots Ian and communicates something with his gaze. No words pass between the two men, just a series of head nods and a few grunts. Wyatt moves off the stool he's been occupying and steps back. The brunette moves to dodge his large body and disappears into the crowd. It's only now that I notice she's not wearing pants—a tank top, thong underwear, and fishnets with stilettos on her feet, but no freaking pants.

"Stay here," Ian says. He turns toward me and directs me onto the offered stool, which I take. Dipping his head close to my ear, he finishes with, "Soda or water. No booze or anything else that might make me unhappy."

His words are menacing, meant to be taken seriously. And I do take him seriously, but I don't fear him like I think he wants me to. He could hurt me in so many ways and I still don't think I'd fear him. He's Ian.

"You're leaving me here alone?" God, I sound like such a freaking baby. His answering smile is all I need to relax a little.

"Club business, babe. Can't avoid it. Chel will take care of you." He nods behind the bar and tips his head to me. I follow his gaze to a barely dressed woman pouring drinks and giving Ian a sexy smile. It's not flirty in an immature way or anything. It's just sultry and sexy and all woman. Her eyes slide to me with a friendly smile. She moves close and leans across the bar.

Her voice is low as she says, "Every man in here saw you walk in with Ian. I'll watch over you, but you don't need it."

"I'm not worried about . . ." I stop myself. I don't really know how to say what I want to say. Maybe I don't even know what I'm trying to say, but either way it's just not coming out right.

"Remember my warning, Melinda," Ian says, his lips brushing my ear. A tingle runs down my spine at the unexpected contact. I should be terrified. I should cringe. I don't. Instead, I just breathe him in and enjoy this perfect tiny moment. And I nod. Because I've suddenly realized that he's waiting for a response.

"Good girl." So tenderly, he places a kiss to the top of my head. My eyes flutter closed in response to his intimate touch. I force them open and watch as he leaves with Wyatt.

From the corner of my eye I notice the vested men we passed on our way in. Their eyes are on me. Some staring curiously and some inspecting, but they're all paying attention. It's not dirty or scary, it's just . . . interesting. If I didn't know better, I'd say it's a look of respect. But that doesn't make any sense.

"Water or pop?" Chel asks from behind the bar.

"Pop?" I turn and try to get into the conversation with her, but it's hard. Everything is so unnerving here.

"Soda." I wrinkle my nose at the foreign term but don't ask. She elaborates anyway. "I'm from the Midwest. I guess some things you never lose."

I give her a genuine smile and decide that I like her. "Water's fine."

She's only gone for a moment before she returns with a bottle of water and hands it to me. I take a large gulp and will myself to chill out. Chel seems nice and Ian trusts her, so that's something. With every sip of water, I feel more comfortable in this space. I wasn't pleased about Holly's relationship with Grady at first, but I can't deny the appeal of this world. I watch idly as Chel serves drinks and chats up different men. Some seem to communicate something deeper than a beverage request to her, and others take their drinks and leave.

Taking a break from my people-watching, I send Holly a text to let her know where I went. I get the notification that she's seen the message, but she doesn't respond. That's okay. I was a jerk for ditching her when we were supposed to hang out, and I can't really blame her for being upset with me. After a few minutes, I give up waiting for a response and shove the phone back in my pocket. The man beside me vacates his stool, and it's not long before another man takes his place. I try not to be fearful of every movement and each noise I don't immediately recognize.

An eerily familiar scent fills my nostrils. It's a decadent combination that smells woody and earthy but clean at the same time. I tense from head to toe and battle to maintain my composure. I used to love this scent, but now it brings me back to a time I'm still struggling to get past. Very slowly, I turn toward the scent, already knowing what I'll find. I'm going to find the owner of the black Mercedes. I'm going to find a man in an impeccable suit, and he's going to be handsome and strong and polite, even when he's in the midst of carrying out a kidnapping.

I've barely caught sight of his olive complexion when he notices I'm staring and turns to face me. His lips form a smile.

"Melinda Mercer. It's nice to see you." He sounds friendly, as he always did pre-kidnapping. Well, he was friendly mid-kidnapping as well. But that doesn't mean it wasn't still scary. It was the beginning of everything that led to *that* night. And whether it makes sense or not, I fucking hate him for it.

"Go to hell."

Chapter 8

"THAT'S NO WAY for a lady to talk, now is it?"

"Bite me." The words slip off my tongue quickly, before consider the repercussions. The last time I saw him, he warned me and Holly that he doesn't like to be yelled at and greatly values compliance. But that's when we were at home, and my nails were wet, and I was caught off guard. I've met bigger monsters than him and lived through it. Still, my hands shake around my mostly empty water bottle. I grip the plastic tighter to make it less obvious, but all that does is create a crunching sound.

"You have no reason to fear me." His dark brown eyes are on my nervous hands. Those eyes and his bright white smile used to make my breath hitch. They used to make me blush. I used to think about all the things I didn't expect to think about again. But that was before. That was when my only concern was that no man worth dating would want to date a junkie. Doesn't matter that I've been clean for four years now. Once a junkie, always a junkie. The only thing worse than being a junkie is being sexually impotent. Put the two together and the only thing left for me is my fantasies.

"You were an unfortunate casualty in a war you have no part in." I think he's trying to comfort me, but I can't really tell. Men in expensive suits with fancy cologne and luxury cars don't grovel. Not that men in dirty jeans and worn leather vests grovel either. Actually, the only man I ever saw grovel was Heath. We were so young then. If he were still here, I don't know if the man he would have become would grovel now. Maybe not.

I quickly pull myself from my thoughts and look around. How the hell did he get in here? How has nobody pulled a gun on him yet?

"What the hell are you doing here?" I practically shout in panic. Peeking down the bar, I see that Chel is busy with a burly, older man with a long graying beard. He says something she must like, because she reaches across the bar and gives him a peck on the cheek with a sultry wink.

"Relax, Bean. We've come to a truce." The confident smirk on his face angers me. It sends shivers down my spine and a vengeful hatred to my heart. This man scared me. He made me suffer in relative discomfort on a sea wall, and my only crime was being home on my day off. He left me there to wonder if I would make it home that night, if the tide would sweep me away, or if I was left there to rot.

"You're not allowed to call me that. Actually, don't call me anything." I could stab him in the face. I mean, I could slap him at least. I won't, but I want to. How dare he call me that nickname. How dare he call me anything.

"Let me make it up to you." Still with the fucking smirk. "Another water?"

Ian's words float into my mind. The warning he gave me at Smirk's house was terrifying. I haven't tried to score since. Still, it's a lot of responsibility he's placed on my shoulders. If there's one thing I'm sure of, it's that Ian doesn't make empty promises.

The next person you try to score from dies. The next person who hurts you dies. The next person who stands too close to you, looks at you wrong, or just bugs me fucking dies.

The man beside me raises his glass of brown liquid, empties it in one sip, and then shakes the glass at me suggestively.

. . . or just bugs me fucking dies.

I can't drink. I can't. I mean, I can control myself. I can

stop myself from falling back into the rabbit hole. I know I can. I don't want anyone else to get hurt. I don't want to cause anyone pain, aside from myself, that is. And yet, the wheels are in motion and I can't stop myself.

"Vodka. I'd love a vodka." I contain my smile and try for relenting to an unfavorable request. Ian won't really kill him if they've entered a truce, would he? He couldn't. I just can't believe he would, and that's how I convince myself this is okay. I rub the black chip in my pocket and force myself to feel the pang of sadness.

Four years, two months, and fifteen days.

Four years of keeping a needle out of my arm.

Leo gets Chel's attention and asks her for a vodka. Her eyes slide to mine and in a bitch move, I shake my water bottle at her innocently. She gives in and brings the vodka to Leo quickly along with a new bottle of water that she places in front of me.

Four years and two months of staying sober.

I turn my body toward Leo and take the glass of vodka in my hands. He shifts on his stool to give me more of his attention. The smile on my face is apologetic, but he might not know that. He might think I'm grateful or that I'm trying to get over what happened between us. He'll soon find out how very wrong he is.

"I don't like you, and I don't want to get to know you."

Four years, two months, and fifteen days of being the new Mindy and now the new broken Mindy.

I hate both of them with equal vigor.

"But thank you for the vodka." *One sip, Mindy. All it takes is one sip.* I force a smile to my face, more of a grin really, and bring the glass to my lips. The vodka smells like regret and self-hatred. It smells like desperation. It smells like the worst mistake I'm ever going to make, because now I know what awaits me at the bottom of the glass.

Be brave.

Tipping the glass up just enough to taste the vodka on my

lips, I fight back the churning in my stomach. Shit. I forgot how repulsive liquor is. I guess that's why people drink to the point of being drunk. It's not like this stuff tastes good. Its real purpose is to numb the world around you—to numb everything until the world you live in is tolerable enough to continue to exist in. And with that thought in mind, I swallow the little bit I manage to get into my mouth. With more confidence than I feel, I lower the glass and stare into Leo's eyes.

"It was nice knowing you, Leo." It wasn't, but it doesn't matter. His dark brown eyes are suspicious and shifty now. The more nervous he becomes, the more inclined I am to drink. It's powerful, holding this man's future in my hands. Intoxicating in a way I don't think even heroin could be. Instead of being out of it and lost to the world, this power gives me a sense of self, an awareness I don't know that I've ever had before. I force another sip down my throat before I give up and set the glass down on the bar. I can't finish it. Finishing it would be going back to where I was before.

Four years, two months, and fifteen days.
And now I'm back to zero.

Tears form in my eyes, my heart speeds up, and there's a sickening lump in my throat. Leo is still giving me an unnerving look. It's the only thing that makes any of this any better—knowing that I can unsettle the mafioso.

"Before we part ways, just tell me one thing. Was it worth it?" As I wait for his response, I dig my black chip out of my pocket and hold it in my lap.

"You're taking my actions more personally than you should."

"But was it worth it?"

"I believe in my cause, so yes."

"Good," I say with a firm nod. I'm so focused on my task that I don't notice the wavy blondish-brown head of hair barreling toward us until I already have my black chip out on the bar top in front of Leo. His jaw ticks as he focuses in on the chip.

"Was it worth it?" he asks.

Worth what? My sobriety? My soul? Is anything worth losing myself? The harsh tang of vodka on my tongue is the only answer I have.

"Yes."

It's barely a moment before Leo is pulled off his stool and he's spun around, facing a familiar face that I barely recognize. There's a vicious snarl emanating from Ian. It's so guttural, raw even, that I shrink back on my stool. Tears well in my eyes that I can't bring myself to wipe away. I should, though. I can't sit here and cry like a bitch after what I've done. I deserve whatever I get. We all do, I guess.

"Did you forget?" The nasty bark of words aren't for Leo—they're for me.

"No."

"I always make good on my promises, Melinda." Ian leans in close to Leo as he spits the words out. The men around us jump to their feet, with Ryan and Duke appearing out of the crowd, each with a gun trained on Leo.

"Give me a reason, asshole," Ryan says. His trigger finger lowers and lifts and then lowers again.

"What happened, brother?" Duke asks and slowly lowers his gun. His angry glare turns to confusion quickly.

"Tell me the rules, Melinda," Ian grinds out. Leo's arms are raised in the air now. He's shaking his head with his angry eyes on me.

"The next person I try to score from dies," I say flippantly.

"Were you fucking confused?"

"No. You said you always make good on your promises." Ian pulls his face back from Leo just enough to turn his attention to me. He stares at me searchingly, like he's struggling to find the logic behind my actions. The entire room is still save for the men rushing in from other rooms, obviously having been alerted to what's happening at the bar. Even Ryan lowers his gun and waits for an answer.

"I hate him," I say with such fire that I surprise myself. I can't punish the men who really hurt me, so I'm going to punish the one who could have. It doesn't matter that the club made a truce with the guy. I didn't choose to forgive him. I didn't choose to let him walk away. I don't get to choose anything except this. The only power I have is the power Ian's given me, and I'm going to wield it as I like.

"Somebody babysit the WOP," Ian says and shoves Leo back down on his stool. He's moving so quickly I don't see him drop low and wrap his arms around my torso until I'm propped up on his shoulder with my butt in the air.

Shit.

This shouldn't be hot, and I shouldn't be okay with this kind of touching.

But it is, and I am.

It's not the vodka giving me the courage—it's Ian.

The crowd parts around us as Ian hauls me off down a hallway lined with doors on both sides. We enter an unlocked room, and he slams the door behind us. His chest heaves beneath me, and I think I can even hear his nostrils flaring. Blood is rushing to my head, making my position on his shoulder uncomfortable. Wisely, I don't voice my concern. He seems like he needs to calm down before talking to me. Or looking at me. Or putting me down apparently.

The discomfort becomes too much. Gently, I place my hands on his cut, toward the bottom right, on top of the upward curving bottom patch that proudly says CALIFORNIA, and take a deep breath as I use my arms to help me lift my head for a better view of the room. Even beneath the patch and the leather and the shirt he's wearing, I can feel the firm muscles of his lower back. Though he isn't as bulky as some of his brothers, he's certainly well-built in all the right places—from what I can tell at least. My face heats at thoughts of the right places I don't yet know. His muscles tick beneath my touch, like he's surprised by it. I guess he has a right to be. Considering he's really the only person I welcome to touch me—and even that in itself is scary—he has a right to be surprised that I would initiate touch in this way. I don't understand why he's the exception, but he is, and I'm tired of trying to work it out in my head.

While I wait for him to set me down, I survey my surroundings. The room is small—with a large bed that's minimally dressed and a worn black trunk on the side that's functioning as a nightstand. There's a few empty beer bottles on top of the trunk and a pile of used matches scattered around the bottles. The wall opposite the door is exposed brick, but the other three walls are painted black. The depth of the darkness makes it feel like the room is smaller than I think it actually is. There's nothing personal about the space at all, just a few strange items attached to the walls. One wall has what looks like leather handcuffs bolted into the black concrete wall. They hang at a curious height with a few feet between them. It isn't until my eyes find the large menacing whip hanging next to the cuffs that I put two and two together and realize what the cuffs are for.

Oh God.

Is this a torture chamber? My eyes drift back to the bed. No, I guess it's for a different kind of torture.

Oh God.

I want to look away, but I can't. I've read books about this kind of stuff—books that I'd never admit to reading—and the participants always enjoy themselves. But I've read books about crazed heroes who do really screwed up stuff and somehow they always come out smelling like roses in the end. The real world doesn't work that way. It just doesn't.

"Um, Ian." I don't really have anything to say, but I feel obligated to say something. I need to do something, anything. I just can't hang here on his shoulder, staring at his . . . whatever they are . . . and not saying anything.

"Silence." He barks out the word with such ferocity that his torso vibrates, and his grip on my legs tightens. Something about the whip and handcuffs knocks me off my game, and I'm nervous. I shouldn't have set Leo up like that. I still don't like the guy. At the absolute least, he's a douche bag. That doesn't mean I should have tried to get him hurt.

I'm jostled from my thoughts when Ian bends and drops me to my feet and takes a step away from me. His brown eyes are searching for an answer I don't have. They're narrowed and unkind. I definitely haven't gotten this look from him before. I've gotten the grimace and even the displeased pout. But this is different. Instead of sorrow or disappointment in Ian's eyes, I see anger. For the first time since I've met him, I see what he must look like when he's taking care of club business. This isn't my Ian. This is Ian, the treasurer of Forsaken. This is the guy who unsettles Sterling Grady. And I start to doubt how well I know him after all.

"Five," he says. His upper lip rises in a snarl, and the raised skin of his scar crinkles near his eye. Shit. He's scary like this.

My hands shake at my sides, so I shove them into my jean pockets as far as I can to hide my fear. For some reason I don't think he'll care much if he knows how badly he's scaring me.

"Four."

My eyes go wide and, like the crazy lady that I'm turning into, I raise my arms in the air and start waving them frantically.

"Why are you counting down?"

"Three."

Oh fuck.

Oh fuck.

Oh fuck.

"No, really," I say and then cover my mouth because, even though he's looking at me, his eyes are unfocused and I'm not sure he's really looking *at* me as much as through me.

"Two."

Suddenly I remember the night at the park.

I own you at one.

Holy crap.

I can't really process what's going on here. I've never been in a position like this before. Holly and I grew up with the club at arm's length. They were always a distant enough nuisance. Even when we were in school, we didn't really cross paths with the club kids. Ryan, Ian, and Duke were a year behind Holly and a few years ahead of me. Nic was a year behind me, and even though we all grew up in the same small town and an even smaller school, I didn't know any of the club kids back then. I hung out with a very different group than they did. I think maybe if I had more experience with them and their world, I might know how to act here.

"One." Ian's eyes shine and the word comes out so slowly. There's a sense of pride in his voice, but it's overshadowed by the predatory grin he's sporting.

"Who do you belong to, Melinda?"

"You."

What the hell did I just say? Why did I say that? I don't even know what belonging to someone *means*, much less if I'm even capable of belonging to Ian. Surely he has expectations—expectations I doubt I can fulfill.

"I gave you a chance to be responsible for yourself, but twice now you've proven to me that you can't handle it. From now on, I make your decisions for you."

What in the hell . . .

Ian's disturbing grin falls as he stares at me, expressionlessly. His brow is smooth and his eyes look bored as he stands there silently. Something has shifted in him, and I can't figure out what it is or why. He's not normally like this with me. He's been so even-keeled and gentle with me, but this isn't gentle. This is a darker side of him that I need to take note of. Holly and Nic tried to warn me for a reason, and even if I don't really know what those reasons are, I can't ignore that they exist.

"Tell me you understand," he says. Despite the rapid-fire freak-out going on inside my head, I can't stop the blossoming excitement that's spreading through me. Ian won't hurt me. He said I'm not safe with him, but being safe and getting hurt are totally different. Aren't they?

"Tell me." His jaw is locked with his demand.

Suddenly I want something from him so fiercely that it takes me by surprise.

"You keep saying I'm not safe with you. Why not?"

He pauses but eventually relents.

"I want certain things. I like certain things. You're never going to like what I want to give you." His voice is strained as he speaks the words.

"Tell me then," I say on a plea.

"When I think about you, I want to fuck you hard and raw, and it would hurt. You're not ready for it. You won't like it. I won't make us both suffer by even trying it, so no, you're not safe with me."

"You can't be gentle?" I ask.

"I've never tried. I don't know if I'm capable of gentle. But I'd try—for you."

My breath catches, and my legs are wobbly. He's trying to scare me—and it's working—but even more than that, I'm intrigued.

"Show me what it's like," I say. "I just . . . I need this . . . I need to see it." If what he wants to do to me, to give to me, is so terrible, I have to see it for myself.

Chapter 9

I LET MY eyes fall closed as I wait in the dark and silent room for Mindy. It's rare that the pleasure palace is this quiet, but I worked it out with Pop. He didn't ask questions, and I didn't give any explanations. I couldn't do this with Mindy in my room. I just couldn't think about hurting her in that space I'll have to return to again and again. And this will hurt her. I know it will.

I'm leaning back against a cold, dirty mirror that lines the entire wall. My head rests on the glass. Thirty seconds pass. A minute passes. Then two minutes, and Mindy is still not here with me.

I gave her a choice. Kind of. She doesn't have to come, but I want her to.

Another minute passes, and I fight back the desire to slam my head into the surface behind me. It's a mirror, not a plaster wall. The painful breaking of my flesh would bring a much-needed and welcome relief, but I'm not here to make myself feel better.

I'm here for her.

Slowly, the door squeaks open. Basked in the light from the hallway is Mindy. Her face is shrouded in the darkness of the room, but I'd recognize her reddish-blonde hair and the curves of her body anywhere.

She reaches into the room and flips the switch on the wall. The light is so bright that it makes me blink. It bounces off the opposite wall that's also lined with mirrors, perfectly showing my reflection. I hate that I can see myself standing here waiting for her.

"You meant what you said?" she asks. I don't ignore the twinge of hope I think I hear laced in her words. Not something I'd give to just anyone. But this is Mindy, and I'll give her what she needs.

"Of course," I say. My own voice doesn't sound like how I think it should. I should sound bored or confident, but I don't. I've never been here before, never promised a woman what I've promised her. Safety. Love. Myself. Even if I didn't say those words exactly, she should know they're what I meant.

"You can't . . ." she says and sucks in a deep breath before she continues. "You can't touch me, but I want you to. One day, I want to be touched. I want to be better.

"I need to see it," she says. Her high octave crawls almost impossibly higher as she takes a single step into the room. How the fuck am I going to *show* her if she won't let me *touch* her? She takes another step in the room and steps aside, showing me a woman standing behind her in nothing but a pair of black panties. I recognize her as Kaz, a nurse who likes to party with us.

"Please," she says.

I shake my head and toss my hands up in the air. "This is too fucked up, even for me." I run my hands through my wavy hair. It feels slick to the touch from all the sweating I've apparently been doing while I waited for her in here. Fucking nerves, man.

"Ian," she says louder now. Her voice shakes as her brown eyes grow wild with fear. "I need this. You promised me you'd help me that you'd take care of me."

In an instant, I've pushed off the mirror and have closed the distance between us. I reach out and wrap an arm around her waist, pulling her close to me. Her body stiffens, tears now stream down her face, and she hiccups.

"Let me have this," she begs, careful not to touch me as much as possible. Mindy isn't good with gentle or kind. I know this. But I can't help the desire I have to give her something that's not entirely fucked.

Leaning in close to her ear, I whisper, "I can take care of you. I can be good to you. Let me show you that I can do more than I have been, just not this. Please not this. Let me show you that I can make love to you."

"I don't want that," she says, slowly stepping back and sliding out of my grasp. "I just want to see it."

"Yes you do," I say. I stay where I am though everything in me begs to reach out for her, to hold her and keep her safe. I'll protect her body *and* her heart. I'll keep every part of her safe even if I have to kill again to do it. "You had good once—you know how it felt. I know you remember the good in life, baby. Just let me bring a little of that back to you."

"*Show me*, Ian," she says. "Show me how you can make me feel."

"I will," I say and reach out for her.

But she pulls back and points to the woman still standing in the doorway. "On her. I can't be touched yet. I want to. I really do, but I keep replaying *that* horrible night in my head and making sex into this huge scary thing."

But she pulls back and points to the woman still standing in the doorway. "On her."

My gut twists, rejecting the idea. It's not like I've never done shit like this before. I've had complete strangers against walls, in bars, on pool tables. I've had them in public and in private, and I've had one at a time and more than I can count, usually with props. But I've never had this. If this wasn't Mindy, I'd already be fucking hard at the idea of some crazy chick watching me fuck. I like an audience, and I like it rough. Not everybody is into that, and a lot of women thought they could handle it only to run away screaming. But not with Mindy.

I don't want that with Mindy.

She's had fucked-up. She's had shit she didn't want, couldn't handle, and won't ever fucking get over.

I won't be another thing she has to get over.

I'm going to be the thing that pieces her back together.

Across the room, the woman loses her panties. Her fake tits don't move, and her too-perfect-to-be-natural tanned skin shows no awkward lines where she's paler. She's the perfect size in every respect, has the perfect face with perfect lips for sucking dick. The way she walks toward me is perfect, too. And I hate everything about her.

I want Mindy's natural breasts that I've never even touched. I want her tan lines and pale skin and her scars— everything that I see but can't feel. Every single one of her scars belongs to me now. She won't admit it, but I own them. All of her damage and her history are on my shoulders for me to take care of for her. To make sure they don't hurt her any more than they already have.

Kaz places her hands over my cut and drags them down to the buckle of my belt. She pulls at the aged leather and slowly pulls it out of my belt loops. I look up to Mindy to find her locking the door and taking a seat on the bar stool there by the light. She gives me a head nod that I guess is meant to reassure me. I don't feel reassured or confident. I feel like a scared child who fears that anything they do is going to get them into trouble. There are no safe choices.

"Show me how good you'll be to me," Mindy says. Her voice drags, making me wonder what she's feeling right now, if anything, or if she's totally numbed everything out.

I allow the woman to slide my cut off my shoulders. She catches it before it hits the ground and tosses it to Mindy. I don't let anybody handle my cut like that. I feel the frustration ease in my muscles when Mindy gives it a little sniff and then slides it on over her shirt. She should look ridiculous, sitting there with my cut draped over her shoulders—she swims in it. But she looks up at me in a sultry gaze that makes my jeans tight. She holds the worn leather between her hands, wrapping herself in it. She takes another sniff, and it's like she's bathing herself in me.

The blonde woman yanks my white shirt out of my jeans and runs her hands across my lower abdomen. She pops the top button of my jeans open and drags down my zipper. Before she can move any further, I lift her chin so that she's forced to look at me, and I say, "There is only one way this can work. You stay silent. I don't care how you feel. You say *nothing*. There are only two people in this room—me and her. You are nothing to me. Don't touch me, don't try to kiss me, and don't you dare fucking speak to me. Do you understand?"

She nods her head and removes her hands from my jeans and stands compliantly. Beside us is a chaise lounge with an inclined head rest. I take a step back and keep my eyes focused on Mindy. Not so deep in my soul I fear that she's not going to want me to do this and that she's going to freak out once it starts. Or worse, she'll feel nothing. But I know better than to try to push her and force her into something she's not ready for.

"Lie down, baby," I say, staring into my girl's brown eyes. She nods again as the woman complies. Stalling, I slowly take my white shirt off and toss it aside. Mindy's eyes travel over my naked chest, slowly surveying the tattoos and scars she's never seen before. "You like what you see?"

"Yes," Mindy says. She forces the word out on a ragged breath as she drags her index finger over the FORSAKEN patch of my cut. Directly beneath the patch is her pert breast and what I fucking hope is an erect nipple. I want to see them, taste them, feel them. But not yet. Maybe not ever.

I keep eye contact with her the whole time. Mechanically, I roll the condom on and fuck the faceless woman slowly and patiently—two things I didn't know I could be capable of. I try to make it good enough for her that she enjoys herself. I don't want Mindy getting the wrong impression, but every time the woman beneath me responds to my touch, my stomach rolls.

The longer it goes on and the more graphic the scene gets, the less Mindy's looking at anything in particular. She stares at me, not in my eyes, but through my eyes. I hate how long it takes me to get to where I need to be, but when I am, I focus myself enough to talk.

"This could be you, Melinda. And it wouldn't hurt. It wouldn't be scary. We could have this together. Tell me you could want this," I say through gritted teeth as I do my best to fight off my orgasm.

"I might want it," Mindy says. The woman beneath me arches her back and moans. I'm certainly not touching her anywhere I need to, but a quick look at her confirms that she's touching herself, rubbing small circles over her clit. Her insolence annoys me, and I find myself choking her as I pound into her more quickly, fiercely. I'm enraged with Kaz for making it about her when this is about Mindy. My hands around Kaz's neck sets off a chain reaction, and I come immediately.

There's a light in Mindy's eyes now that wasn't there before. She chews at her bottom lip and lowers her eyes. So quietly I almost miss it, she says, "I could want that, too."

Chapter 10

My arms are stretched out in front of me and my focus on-point as I unload the clip of bullets into a distant redwood. It's all I can do to distract myself from what I really want to focus on.

Mindy.

Christ. Mindy is a pain in my ass. The best kind of pain in my ass. I don't know what the fuck I was thinking. I have no business owning a woman like Mindy. I have no business owning anyone, but especially not a woman like her. She's good—too good—and she has no idea what being owned means. And I have no idea where her head is at. We haven't really spoken since that bullshit at the clubhouse. First, she went and tried to get me to hurt Scavo and then she begged me to fuck a lost girl. The whole night was fucked and when I dropped her off back at Grady's, she was acting fucked too. She seemed fine which is why I think she was acting strange. How could she not be fucked over that?

I empty another clip into the same tree before moving to another tree and changing my target. Too many more bullet holes and the redwood might not be able to take it. I don't like destroying things. People, sure. But not this tree. Unlike people, trees just exist and grow without intent to harm anyone.

Unlike Carlo Mancuso.

My hands make quick work of discarding the empty clip and sliding a new one into place. Taking a deep breath, I spin around and face the woods behind the house I'll always call home. In a matter of seconds, I fire off round after round into the trunk of the redwood until this clip is also empty. Again, I pivot and grab another full clip from the bench behind me, load it into the hand gun, and spin back toward the woods, ready to fire.

I hate him.

I hate him.

Ma always says the choices we make are a reflection of either what we fear or what we love. Giving up her twins in their infancy, in her words, was a reflection of her love for me. But she's full of shit. Giving them up was a reflection of a mother's ultimate fear. She couldn't stomach allowing one of us to die so she could keep the others—not that Carlo would have allowed her to live. In light of her fear, I choose love. Which is why I'm going to carve Carlo Mancuso's heart right out of his chest and hand deliver it to her. This war isn't about justice or revenge. It's about love—loving someone enough to kill for them.

My index finger slowly presses against the trigger just as a bright red figure comes into view at the tree line, hands raised in the air. "Please don't shoot!"

Alex.

Fuck.

What the hell was she doing in the woods? I'm not in the mood for this shit. Not that I ever am in the mood for this, but especially not now. Images of Carlo, her father, flash in my head. Sometimes it's easier to forget the man who raised my sister, and sometimes it's harder. Like now. She crosses the field quickly and comes to stand beside me. She's wearing a red leather jacket that's bright enough to make her a walking fucking target.

"That jacket bright enough?" I shouldn't be a dick to her. I'm trying not to be a dick to her.

"You think we need to worry about aerial snipers?" She smooths her long dark-brown hair down and pulls it up into a messy bun atop her head, using the hair tie on her wrist to secure it.

"Guess not." I click the safety in place and then shove my gun into the waistband of my jeans. "Something you need?"

Alex raises her eyebrows, her eyes bob around me, and she nods her head. Shit. Trying to not act like a dick has me doing exactly that. We're going to have to talk sometime, but does it really have to be now?

Alex turns around and heads for the tree line toward Ma and Pop's house, but she stops a few feet away and blows out a heavy breath.

"Why does this have to be so awkward between us?" She turns around and shifts from foot to foot. "It's almost been a year."

"Because I fantasize about killing your father." There. Honesty.

"I don't blame you," she says. Her cheeks redden and she looks away for a brief moment before meeting my eyes again. She lifts her chin and clears her throat. "I was raised to be seen and not heard. My father never asked me what I wanted for myself. He just made my choices for me, and I hated it. I can't hate him even though I want to. So even though I love my father, because he's still my father, I don't blame you for wanting to kill him. I don't know if I could blame you even if you do end up killing him."

I guess this is the most I can ask for from her. I still don't know how we're going to have a relationship when I want her father dead more than anything else on this planet. How could she ever forgive me? And Michael? I doubt he could move past it either.

"I will kill him. He deserves much more than death, but even I'm not sick enough to make him watch his children be sliced to pieces." She stands stock still at my words but doesn't break eye contact. I force myself to be as honest as possible because regardless of how I feel about the situation, regardless of the memories she stirs, she's still my sister. "I would never hurt you or Michael. Not just because it would hurt our mother, but because you're my sister. Michael's my brother. I won't hurt either of you."

Tears well in her eyes. Oh, for fuck's sake. No fucking crying. They don't fall down her cheeks, but they're there.

"I don't deserve this. I don't deserve any of it," she says. "Chief would be alive, so would Tegan, and Tall, and Michael's friends. Mindy never would have gotten hurt if it weren't for me."

"That's not on you. That's on Pop," I say with a nod. Because it is. If Alex has been carrying around this guilt, then it's time she drops it. My dad put the wheels in motion long before this war started.

"I like talking to you. I want to get to know you."

"What's the point in getting to know me when you're just going to end up hating me eventually anyway?" This is why I don't want to bond with her. I don't want to let her in and to love her the way Ma does, the way Michael does. Even Ryan loves her, and I'll be damned if Pop doesn't love her, too. She's squirrelly like that.

"I can't hate you. If I can't hate my father, then I can't hate you either. I won't ask you not to hurt him, and I can't tell you how I'll feel when he dies, because I don't know how I'll feel. But I can tell you this—he stole you and my mother from me. My father hurt you, and he hurt me in a different way. He hurt Michael, too, but he might be too proud to admit that just yet. Carlo Mancuso has his family, and I have mine."

She takes a step closer and reaches out, grabbing my arm. The tears she was holding back slide down her cheeks as she stares up at me.

"I don't like violence, and I hate to see people get hurt, but no matter who I am today, I was a principessa, a Mancuso. I understand the need for justice, and deep down, I know this war goes back further than last year and that it's only a matter of time for my father to get what's coming to him."

"I don't want to hurt you," I find myself saying. My chest aches and my jaw is tight. I reject the emotions that make me weak and force myself to think about anything but how good it feels to get this gift from her. "Every year on your birthday, we have a party. It used to be just me and Ma, and then when Pop and Ryan came around, they'd join in. It was always just something we did. Ma never wanted to forget either of you, and she made sure I never could. I don't want to hurt you, but I have to make this better for her."

"Will killing my father really make this better for her? Is that really going to help?" It's not judgment in her tone, I don't think. It's a young woman finally understanding why a man she loves has to die.

"Ma's never killed anyone. She came damn close once when I was a kid, but she stopped just before finishing the guy off. Motherfucker deserved to die, but she left him paralyzed. What that man did was far less brutal than what Carlo did to her. You might not understand the need for his death, but I do. I know a side of Ruby that I hope you never meet."

"What did the man do?" Her words come out so damn quiet that part of me wants to fucking hug her. Hugging usually makes women feel better. At least it does with Ma.

"Not important, but he deserved worse than he got. Everything that I am is because of our mother. I don't want her to go back to that dark place she was in before Pop came into our lives. I won't let her suffer any more. If taking out Carlo Mancuso gives her even an ounce of peace, then that's what I'll do."

"There's so much I don't know about your lives before I got here. I feel like I barely know you, and yet I feel like I know you all so well."

"You know us because you're one of us. You can't bring yourself to want Carlo dead, so that's why I'm here. I'll take care of what you don't want to do."

"You're more open than I expected," she says.

I let out a heavy sigh and swallow the lump in my throat. I'm more open than I expected, too. Fuck. When I don't say anything for a long while, she lifts her hand from my arm to the side of my face and softly brushes the scar her father put there. I flinch at the contact. It doesn't hurt, but I don't like people touching it. I'm selfish like that. This pain, this memory, is all mine, and I refuse to share it with anyone else.

"Anyone would be considered open compared to Ryan."

She laughs lightly, but her amusement doesn't reach her eyes. She drops her hand and folds her arms across her chest.

"Now that we're over the awkward sibling bonding thing, can we talk about letting me see Michael?"

"No. I'm not getting into a fucking fight with my brother over that shit." I will, but I don't want her thinking she can play me like she plays Ryan.

"Then can we talk about Mindy?" Her eyes are shining now in a mischievous manner as she says Mindy's name.

"Call her if you want to talk to her," I say. She won't, and Mindy won't have anything to say to her, not really, anyway. I have her under orders to not talk to anyone about what I have her doing. People won't understand.

Alex's knowing smile is all I need as she tries to look innocent. "I heard you're interested in her. She's pretty."

"That asshole of yours has a big fucking mouth," I say and head for Ma and Pop's house. Alex trails behind at a slow pace. I move quickly to put distance between us and try to block out her quiet snickering. I knew I never should have told Ryan a fucking thing about Mindy.

"Thank you for this," she says from behind me. I stop walking. She catches up quickly and stands beside me, just yards from the house.

"Didn't give you nothing."

"You know, Ryan is a pain in the ass."

I can't stop the laugh that escapes me. She knew this before they hooked up, so I'm not sure why she's bringing it up now.

"But he's loyal to the people he loves. He says you guys learned that from Mom and Jim. He's told me stories about when you were kids. I know how much he loves and respects you. It makes me jealous—the relationship you two have. I've spent the last year just wanting to get to know you, wanting that kind of loyalty from you. Ryan doesn't respect much, so the fact that he respects you means a lot. So thank you for giving me that."

She walks into the house without another word, and thank fuck for it, too. I've done enough of that sharing my feelings shit. The last thing I want to do is stand here and tell her the truth. I've always loved her. She's my sister. I guess I've always loved Michael, too, but it's different with my brother. Where Alex walks around with this desire to be accepted and needed, Michael carries a detached confidence with him that's a little too similar to his father. No doubt it's how he was able to beat the crap out of her when he thought he was saving her. He just did the job he felt he had to do and didn't stop to think about it. He's a real company man in that way.

I've been standing outside the house for so long that Pop strides out the front door with PJ on his heels.

"Heard part of that conversation," he says.

"Nosy fuck."

"Eh, your mom's rubbed off on me. Got to have her nose in everything."

I don't say anything because I'm pretty much talked out. Too much talking and feelings. I don't like it. I want to go back to my safe place. Somebody needs to be late on payment or give me lip so I can release some frustration.

"Glad I got you alone. We need to talk."

"Least favorite words, Pop. The kid just talked my fucking ear off." I scowl, but it doesn't pass muster.

"You like her. She's difficult not to like. Even with the crying shit." Pop and Alex have a weird father-daughter bond going on. Sometimes he says offensive shit just to see her spin her wheels and try to figure out how to respond. I admit, it's funny as fuck to see her figure out how to mouth off to our patched president.

"Better be club-related. I'm too sober for any more talks about feelings."

"It is." He points to the bench by the front door. We sit down awkwardly, our big bodies filling up the space. "Been a hard year. I'm tired."

"Yeah." There's nothing else for me to say. We're all tired, and we've all suffered in different ways.

"I've been thinking about where I went wrong, what I did to get this all fucked up."

"Sometimes shit just goes sideways, Pop, and it's nobody's fault."

He runs his fingers through his graying hair and tucks the long strands behind his ears.

"Fucked up more than I think if you're lying to me."

He knows I'm lying. Of course he knows I'm lying—he's my dad. Now I'm the one nervously tucking my hair behind my ears and delaying the speech I know he deserves. Jim Stone is more than my father—he's my patched president. Questioning his leadership is a big fucking deal. It's like spitting on the patch and should only be done when absolutely necessary.

"Out with it, boy."

"We've been too complacent. We're like sitting ducks out here. It's almost been a year. We should have done something by now. As a husband, you want to give your wife what she needs by protecting her kids. As a father, you want to give your kids some peace. But by putting in that marker, we started a fucking war with the Italian mafia. Every man at the table looks at the gavel for direction. Instead of playing offense, we've been playing defense, and it's getting us killed."

He nods his head slowly, thoughtfully, as he lets it sink in.

"Wanted to tell you before I talk to your brother. Just had to make sure I'm doing the right thing first."

My entire body tenses as I wait for him to finish. In a way, I don't think I need him to say it. I already know where he's going with this little talk we're having, and it makes me feel sick to my stomach. Men patch in and they don't patch out. In most charters, presidents hang on to the gavel until they can't ride anymore. Our charter does a lot of physically exhausting work, and it's important that our men are able to handle that work. Pop's nowhere near being unable to take care of his end, but it's not the day-to-day that's bringing him down. Shit. I'm not ready for this.

"You don't have to say it." If he doesn't say it, then maybe I can pretend for just a little longer that this isn't really happening.

"Got to. Otherwise I'll probably change my mind."

Fuck. Don't say it, Pop. Don't say it. I fight the urge to cover my ears and rock back and forth with my eyes closed like I did when I was a little boy and he would get to screaming at Ryan or vice versa. I hated the noise back then—still do, actually. But back then I didn't know what kind of man Pop was. My experience with Ma's men up to that point hadn't ever been good. I didn't know men could be good until this pushy fucker came along and forced himself into our lives. He changed me, us, for the better.

Fuck. Now I'm having mushy feelings I'm not comfortable with.

I hate feelings.

"You don't have to."

Please, don't.

Fuck.

"I have to step down, son. It's time." His voice is gravelly, and it skips as he pushes the words out. "You were right. I've held back because this shit is personal for me. I've acted like a husband and a father when I should have been acting like a president."

"I get it. I just don't like it. I don't want Wyatt to be president just yet."

Pop breaks out into a grin and shoves his shoulder into mine.

"You're whining. It makes you sound like your brother," he says.

Oh, fuck that.

Fuck that.

"On second thought, go ahead and retire, you senile bastard," I say in the same grouchy tone that had him telling me I sound like Ryan.

I do not sound like Ryan.

Chapter 11

IT'S BEEN A little over a week since that shit went down at the clubhouse with Mindy and Leo. Nobody's brought it up, and thank fuck for it, too. After Pop unloaded that shit on me a few days ago about him stepping down, he hasn't said another word about it. Basically, I've spent the past week avoiding people and their bullshit—even Mindy. That's why I'm holed up in the chapel all alone and long before we have to be in here for the meeting with Leo and Michael. So far, their stories check out, and we're mostly confident that working with them won't backfire on us. It's not like we have many other choices anyway.

Before I forget, I shoot off a quick text to Mindy reminding her that she's due at Duke's house for babysitting duty in an hour. This is the most I let myself have of her. I don't have to remind her, but it makes me feel better to be a little more in control of what she's doing. Spending time with her is dangerous—I always want more of her—but I won't do this to her. The only thing that makes me feel good now is that she doesn't fight me. I've wanted this for a long time—a woman who submits herself to me without question. I think Mindy could be this woman for me.

No. I can't let myself go there. I want more than she can give, and I need to stop thinking about keeping her. Maybe if I were normal, I could help her get to a healthy place. Maybe if I didn't feel this violent thirst. Maybe if I were normal or safe or even capable of giving her the kind of love she deserves. Maybe then she could be mine.

But that's not the case, so I need to let it go no matter how bad it burns. Not even the nastiest whiskey burns as bad as the idea of letting Mindy go.

Boots slap against the concrete, jarring me from my thoughts. I look up to find Ryan walking in, a grimace on his face. He plops down in his seat beside me but doesn't say a word. He's acting weird with his silent he is. Not that Ryan is ever very talkative, but he isn't prone to holding back, and I can tell that he is holding something back.

It's a long while before he speaks. While I wait, we sit in silence and I act like he's not even there. There's nothing pushing Ryan to talk.

"Talked to Pop," he says.

Now I know why he's being quieter than normal. It fucked me up pretty good when Pop told me he was stepping down, so it has to be fucking with Ryan, too.

"Yeah." It's fucking stupid. We're grown men, but here we are acting like kids whose parents are getting a divorce. I never really thought about how I'd feel about Pop stepping down before. It's not something I wanted to think about.

"Might be good, not having that asshole be pres," he says. "Bad enough he thinks he can still tell us what to do because he's our dad, no matter how fucking old we get."

"You mean that?" Even if Pop does get carried away with his controlling bullshit at times, I just don't buy that Ryan is cool with Wyatt taking Pop's place. Not that Wyatt isn't a good man and not that he can't do the job well, maybe even better than Pop. It's just weird thinking about Pop not being president.

"Yes," he says quickly. Then he curses under his breath and kicks at the floor. "No. I don't fucking know. Won't be able to tell me where to stick my dick anymore."

I clench and unclench my fists on the table and take controlled breaths to keep my temper in check. I really don't need to be reminded where he's sticking his dick.

116

"Pop's going to tell you what to do until one of you dies. Holding the gavel has nothing to do with being your father."

"So there's no upside here, then?" He's sulking and so am I, so I decide it's not worth calling him out on it.

"Basically."

Just as we finish our bitching over Pop's decision, our brothers start to wander into the room. Duke and Diesel have Michael and Leo walking between them. When the four of them get to the open doorway, Diesel stretches out his arm with his palm in the air. Michael and Leo hand over three mobile phones and two knives. I don't know who the fuck gave them permission to carry a weapon, but I guess they have it. It's not my fucking business to question the decision, so I keep my mouth shut.

Diesel sits down beside Ryan with Fish and Bear across the table from them. Nobody really sits in Chief's old seat. It's not some kind of rule or something, and it's been eight months since his death, but none of us seem to be ready yet. We're going to have to patch one of our prospects in soon, though. We function best as a ten-man charter, and with everything going on, it's dangerous for us to not replace Chief's spot. There are just some things the prospects can't do. Pop hasn't talked about it, but I think he's been holding off patching Squat in because we're still waiting on word about Torque's release. He was supposed to be out a few months ago, but a couple minor infractions earned him extra time.

Leo and Michael stand off to the side and wait for direction. Jeremy strides in with two wooden chairs from the main room that he sets down at the empty end of the table, moves Chief's chair out of the way with his foot, and puts the chairs from the main room in its place. Michael takes the seat next to Diesel and Leo sits between Michael and Bear. This isn't an official Church meeting because of the visitors in the room, so I'm not surprised when Pop signals to Jeremy that he can stay. Baby Boy nods his head and moves to stand against the wall behind Michael and Leo.

Michael's wearing a pair of jeans and a dark-red long-sleeve waffle shirt, and Leo's wearing a black suit. I withhold the snort that bubbles up. It looks like Ma dressed Michael today. Grady's chilled out some since shit went down at Ma and Pop's house. I can tell he doesn't like working with Leo in particular—and I don't blame him—but he sees the value in the arrangement. Just yesterday we let Leo go to a hotel in town instead of forcing him to hole up in the extra bedroom at Wyatt's house with Michael. We haven't released Michael, though. We talked it over, but Pop likes to be able to keep an eye on him, which really means that Ma doesn't want her baby boy too far out of her sight. The more I think about it, the more I realize how right it is that Pop steps down. It's no secret that a brother's old lady has his ear at home, but Ma's got Pop's ear way too often. Her heart is in the right place, but sometimes her priorities are different from the club's.

Pop takes his seat and stretches his arms out to the corners of the table. His eyes slide to his right and fix on Wyatt. With a nod of his head, he gives his successor the floor and leans back in his chair. Wyatt straightens his back and clears his throat.

"ID on the car at the 101 Club checks out and leads back to the Italians in the city," Wyatt says. Leo nods at the other end of the table. He told us it would, but we had to check. I settle in my chair a little more, knowing that he's been straight with us so far.

"What I don't get is why the WOPs in the city got a problem with us," Ryan says with a taunting smile in Michael's direction.

Michael's jaw ticks as he fights back a response that will no doubt make everything blow up. Ryan's not been quiet about how he feels about Michael, and his insistence to remind everybody of that fact has created a pretty severe rift between the two. Not that I like what Michael did to my sister, but if she can get over it, then maybe we should too. Then again, if it were Mindy . . .

"Good question. Guess we should pay Segreti a visit and have a little talk," Grady says with a nod and a dark smile. Half the table grins, getting excited at the idea of busting into the city and fucking with Segreti's shit.

"Wait, Segreti?" Michael's brow is furrowed. He looks to Leo in confusion. "Is this the same family?"

Leo nods and folds his hands in front of him on the table.

"But how? Segreti's not strong enough."

"He used to be. The more business Mancuso scooped up, the less Segreti invested in New York. Took his business west and started building in San Francisco. Now he's got the city."

"Great. So a dude our friends in New York pushed out has a beef with our new friends in California. Fucking fantastic," Michael gripes and rubs his hands over his face.

"Watch your fucking mouth!" Ryan is tense beside me and shakes his head.

"You're starting to piss me the fuck off, dude. First, I know you're the one who's stopping me from seeing my sister. And second, I know she's over the shit we went through, so maybe you need to fucking let it go already."

Ryan stands up quickly, his chair sliding back and hitting the wall behind him. If I thought he was angry before, I was wrong. I don't stand up, because I'm tired of my brothers fighting. Plus, maybe if they beat the shit out of each other, we can move the fuck on already. Instead, I look to the middle of the table and grab the full bottle of whiskey and a glass. I pour myself a sizable amount as I watch the action. It's all so predictable. Michael stands up, and then Diesel does since he's in between the two morons.

"Be clear about one fucking thing, little boy. The woman you beat the shit out of is my woman. She's under my care, my protection, and my fucking body every night. Somebody fucks with what belongs to me and I'm going to get pissed. Don't like it? Maybe you should take your anger out on your daddy's dick instead of mouthing off to me in my fucking clubhouse."

Oh, for fuck's sake. I take a sip of the whiskey and eye Michael carefully. Just when I think all hell is going to break loose, baby brother breaks out into a smug grin.

"If you know your woman as well as you think you do, then you at least know not to say that shit to her face. The last thing my sister appreciates is being treated like property. And make no mistake about it, you white trash asshole, if you fuck her over and treat her like she's something you own rather than treasure, you answer to me."

"Enough!" I shout as loud as I can. Most of the men in the room look bored and annoyed by this little dick-measuring contest, but I can tell by the looks on Pop's and Leo's faces that they're not enjoying the show. From my right side, Grady snorts.

"You're adults, not fucking children. Sit down, shut the fuck up, and learn to get along." Both Michael and Ryan narrow their eyes at me and open their mouths to speak, but I slam my fist into the wooden table top so hard that my fucking arm throbs. I can't even feel my hand. "You're both my brothers, and you both love my sister. This family is incestual enough without you two shoving your dicks up each other's asses. Now knock it the fuck off. We have a call to make. Fuck."

"Not so easy dealing with a couple of immature assholes, is it?" Pop says from behind me. I turn to the head of the table and shake my head. I know he's referring to how difficult Ryan and I were when we were kids, but now is so not the time. Asshole. Shit. No wonder Ma stays high all the time. She'd have to be high to put up with this bullshit.

Diesel pulls out the three phones he confiscated from Michael and Leo and Leo tells him which one to use. Leo directs Diesel which contact to pull up, and while they get the phone ready, I set up the speaker system I just acquired. It's nothing fancy, just a one-way speaker that allows the entire room to hear the conversation through the headset Leo will use. It's not fool-proof. If the room gets too loud, the person on the other end will surely hear the commotion, but it's the best we can do while not fully trusting Scavo's motives. Once Leo has the headset hooked up into the phone and adjusted to his liking, he lifts his head and looks to the other end of the table.

"When I talked to Gloria, Carlo and Emilio still hadn't been released from Rikers. Because of my prior convictions, I was unable to visit them. Neither have contacted me, but according to Gloria, Carlo got himself in the hole for a while. My only point of contact since this whole mess went down with the lab bust has been Carlo's consigliere, who is also my uncle Carmine, and Tony. Carmine has been shut out by Rico, Emilio's younger brother. The stupid fuck is just a capo, but he's been running around like Tony thinking he owns the streets while he owns nothing. I hate that prick."

"Just find out what you can. We're not so desperate that we want anyone in the organization figuring out we're working together," Pop says.

"Uncle Emilio has a thing about checking in. He likes to know where his capos are at all times," Michael says. He's speaking to Leo, really, but he's loud enough for the whole room to hear. "I know you know this, man, but better to be reminded than to fuck up. Best thing to tell him about Tony is that he's trying to run shit and he's pissing everybody off, including his own capo. Tell Uncle Emilio his boy's got a big head and, as far as you know, Alex found out about Ruby and company on her own and she'd been in contact with the club for months."

"Smart. Takes the heat off Princess about the whole ratting thing," Duke says with a nod and a proud smile to Michael. "Nosy little girl just wanted to meet her aunt. She had no fucking clue what she was stirring up."

"Yeah, but is Uncle Dick-Sucker going to buy that story?" Ryan asks Duke, totally ignoring Michael.

"What other story is he going to believe? Either we tell the truth and make the target on Princess's head even brighter, or we play up the raging Mama Bear angle," Duke says.

"He'll buy it." Michael chimes in, nodding his head. "Al's always sticking her nose in things she shouldn't. I talked to

Aunt Gloria a few days ago. She and Dad have been in a pissing match since we were born over telling us the truth. She thinks it's unfair that we never knew, and for obvious reasons, he never wanted us to. Once I knew the truth, a lot of shit from childhood started to make sense. Nobody can keep a secret this big forever. Tell him I'm refusing to bring Al home. We're getting to know our mother and Tony's just pissed because he sees Forsaken turning the Boss's house into Swiss cheese as disrespect that can't be ignored. The Boss and Underboss getting sent away was the perfect time to prove himself and move up the ranks."

"And if Tony's told Emilio the truth?" Duke asks.

"I stick to the story. Either way, it buys us some time and gets us some info," Leo says.

Finally it seems the room doesn't have any more questions or comments and we can fucking get to the reason we're here. Diesel gets the call going, and I hold my breath, hoping nobody fucks this up. Leo adjusts the earpiece that's attached to the mobile and settles in.

"Vescovi." The prick answers his phone with his last name, like the asshole calling doesn't know who the hell he's trying to reach.

"Sir," Leo says. "Scavo checking in."

"You calling from a comfortable place?"

"As comfortable as can be," Leo responds. Each organization or club has their own code words and language they don't explain to outsiders, but for the most part it's all the same.

"Good. Then you want to explain what the fuck you're doing out west with Michael?" Emilio's voice booms through the speaker. Half the men in the room roll their eyes at Vescovi's dramatics.

"Things became . . . complicated when Tony was released from the hospital. Most of our friends have remained interested in keeping company policy, but a few co-workers have been . . . less than cooperative."

"You're saying Tony's been, uh, uncooperative?"

"I'm saying that a misunderstanding at home lead to a misunderstanding in the workplace and has since resulted in a disaster on both fronts. Tony's felt his boss's absence a little harder than most men in the office. He's, uh, blazing his own trail so to speak." Leo's a smart man, and this conversation proves it. Emilio may be the underboss, but he's also Tony's father. Disrespecting the man to his father outright isn't wise, especially when we need to remain on his good side long enough to find out what he knows.

"What does that have to do with your visit to California?"

"Apparently Alexandra has had an interest in her mother's family, and when she found out about her aunt Ruby, she hunted her down. Being unaware of the wounds she was opening, Alexandra turned to Ruby for comfort when she was scared. I'm aware of how unfriendly Ruby's husband was upon his arrival. It's unfortunate and a disrespect, certainly, but given everything, it's personal. Tony was unhappy with this and made it a work issue, sending Michael to retrieve his sister. When Michael didn't return, Tony sent me."

"How are the twins?"

"Happy to be getting to know the other side of their family. As far as Ruby and her husband are concerned, the debt is paid. There is nothing further to settle. The twins are free to leave when they so wish, but as it stands, neither appears interested in returning to New York."

"That's more information than I've gotten out of a single man face-to-face since I've been out," Emilio gripes.

"And how are you and Mr. Mancuso? The last time I called the house, your beautiful wife explained that you were otherwise occupied and unable to come to the phone. I'm pleased to be hearing from you."

"I'm on house arrest. It's terrible. My beautiful wife, as you call her, won't get off my ass. The woman can cook for twelve hours straight without taking a break—the only thing she can do for longer than that is bitch. Carlo was in Rikers until a few weeks ago when he got transferred to MCC. He's got a two-year sentence, and they're not crediting him for time served. Fucking assholes. I asked Tony to visit him, but he's been too busy. Now I know why. That fuckin' kid is starting to piss me off." Emilio's angry New York accent slips into Italian full on, and only two of the men in the room understand a fucking thing he's saying. I press the mute button and give the signal to the room that they're free to talk.

"He's such a douche," Michael says and rubs his temples.

Leo snorts and nods. "Mr. Vescovi is wishing he deposited his sperm in a better uterus. He thinks he would have a more intelligent son had he chosen better."

"Maybe he should've stuck his sperm up his little brother's ass. I'm sick and fucking tired of the way this asshole bitches about my aunt. She's a good woman," Michael says.

Ryan looks almost pleased with Michael's frustration.

Emilio calms down and starts speaking in English, so I give the signal for the room to shut up and then un-mute the speaker.

"That boy. I told Carlo he was too young to apply for a position. Too immature. Carlo insisted. He knows his place, but maybe I need to remind him of it."

"How should I move forward? My guys have been having trouble with their daily routes. People seem to think the company takes late payments. Too many to count. Tony's got everybody questioning their contracts. They're saying that if the company is sloppy enough to allow this embarrassment, then they shouldn't retain the offered services."

"I'll reach out to your guys and get them back on schedule. Don't worry about that, son. Carlo is unhappy with the way Ruby and her husband went about meeting the twins, but he's agreed to temporarily let bygones be bygones. He's a wise man. He sees the value in keeping the peace. You stay with Alexandra. She's to be your wife after all."

I shoot Ryan a deadly look that promises severe pain if he opens his mouth. Emilio thinking Leo is still betrothed to Alexandra is a good thing. It means that Tony is keeping his shit close to the vest. It's the best scenario we could have hoped for. Ryan's jaw ticks and his shoulders tighten as he grips the edge of the table. Fucking temper tantrums. He knows damn well, and every man in this room knows damn well, that Alex belongs to him. Even Leo knows Alex didn't want to marry him, and he's fine with it. He's a smart man and knows that a wife who doesn't want him isn't much of a wife at all.

"And Ruby's husband? His display in Brooklyn can't be forgotten," Leo says. He carefully eyes Pop, making sure he knows this is an act. We don't have guns in Church. We never did, really. Only a few times, and when Ryan pulled his piece on Grady, we stopped. Didn't matter how dangerous shit was at the time. No amount of safety planning is worth having to put a brother down for taking out another brother in the only fucking place we should be able to feel safe. Fuck that.

"Don't let that bother you. Carlo has had his eyes on Mr. and Mrs. Stone for many years now. Though the grapevine has been unreliable at times, it's proven worth the investment." What.the.fuck.

"Is this something I should be aware of?" Leo asks.

Emilio scoffs. "No. Take care of your bride, son."

The men say their goodbyes and agree to catch up with one another in a few weeks. When the call has been disconnected, we sit there in silence.

"Did he just say we got another fucking rat?" Grady asks. His eyes are menacing and his growl fierce.

My body is tense, and from what I can tell, there's not a man in the room who isn't about ready to fuck something up. Another fucking rat? The anger that's always just barely concealed in me is threatening to bubble over as I eye each one of my brothers. It couldn't be one of our own, could it?

Mindy

Chapter 12

DID YOU RUN? the text reads. It's like he's baiting me, and I'm starting to hate him for it. Okay, maybe hate is too strong of a word, but he's getting on my damn nerves. I took care of myself long before he came along. I don't need an owner or a master or whatever the fuck he thinks he's doing—I just need a freaking friend. And I thought we were friends.
YOU WOULD KNOW IF YOU WERE HERE.
There. I said it.
I haven't seen Ian in several days, and it's pissing me off. Actually, the only thing pissing me off more than his not being here is him deciding that he's going to act like he's my keeper. He's not, and he's not going to be as long as he's hiding from me. I'll play his crazy little game as long as he shows up, but he's not showing up, so screw it. I don't want to irritate him, but I'm way too frustrated to bite my tongue right now.
I miss him and I thought—just maybe—we could have had something. But he doesn't want from me what I want from him. He told me I was incapable of making my own choices, and I thought that meant more than daily text messages and acting like my human day planner.
THE RULES, MELINDA.

God, he's annoying. My stomach flips. I'm grinning like a silly fool. I'm hopeless.

BITE ME, I text back. I can't help but giggle. Ian's not a man to be toyed with, but all that nonsense doesn't stop me from baiting him the way he's baiting me. Maybe I'll suddenly remember the rules if he takes me for a ride on his Harley. Until then, I seem to be experiencing a random bout of memory loss.

YUM. WHERE?

I stare at my phone blankly. What does he . . . oh, hell. I'm not stupid. I know damn well what he means. My cheeks heat at the thought. Where is such a loaded question. I fumble with my phone until I settle on a response and start typing it out. No sooner than I have it ready to send do I decide against it and delete the entire thing. I can't say that. I shake my head at myself. If I had actually told Ian to bite my ass, he'd probably be angry with me. I don't mind annoying him, but I don't want him angry. I've seen Ian angry, and I don't like it. Maybe he's trying to get over what I asked him do? He was so mad after, maybe because I wasn't upset about what I saw. If anything, it gave me hope and a new mission.

DON'T PLAY WITH ME, M. THE RULES EXIST FOR A REASON. GO RUN!

I clench my jaw shut to suppress a scream. He takes all the fun out of being difficult.

ALREADY RAN, BOSS, I say. I stare at the screen for a long moment and then toss the phone on my nightstand. He never lets me have the upper hand, like ever. Feeling defeated, I give up on him for the night. Just because he's getting on my nerves doesn't mean I have to spend the evening sitting and sulking. I don't want to be that woman whose life is dictated by her relationships. I always hated those girls growing up. When they had a new boyfriend or something good happened, they were in insufferably cheery moods. But if something bad happened or they broke up, they would spend at least a week moping and forcing everyone around them to be just as miserable as they were. Those are the girls Holly and I used to mock for being so needy. I refuse to be one of those girls, even though I know I'm one pathetic sigh away from being one of them. I love how Ian makes me feel, but I really hate how needy I become when he's not around. It can't be healthy.

I throw myself onto my bed and shove my face in my pillow. I know what I need to do, but I'm scared. I don't want to try only to find out I'm not ready. It's been five months. If I'm not ready now, when will I ever be? In the back of my head, I fear that I already have the answer—that I won't ever be ready. But that's not acceptable. It's just not. Maybe I won't ever be totally healed or normal, but I have to believe that I can have some things back. Those assholes don't get to take everything from me. They just don't. I didn't feel much when I watched Ian, not sexually anyway. A little tingle, maybe a bit of excitement, but that was it. Emotionally, I felt so much. Thankful to Kaz for doing as I'd asked. Thankful to Ian for playing along. Maybe I should have been jealous because I was watching the man I want with another woman, but I wasn't. I just kept thinking how lucky she was to be able to be with him. Those thoughts verged on a tinge of sadness when I started to think that I might never heal enough to be with him in that way.

Summoning the courage I've been faking for weeks now, I crawl off my bed and go to my bedroom door and lock it. The absolute last thing I need is for either my mom or dad to walk in while I'm trying to reclaim a tiny bit of normalcy. In my closet, in an old shoe box that's hidden in an old suitcase I haven't used in years, is the bag I'm looking for. I pull it out and stare at it wearily. It's really just a few pieces of plastic and metal with a silicone shell. The damn thing isn't demonic, and it's not going to hurt me. I know that, but its purpose terrifies me half to death.

I want this.

Maybe Ian doesn't want me the way I want him, and maybe he never will. But right now it's unfair to want him to want me since I can't give myself to him. If I really want to have Ian in a permanent way, then I'm going to have to get over this. No man, especially not a Forsaken man, wants a woman who can't fulfill his needs. If I can't touch him and he can't touch me, there's absolutely no hope that I'll ever be able to turn my fantasy into a reality.

Maybe that's why he's avoiding me. He knows I can't meet his basic needs and sees no point in trying to form a relationship because of that. The idea that he could want me, if only I can get over this one thing, fills me with a new determination to get better. For him, for us.

The adult toy inside the bag feels so heavy as I pull it out. I borrowed my mom's car a few days ago and drove down to Santa Rosa to buy the stupid thing. I was not about to find a place in Willits to buy something like this. We're kind of isolated out here, and even though the people there may not know me, I know me. I know how close I am to home, and I know they could recognize me from the newspaper article about my attack. Even if they don't recognize me, the very thought of buying a sex toy so close to home is too nerve-racking. I could have ordered the stupid thing online, but my mom is nosy and would want to know what's in the package. This was just easier, even if it did take half a day to run the errand and more money than I would have liked to spend. I push the guilt away and rationalize that even if it is Ian's money I spent on this, it's also for Ian, so it's okay. Not that he cares.

When I was in the hospital, he stayed in my room as much as he could, and when he couldn't, he sat outside my room. I was half out of my mind at that point, but I always knew he was there. He told me I didn't have to work, that he would take care of me. In a moment of pure, selfish pity, I accepted the arrangement. Now, every month, like clockwork, he brings by a wad of cash. I've tried to refuse it, and I've tried to give some back because it's always way too much. He never accepts it. I gave up trying to argue when Holly told me the truth about how she and Grady got together. He tried to force that twenty-five grand on her, and even though she fought not to take it with everything she had, he still managed to make her accept it. It's in a hat box in their closet now. She says she's hanging on to it until he dies so she can bury him with it. In the same spirit, I use the money I need and put the rest away. Not in the bank, though. I know enough to know that cash deposits of random amounts with no traceable source are suspect, and I don't want to get anyone into trouble. Especially not Ian.

Ian—that's why I'm doing this. For Ian.

The device is already loaded with batteries. I did that they day I brought it home. I also tried it out on my arm. I spent a little extra on it because it has four setting levels, each one more powerful than the last. The lowest setting barely buzzes, but the woman at the store swears that the little extension on its side ensures even the low setting is pleasurable. I don't know what I can handle, if anything, but I'm determined to push myself to find a way to eventually enjoy this. Even if it's only ever with myself.

With shaky hands, I toss the vibrator on my bed and remove my clothes. Even my socks get tossed on the floor. Being naked isn't much of an issue as is being naked with the intent to pleasure myself. I'd never experimented with touching myself before I met Heath. Then we were together and there was no need to. It wasn't until he went away and some of the other Army wives were talking about their favorite toys that I gave it a try. I thought I'd feel dirty by touching myself so intimately and all alone, but I didn't. Getting off became a part of my routine. Talk to Heath, touch myself, go grocery shopping, study for finals. After a while, I even stopped buying ibuprofen, because having an orgasm was better than taking pain killers any day.

I just hope I haven't lost that forever.

Getting back into bed feels like a chore. Most of me doesn't want to do this, but a small part of me is excited at the possibility that I can do this and maybe even enjoy it. I do it anyway. I crawl into bed and go about my actions mechanically, waiting for the sheer terror to creep into my lungs and make it impossible to breathe. If I were trying to seduce myself, I would start by running my hand down my chest to the apex of my thighs where I would lightly drag my nails along my inner thigh and then back up. My fingers would slide between my lips. It would be just enough to make my breath hitch. My fingers would pinch at my nipples, twisting just enough so that I whimper.

I would imagine Ian running his scruffy jaw along my inner thigh as he breathes heavily. His hot breath would wash over my wanting pussy. I would bring the side extension of the toy to my clit and turn it on the lowest setting. It wouldn't be enough, but it would send a sweet little tingle down my spine. It would be delicious as I turned up the power to the second setting and made myself wait in agony as I deliberately intensify the vibrations and then lower them. I wouldn't want to come too soon. I would want to draw it out just like Ian would. He would want me panting, I'm sure. So I would torture myself until I'm so needy that my swollen, wet pussy is begging for release. Then and only then would I slide the thick silicone-covered device into my core. In and out. In and out. It would be incredible. I would be breathless, wanton, crazy with need and desire. I would be high on the feeling of it rather than high because of the needle in my vein.

But I'm not trying to seduce myself. I'm simply trying to get over something I can barely name. I don't run my hand down my abdomen. I don't tease my inner thigh or my core. I just close my eyes and bring the still device to my clit, where I place the side extension, and suck in a terrified breath. I'm actually doing this, and as much as I know I want to, I'm scared of pressing the button and turning the fucking thing on. An orgasm shouldn't be this scary. Nothing should be this scary.

But it is.

Tears slide down the sides of my face and pool in my ears. I hate the way the wetness tickles, but I don't move to wipe it away. There's so much about this—and about the entire world—that I hate, and I can't wipe any of it away. Every terrible feeling, every awful moment, and every single fear refuses to be scrubbed away. I could peel off my own flesh, and the terror would still remain.

My lungs strain to breathe. It's such a simple task, one we do several times a minute. Every day. For our entire lives. I tend to forget I'm breathing at times—I think we all do. It's only when I can't get my lungs to suck in air that I realize how important the simple act is. Focusing on the action, I manage to loosen up enough to get a little air in my lungs. And again. The discomfort in my chest lessens, slowly but surely, with every breath I take. I don't move the toy from its position. If I do, I might not put it back and all these shot nerves will be for nothing.

Be brave.

I move the silicone piece in a slow circle on my clit. Even just being naked here like this is a little exciting. There's a flutter of anticipation that gives me hope the memories will subside. I haven't touched myself since well before that night. I've been too afraid to feel anything even remotely similar to what I felt then.

The barely there, pleasant hum shivers through me at the contact. They didn't touch me here. They didn't care about my comfort or pleasure. Actually, they tried to make it as painful as possible.

Shut up, whore. I didn't say you could talk.

My body tenses at the memory. The hard plastic gun slams against face. Pain radiates out from my cheek, throbbing and crashing into my brain and neck and even down my spine. I don't know how, but it does. It just hurts. Everything hurts. More tears fall from my eyes as I make another circle with the toy and then another. Every memory that hits me is more and more vicious than the last, just like that night.

His lips on mine hurt. He's pressing into me so hard. I could bite him. I think about it, about biting him, but I'm too scared to do anything. He's bucking against me, painfully squeezing my breasts. He's so hateful, so violent, and so mean. I hate it. I hate every second of it. I'm crying so hard, still rubbing the toy against myself, and way too afraid to stop what I'm doing. I'm not entirely sure I know the difference between what's happening now and what happened then. It's blurring together in the most terrifying way. My head is slammed into the wall behind me. Everything feels hot and painful and just . . . too much. Somewhere, in the back of my mind, I know that this isn't happening. I know I'm in my bedroom at my parents' house. I know I'm naked in my bed and touching myself with this stupid silicone toy.

But it feels so real. Every time the memories surface, it feels like I'm right there. I'm feeling every hit, every excruciating thrust inside me. Every tiny movement. Skin against skin. Men I don't know. Hands I'm unfamiliar with. They're not Heath, and they won't ever be Ian. And the smells. The putrid smell of hot, sweaty, dirty skin. A smell so vile, so distinct that I may never forget it. Even now, a lump forms in my throat.

I'm unexpectedly pulled from my thoughts by a slow but unmistakable pulsing in my core. My legs are tingling, my blood pumping faster now than before. I feel like I do when I've been running awhile and I'm about to give up and turn around. Only, my lungs aren't straining for air, and my head is foggy. I can barely hear anything around me, and even though my eyes are open and my vision is fine, it's like I can't focus on any of it. Forcing myself to pay attention to my body, I realize what's causing it.

In my anger at the surfaced memories, I'm rubbing my clit harder and faster, aided by the dampness between my legs. The memories have fueled something inside me that's taken over. In this moment, I don't feel like a broken down woman. I feel powerful.

Powerful.

So I turn the vibrator on its lowest setting and have to fight back a moan at how delicious it feels. My heart rate spikes. The increasing throbbing takes me back to that night when, despite all of the pain and abuse—and perhaps worst of all—when what they did felt less than awful. Good, even. Doctors tried to talk to me about it. They said it happens. Even if you don't want it, sometimes your body responds anyway. And I hate myself for feeling something then. And part of me hates myself for feeling something now.

It gets old—feeling so inept and incapable of moving on. I've never met a person more resistant to letting go of awful memories than me. It's just another thing to hate about myself. It's the final straw in an intricately designed straw hat that's too worn to really be useful. My complete refusal to let go of my bad memories is the only straw that's holding the entire thing together. And when it breaks, I find myself unable to suck in a breath. With my lungs stalled and my nerves about to break, my legs shake and I open my mouth to scream. It's a silent cry for help that jolts my entire body, but it's not enough. I can't make noise with anybody else at home—or any of my neighbors at home either. When I run out of breath, I gasp for what little air I can manage and let out another silent scream.

And I turn the vibrator up to its highest setting, and without another thought, I reposition the toy so the silicone shaft is positioned against my wet, aching pussy. I shudder at the feeling of almost—just almost—having what I want.

What I need.

What I hate.

And there are no more straws. And in place of what used to be a beloved, well-worn hat is nothing. Just a pile of straws that have no purpose. That do nothing. And mean nothing.

And I've had enough.

Be brave.

I slam the vibrator into my core as hard as I can and fight the enclosing panic.

I can almost feel him punching me in the stomach and then in my nose. There's so much blood. I hate the blood. It's not really happening, I know that, but it feels like it is happening all over again. I pull the vibrator out and slam it in again. This time, the side extension presses against my clit. It's exactly where I want it to be. Perfect. My legs shake and my eyes cross. It hurts in a way that feels right. Like I deserve to feel the pain again. I deserve a lot for throwing away my sobriety because of spite. The vibrator is bigger than they were. It's bigger and more pleasurable and just the right amount of painful. I can't focus on anything but the sweet ache and brilliant shocks that ripple through my body.

For a moment, I forget that I'm in bed. Instead, I'm bent over Eileen's desk at Universal Ground and it's not me touching myself. Every bone, every inch of flesh, and every muscle in my body hurts. Holly is across the room with the phone to her ear, forcing herself to tell Ian what they're doing to me. How they're enjoying it. She reaches forward and wraps her hand around mine, and it's the absolute most important thing in my world. I can feel her hand on mine, like I really am still there. She holds on to me—the way she always has—fiercely and without fail. She doesn't let go even when his thrusts are so hard that they slam me painfully into the edge of the desk. I nearly bite straight through my lip with how hard I'm biting down.

I'm here, Minds.

I love you, and I'm here.

And in an instant, I'm back in my bed, clearly, fucking myself. It's nobody else and I'm safe.

And I'm come savagely, gasping, and bucking against the bed.

When it's over, I can barely move. My body is so heavy that I feel like I did then—almost dead. The only difference is that now I'm not praying for death. I don't welcome the blackness that will swallow me when it's time. I don't beg an invisible being I doubt exists for release from my torture.

No, instead I'm left with the bitter, desperate, hate-filled need for revenge. I'm tired of being a victim of rape, a dope-sick junkie, an alcoholic, a fucking failure. I won't be a victim anymore. I refuse to be afraid.

If I can't shake the monsters, then I'll become one of them.

MAY

11 months to Mancuso's downfall

Chapter 13

IT'S BEEN SEVENTEEN days since I last saw Ian. Seventeen days of bossy-ass text messages and his little warnings. Seventeen days of running harder and faster and longer. The first few times Ian disapproved of my responses, I was wary of pushing him further, but then he sent more texts. He checks up on me more regularly and about everything. He isn't playing fair, with all his warnings and bullshit. I don't care, though. He can only yell at me so much in text form. Eventually he's going to have to face me.

I want him to face me more than I want him to like me. I can't deal with his craziness without seeing his face or hearing his voice. The sound of his voice in my head pushes me to get to the house in record time. The more frustrated I get with him, the faster I am. I've shaved minutes off my loop around town by driving myself to be better. I don't tell the asshole that, though. He wants to send me lame-ass texts that reek of obligation and his self-sacrificing bullshit, so I give him what he wants and nothing more. Sometimes I argue or don't answer until I feel like it. Sometimes I answer right away because I can't help myself. And sometimes, late at night, I have to put my phone across the room from me when I feel myself giving in to texting him first. I miss hearing his voice. I miss catching his eyes on me. I just miss him, but most of all, I miss his touch. By now, everybody else knows not to touch me. It's isolating, not being touched—only I didn't realize how isolating until I had his touch and then lost it. He doesn't even have to talk to me. Maybe if even he could just hold my hand once in a while. That might be enough. It would still be too little, but I could settle for it.

It's the least he could do—to boss me around in person. And since I can't irritate him into showing up, then I guess I'll have to be the one doing the showing up, and the best way to do that is by finding a job with the club. If I'm at the clubhouse, he'll have to talk to me. I intend to make sure of it.

Step one in getting a job with the club is talking to the person in charge, which according to Grady by way of Holly is Ruby. She says he's always bitching about how much influence she has over Jim. I've done my best to try not to be too obvious with my questions. Holly's made her feelings about me and Ian clear, and honestly, I can't tolerate another round of judgment. Ian doesn't deserve that after everything he's done for her.

I let it sink in—my anger with Holly—and I focus in on it until I'm flying so fast down Sherwood Road that I'm barely making out anything around me. My muscles burn and my lungs ache from the strain of my speed. Three months of running as far and as fast as I can have given me a bit of an advantage. My body is used to the abuse, and my mind welcomes it. I've learned how to breathe through my mouth, not my nose. I've learned that when the aching starts is right when I'm hitting my stride. I've learned how much my body can take before it gives up. But most importantly, I've learned to take my life in my own hands.

The last quarter mile to Ruby and Jim's house is on a slight incline that isn't very noticeable if you're in a car. Right now, miles from home and pushing myself to my limit, it makes all the difference. I try slowing down to make it to the driveway, but with every step, my body feels heavier and heavier. On weakened knees, I stumble into the weeds and brush that edge the paved road. My upper body is pulled forward, and just before I fall on hands and knees, I regain my footing and am able to come to a safe stop. With my hands on my bent knees, I keep my feet shoulder-width apart. I'm sucking in desperate breath after desperate breath, my eyes watering, and my chest heaving, sore from my maniacal sprint. My eyes cross, my vision blurs, and once again I nearly lose my balance. I shut my eyes and try to focus on regulating my breathing before I move. Losing track of time, I stay bent over like this until my lungs are no longer straining and I feel steady enough to continue my journey.

When I straighten I find a familiar figure at the end of the driveway. He's standing in black jeans and a black short-sleeved shirt. His leather cut covers his broad chest, and his black hair gleams in the late-morning light that's breaking through the redwoods. I've never spoken to him before, but I'd recognize Ryan Stone anywhere.

"Crazy bitch," he mutters with a shake of his head.

I don't respond and approach him. Getting in an argument with Ryan, or worse, being sent away, won't do me any good. If he doesn't let me see Ruby, then nearly passing out on the side of the road was all for naught.

"My brother know you're here?" he asks. I'm close enough now that I can see the slight smirk on his lips.

"I'm not here for Ian." I wipe the sweat pooling at my brow and straighten my back. He makes no move to stop me as I turn onto the long driveway and begin my walk to the house. "Is Ruby home?"

"You're here for Ma?" He chuckles and catches up with me, then slows us down to a leisurely pace.

"Yeah," I say. If I've learned anything from my time with Ian, it's that these guys value directness.

"Wow. Tattling on the boyfriend to his mommy, huh? That's cold, lady." He's nearly grinning at his own humor now. His casual suggestion that Ian's my boyfriend nearly makes me blush. Fighting off the embarrassment makes me feel even more juvenile than I already do.

"Someone sounds like he's afraid of his mommy."

"Damn straight. The woman's fucking insane," he says with a scoff. I can't help but laugh at that. Holly's told me a few things about Ryan—mostly things she's heard from club members in passing. Ryan is supposedly this grouchy, badass who likes to torment people. Holly says that the little bit she's heard about him from when Grady thinks she's not listening to his conversations with his brothers is that the only time they've ever seen Ryan vulnerable is when Alex was missing and then hurt. Until he met Alex, they all had pretty much given up on him ever opening himself up to a woman. Maybe love really has softened him up.

"So, tell me what he did," he prods.

"Why do you assume Ian's done something wrong?"

"Nobody runs like that if they're not pissed."

"I'm pissed, all right," I say. I don't intend to be that honest with him, but it just flies out, and now I'm left to deal with the consequences. We're only halfway to the house, and with how surprisingly chatty he's being, I have no doubt I'll be singing like a canary by the time we get there. Best defense is a good offense. "I'm pissed because I threw away four years of sobriety on a revenge plan that didn't pan out. I'm pissed because I have nothing better to do all day than to wallow in my own sorrows. I'm pissed because everybody's moving on with their lives and I'm not, and now I'm pissed because you're supposed to be the strong, silent type and you're anything but silent."

"Damn, you *are* pissed," he says. He's still finding humor in our conversation that I don't see.

My face is heating for a whole different reason now. I pick up my pace and force him to catch up. Not that I want him catching up. I'd be perfectly happy if he were to stay where he is. I don't want to ask Ruby for a favor when I'm in a bad mood, and all Ryan's doing is antagonizing me.

"What in the hell is so funny?" I snap.

"You got this vein," he says and gestures to my neck. "It's popping out."

"How is it possible that nobody has smothered you yet?"

We're close to the house now. So fucking close to the house and to me losing my shit. I can't figure out what's pissing me off more—the fact that Ian *isn't* my boyfriend and Ryan's casual comment just throws that in my face, or if it's my fried nerves at over explaining myself to him.

"I'm too charming to smother," he says with a shrug. "But you're not. Good thing you got yourself hooked up with my brother, or I might take your attitude personally."

"I am *not* hooked up with Ian!" I turn and end up yelling the words. And once I start, I find it impossible to stop. "He's not my boyfriend. I haven't even seen him in a couple of weeks."

"But you want to," he says. Ryan doesn't even so much as shrug his shoulders or raise a brow. He looks totally calm and in control. I know better than to think his relaxed appearance means he can't or won't snap at any minute.

Instead of responding, I fold my arms over my chest and huff. It's the most mature thing I can manage to do at this point. Why in the hell is he even talking to me, anyway?

"Good," he says with a nod and strides toward the house. Now I'm the one working to keep up with him, utterly confused by the sudden turn and annoyed at myself for even caring for an explanation.

"I didn't even say anything."

"Didn't have to." He stops at the deck, just feet from the front door. I have to back up a step to keep from literally stepping on his toes. "You get away with a lot with me because of shit you don't even understand. I'll tolerate whatever crap you want to throw my way as long as you remember your place with the club and with my brother."

"I don't understand." I feel like I've been dropped into the conversation halfway through, because I'm pretty much lost now.

"He likes you," is his blunt explanation. When my eyebrows pull together in confusion, he shakes his head and purses his lips like he's thinking about what he wants to say.

"More than likes you. Don't take it for granted, and don't fuck it up. He chose you and I respect that, but make no mistake about it, babe—you do him dirty and you'll answer to me." I narrow my eyes, and he leans in closer. His rank breath washes over my face.

"I won't hesitate to slit your fucking throat if you fuck my brother over."

I tilt my chin up, closer to his ear and lean in so we're chest to chest. He's taller than me by several inches, but I don't care. He's going to hear what I have to say, and that's all that matters.

"Threatening somebody with death only works if they're afraid of dying." I say the words slowly and with purpose, meaning every single one. If he wanted to scare me, he should have threatened to take away something that matters to me— like Ian.

The front door opens just as I shove past Ryan, clipping him with my shoulder as I make my way to greet Ruby. She's got on a faded black shirt and cutoff jean shorts. Her hair is up in a messy bun, and she's holding a coffee mug in her hands. She narrows her eyes at Ryan but then redirects her attention to me. She softens her gaze as I approach and ushers me inside, shutting the door behind us.

Chapter 14

EVERY CAR SOUNDS the same. Either that or I'm half-deaf, because as I've been standing at the edge of my parents' front lawn, I've mistaken a pickup truck, a Harley, a Prius, and a minivan for Ruby's SUV. Well, in all fairness, I didn't really hear the Prius. Those things are damn quiet, but when it drove by, I had a moment when I thought it was Ruby. It didn't matter that the Prius is less than half the size of the damn Suburban.

I should have told Ruby that I'd drive myself to the clubhouse. I can drive. I just usually choose not to. After *that night*, it was more or less because the idea of having the ability to drive off a cliff was far too tempting. Everybody said the feeling would pass. And I guess it has. I no longer want to find a way to end the pain. Now I just feel too uncomfortable with the disturbing thoughts that invade my brain.

Somebody didn't use their blinker the other day, and I had to fight back the knee-jerk reaction to slam into their bumper. A man honked his horn at me when I was on my way to the grocery store yesterday because I'd taken too long responding to the light that had just turned from red to green. I flipped him off and sat there, refusing to move. He had to back up because he was so close up my ass and then moved around me to make the light before it turned back to red. He screamed a few obscenities at me, but I couldn't bring myself to get angry. So I smiled as he glared at me, red-faced and nearly out of breath with his anger. My anger may have been hidden beneath the surface, but it scares me.

It terrifies me how easy it is now. The terror and frustration gave way to sadness and self-pity at some point. The self-pity and fright were all-consuming. Once I fought my way through it, I thought I could level out. I thought that maybe I could be normal again. But that hasn't happened. Sometimes I don't like what I see. I'm spiraling out, becoming somebody I don't recognize, and she's not somebody my mother would be proud of. But when I have those thoughts, it's never my voice in my head. It's my mom's voice. Other times, I feel empowered by my anger. I don't recognize myself, but that just excites me even more.

It's freeing, being so angry, so fed up. In those times, when I can't bring myself to give a single fuck, I find myself thinking more clearly than I ever have before. All of life's little gray areas either darken or lighten, and everything is black and white. There is right and wrong, but none of it matters. The only things that matter are what matters to me. It's selfish and hateful. And I love it. I want more of it.

So I choose not to drive. Because one day, I'm afraid of really hurting somebody. And I'm afraid when I do, I won't care. And when that happens, who am I? So I accepted Ruby's offer to drive me to the clubhouse for my first day of work. It's not like she gave me much choice in the matter. Our entire conversation consisted of her giving me a single line of advice and then asking what I wanted. I don't know that she was happy to see me. I couldn't tell. It was just awkward.

From the corner of my eye, I see the red Suburban pulling up. Ruby's in the passenger seat with Aaron behind the wheel. She's got her caramel-brown hair held back in a butterfly clip, and she's smoking a cigarette with the window down. She doesn't smile or wave, even though her eyes are fixated on me. Instead, she just finishes her cigarette and rolls up her window. I open the back passenger door and climb in.

"Thanks for picking me up," I say. Maybe Ruby's in a mood and it has nothing to do with me. In the seat next to mine is Alex, who has a big smile on her face. I return the gesture and settle in.

"No worries. You're on the way," Alex offers. I attempt to shrug off Ruby's silence, but it's difficult to do. Alex's eyes meet the back of her mother's head, and even though she's not saying anything, the action says everything. Something's going on that I'm not aware of. Or maybe—just maybe—Ruby doesn't like me.

Ugh. Perfect. Ruby disliking me is so not the thing I need. She doesn't have to love me, I guess. I have enough issues to work through without Ian's mom hating me on top of it.

Before I know it, we're at the clubhouse and Ruby and Aaron are out of the SUV, leaving me and Alex behind. I move to get out when Alex leans over and places her hand on my knee. I jump in place and try to calm myself down. It's just Alex. She's not trying to scare me. Damn it. I should be over this shit by now.

"Sorry," she says and tucks her dark brown hair behind her ear.

"It's okay." I might not be over it just yet, but one day I will be. I have to believe that.

"My mom's attitude isn't personal. She's having a hard day. She and Jim got into a fight last night."

"Thanks for that," I say. We get out of the vehicle and walk into the clubhouse. It's quiet and well-lit, which is a far cry from how loud and dark it was the last time I was here. There are a few people walking around, though not many. Aaron has disappeared somewhere, but Ruby certainly hasn't. A few of the members of the club are sitting at the bar with bottles of beer in their hands, and others are munching on cookies.

"Bar needs wiped down, fridge needs everything that's expired or just looks nasty to be tossed out, and the floor needs to be swept and mopped. All supplies are in the closet behind the bar," Ruby says. I'm careful to pay attention to what she's saying. She's not looking at me, but there's nobody else in the room who's going to actually clean something around here, save for maybe Alex.

"Got it." Excusing myself, I walk past Ruby, who's got a hand on her hip as she stares at the men at the bar. Her lips are pursed, and she's got a severe pissed-off look on her face. Thankfully it's not directed at me. Unfortunately I recognize the large body sitting on the stool that has her attention as Jim. Damn, that must have been some fight they had last night if she's giving him a look like this and he's ignoring her.

The bar is backed up to an exposed brick wall that's decorated with a long shelf that holds a variety of bottles of liquor. Around the corner from the bar is a large room that's mostly filled up by a pool table and a few pieces of random furniture. It's tucked back from the main room, but not closed off. Just enough to separate the spaces. Around the corner from the back wall of the bar are three doors. One is open and appears to lead to a bathroom. The other two are closed, but one is missing its doorknob, so I narrow it down to the door closest to the bar.

Opening it, I find out I'm right. There's little rhyme or reason to the mess inside, but I find the necessary supplies and pull them out, deciding I'll start with wiping down the bar top. I spend more time than I need to poking through everything. The tension at the bar is just too much. Eventually, though, I give up and walk back to the bar with my supplies, keeping my eyes on my surroundings and not the men at the bar. Aside from Jim, I don't even know who is there. With laser focus, I wipe down the back of the bar and try to keep my ears closed to anything going on around me. There are a few bottles lying around that I place on the shelf wherever I find room. The sink is full of dishes that don't look like they've been touched in a week. Food is crusted on the silverware, and the odor emanating from the sink is pretty bad, so I decide to avoid it until I can't anymore.

I've barely gotten the bottles of liquor put back on the shelf when a scuffle breaks out behind me. I jump at the sound of glass being slammed into the bar top and spin around with my hands clutching the counter behind me. Duke is beside Jim, and judging from the look on his face, I think he might have been the one to slam his bottle into the counter. His eyes slide to Jim, who gives Duke a slight shake of his head.

Ruby is still in the same spot she was when we first walked in. Alex is at the very end of the bar, up against the exterior wall, with a large hardback book open in front of her, the back flap tipped up so nobody can see what she's reading. Even as the argument breaks out, she doesn't move or acknowledge the noise. God, she must be used to it.

I want to move from my position, watching the chaos about to break out, but I can't bring myself to. I'm frozen in place.

"What was that, Ma? I fucking heard you, so answer me." Ryan says from across the room. His shoulders are heaving and he's glaring at Ruby, who is valiantly ignoring him. Her eyes are still fixed on Jim's back, but he's still facing the bar—facing me—and sipping his beer like it's second nature. At his age and for how long he's been in the club, he's probably able to open a bottle of beer from a dead sleep and suck the entire thing down without even waking.

"I know damn well that you can hear me," Ryan barks. He takes a few steps forward and places his hands on the back of a wooden chair, leaning into it. Ruby's jaw ticks, but otherwise, she doesn't move. "Fucking answer me!"

Ryan's yell startles Alex, and she slams her book shut and spins around in her chair to glare at him, and what a glare she has. Jim sets his beer down slowly and gives me a tired look. I force a smile to my face that I don't even believe myself.

Ruby *still* doesn't move—even as Jim slides his stool back and turns around to face his bickering family. I guess he has to address what's going on—both as Ruby's husband and Ryan's father as well as the president of the club. He takes his time standing from his seat and closing the distance between him and Ryan. It's only when Jim lunges at Ryan that Alex and Ruby react, which sets off a chain reaction in the room. I watch in horror as Duke jumps from his seat and rushes at Ryan. He's followed by Bear, who was sitting next to him. Fish and Diesel, who were on the other side of Jim, follow suit, but they head for Jim. Diesel pulls Ruby back from the growing mass of testosterone while Fish tries to get in between Ryan and Jim. Diesel's efforts are rewarded with Ruby turning and cussing him out and trying to shove him aside.

I can barely tell who's helping who and who's on whose side. The mass moves, and Fish gets shoved aside. He falls onto a nearby table with a heavy thud and a scream and then tumbles to the floor and lays there for a moment with his hands on his lower back. Shit. He looks really hurt. Quickly, I grab a nearby rag and frantically search for the fridge, thinking that maybe there will be a freezer and some ice in there. I jump into action when I find something better—an ice maker. It's about the size of a dorm room fridge, but it's plenty full. I pile the ice into the rag and rush around the bar to Fish, doing my best to avoid the fight. With my arms hooked under his arm pits, I try to pull him away from the crowd. He arches his back and screams out in pain, but I don't stop. The crowd is getting shoved in our direction, with Alex on the outside, nearly falling on her butt as she dodges a wayward elbow. When I have Fish next to the exposed brick wall and far enough away from the crowd, I give him an once-over.

"I'm fine," he says through gritted teeth. His face is red, and a line of sweat is breaking out above his brows. He doesn't look fine, no matter what he says, so I proceed with inspecting the way he's lying and attempting to straighten his back out, though it's of no use.

"Can you sit up?" I ask. He narrows his dark brown eyes at me and spits out a curse. He tries to move into a sitting position but stops and grunts in what sounds like pain. Frowning at him, I move around to his side, near his back, and place the rag full of ice against his spine. "Just tell me what I can do to help."

"I said I'm fine," he says on a shout. "I don't need your fucking help."

I don't need this kind of abuse. Especially not from someone I can't yell back at. Instead of making sure he's okay, I stand and survey the scene before me. The crowd is bigger now, with people yelling all around. Through the crowd, I can see Wyatt on the other side, fighting through his brothers to get to the center. Ian's even joined in, too. He's got his arms around Jim, and he's slowly making progress, dragging him out of the chaos. I was so busy with Fish that I didn't even hear anyone else come in, but here they are. Grady is in the thick of the mess and so is Diesel. I see a flash of blond hair from the other side. Duke's got Ryan around the neck and he's pulling him back. It seems someone else has gotten himself in a fight with Ryan now since he's still putting up a pretty hard fight despite the fact that Jim's on the edge of it all.

From the corner of my eye, I see Leo standing in the entrance to the clubhouse. He's got his standard-issue black suit on, and he looks as calm and cool as can be. He takes one step into the room before stopping. His eyes widen, and he turns his head to the doorway, speaking to someone I can't see. Waiting a minute, and then stepping into the room, he heads my way. He's followed by a younger man who has dark brown hair that's parted on the side. There's no gel in his hair, and he doesn't wear a suit, but he has the same confident stride that Leo does. The young man's olive complexion is set off by his gorgeous brown eyes and the slight widow's peak at the top of his forehead, just barely off center. It takes me a long moment before I realize this must be the elusive Michael Mancuso.

Chapter 15

MICHAEL STOPS IN his tracks when his eyes fix on something, and his body straightens. His muscles bulge under the short-sleeved shirt he's wearing to the point that I can see the veins in his arms clearly. Even mad, he's a good-looking kid. And right now he looks downright deadly. Leo catches sight of whatever Michael's looking at and moves to run in that direction, but Michael shoves him back and takes off running. My eyes follow his movement as he rushes to where Ryan is being pulled back by both Duke and Wyatt.

I take a step to my right and see Alex, who's behind Ryan now and whispering in his ear. She's trying to calm him down, I think, but it's not working. She's being pushed and shoved by the collective crowd, but she's vigilant in her task. She takes a heavy black boot stepping on her foot and an elbow to her head, but she keeps on. It doesn't look like any of the offending body parts belong to Ryan, but rather men who are trying desperately to avoid getting the crap kicked out of them.

Michael stands back a few feet, reaching out with his arms but then lowering them. Nobody besides me and Leo even seem to know he's in the room. I know only a little about Alex and Michael and their history. I know she came out to California and he came after her to try and help but ended up hurting her pretty badly. Ian doesn't bring either of them up, so neither do I. Until I have a better idea of where we stand, I can't just go around asking about reappearing siblings and family squabbles. Even if I did know where we stand, I still don't think it would be my place to ask. Everything I know, I learned from Holly. Holly says the club hasn't allowed Michael to see Alex since he hurt her, which would explain the weird arm thing he's doing right now. It's like he wants to reach out and touch her, but he isn't sure if he should. Like he's scared to try to repair that relationship—a feeling I completely understand, but wish I didn't.

A man stumbles back and right into Alex's side. She falls backward and nearly hits the wall behind her but is saved by Michael stepping into action. The man who fell picks himself up and gets right back into the fight, but this time he seems to be trying to break it up by pulling each man out individually. I don't even know how it got this big or violent, much less what it's about.

"You're okay, *miele*," Michael says.

I move closer, around the crowd, so I can hear them better. I don't know why, but I want to see this. I know Ryan doesn't want Alex around Michael and that's caused some issues in the club, so this is probably a big deal. It feels significant.

"Oh my God," Alex says breathily and turns around in his arms. She stares at him with tears in her eyes and then throws her arms around his neck. He gives her a smile that feels too personal, like I shouldn't be watching them. I don't care, though. The confident man who walked into the room is now gone, and in his place is a happy little boy who looks like he's been reunited with his favorite toy.

I'm pulled from Michael and Alex by the quiet that descends upon the room. The man who fell into Alex has effectively broken up most of the fight. Ryan and Grady are still bitching at each other but slowly come to realize that something else is going on around them. Grady pushes Ryan off of him and redirects his attention. Ryan's quizzical look moves to what's caught Grady's attention. It's Michael and Alex, being unwittingly reunited, that has the entire room falling into a hush. Ryan's pained expression shocks me. He looks like he's at war with himself, trying to keep himself in place, when he really wants to rip Alex out of Michael's arms.

"Michael?" It's Ruby. She sounds softer, quieter right now. I search the crowd and find her coming out from behind Ryan. He doesn't move to stop her, but he does reach up and place a hand on her shoulder as she passes. When she's out of reach, it falls back down to his side. The pained expression on his face gives way to a somber one, and I realize that what I'm seeing is more significant than I thought. Michael and Alex didn't know Ruby is their birth mother until recently. They never even knew she existed until Alex got to town. The pieces start to fit together in my head, and I come to the conclusion that if Alex hasn't been able to see Michael in almost a year, then that means Ruby likely hasn't either.

Ruby's eyes are filled with tears as she takes a wobbly step in the twins' direction. Alex pulls back from Michael and moves to stand beside him. Her face is red and wet with tears as her eyes volley between her mother and her brother. Michael stands unflinchingly as he stares at the woman who gave birth to him. His eyes aren't wide exactly, but they're searching her face for something. Maybe recognition, or to see if he thinks he looks like her at all. I don't know, but it's difficult to watch. I barely know these people and I'm nearly moved to tears by being witness to their reunion.

"So, you're my mom, huh?" Michael tries to smile, but it falls flat. The sheer magnitude of the situation appears to have hit him.

Ruby nods and tries for a *yes*, but it doesn't really come out. She takes another step, this one even less steady, and places a hand over her mouth as a guttural sob rips through her. I want to do something, anything to busy myself from this intimate moment, but like everybody else in the room, I can't stop myself from watching. Michael takes a small step forward and pauses. He goes to reach out to her but stops and lowers his arms. He's both awkward and vulnerable, a combination I couldn't have guessed he's capable of.

Ruby's knees give out, and she falls to the floor. Jim moves to crouch down behind her but doesn't obstruct her view of her son. He whispers something in her ear and rubs her shoulders. It's only a few seconds, but it feels like forever as Michael takes one step after another and meets his mother on the floor. There are unshed tears in his eyes, and his chest is heaving. I can't be sure, but I bet his heart is racing a million miles a minute right now. Mine is and this isn't even my family or my moment. Ruby cries harder when Michael crouches down to her level. He barely has his arms open before Ruby throws herself into them and hugs him so fiercely I'm afraid she might break one of his ribs.

Finally I take my eyes off of mother and son and look for the man I know has to be watching this. This is Ian's family and his history. I look around but don't find him at first. Behind the crowd, I see him moving through the room with the pool table and toward the back of the clubhouse. I don't even think about it as I'm following him. He opens a door and steps out into the bright sunlight, not bothering to close it behind him.

Outside, the sun nearly blinds me. It takes a few moments before my eyes can see normally again. I've never been behind the clubhouse, so I take a moment to look around. There's a basketball hoop attached to the tall fence and a few picnic tables that look no worse for wear than the ones out front. Ian keeps moving, so I stop surveying my surroundings and get a move on. He walks through a gate in the fence at the very back and disappears from my line of sight. Just like out front, the chain-link fence back here has black privacy slats that are spray painted with white paint that reads WHERE SOULS SPOIL AND HEARTS ROT in bold lettering.

Through the gate now, I find that we're standing near the edge of a cliff. The clubhouse sits on the ocean side of Main Street. Much of the coast is federal property, so I didn't expect to be standing so close to the water back here. The chain-link fence the government has up to restrict access is a couple hundred feet away and partially shielded by the occasional redwood. I can't imagine we're supposed to be out here, but I don't care. It's gorgeous the way the jagged cliff looks with the blue-gray sky as a backdrop and the sounds of the ocean meeting the shore. The only thing that competes is the man standing on the rock, at the very edge, with his hands shoved in his pockets and his head hanging down.

"View's better up here," he says. A smile creeps to my lips. He knows I'm here and he doesn't care. As much as I'd prefer to not plummet to my death via a slippery rock, I walk to him and move to step up beside him, but I'm stopped by his offered hand. I can't resist his touch, so I take it and let myself enjoy the warmth of his skin wrapped around mine. It's so little compared to what I want, but it's a start.

"Thought about it a lot, what it'd be like for Ma to meet Michael," he says. I'm on the rock now beside him, but he doesn't let go of my hand while he shares this with me. I don't know what it means to Ian, but it means the world to me. "Club fought about it. A lot. Talked it over. We couldn't decide how to handle it." He blows out a breath and gives my hand a squeeze like he needs the strength to get through this. "And this is how it goes down."

I don't know enough to know why he'd rather be out here than inside with his family, but it's clear that he needs this time, so I don't ask. I just stand here and try to give him whatever comfort I can.

"Say something," he pleads. "You're always talking except when I need you to."

"I've missed you," I blurt out. It's the first thing I think of. "Your texts are pissing me off. If you want to boss me around, you're going to have to do it face-to-face."

He straightens his arm and brings it closer to his side. Instead of staying in place, I take the opportunity to move closer to him and rest my head on his upper arm. He doesn't say anything, so I go on. It doesn't matter how stupid I sound. It only matters that I help him work through whatever's going on in his head, even if it means more uncomfortable honesty.

"I don't like how you keep disappearing on me. You're not doing that anymore. You're also going to start ordering your coffee how you like it so you'll actually freaking drink it."

"My coffee?" he says quietly. He turns so that we're not side by side anymore. I miss his touch for a moment before he's facing me, his hand cupping my jaw. Not like before when he would wait for me to instigate touching. No, his warm hand just cups my cheek, and it feels right. It feels perfect.

"You always get black coffee, but you don't drink it unless it's sweet and creamy."

He smirks and lowers his face. He's so close that our noses brush against each other. I suck in a deep, excited breath and hope beyond hope that this is really happening. He doesn't respond to my coffee comment. Instead, he purposefully brushes his nose against mine. My stomach flutters in response.

"Are you giving me rules?" His breath is hot and chocolatey in smell. I bet he tastes delicious. I love chocolate and I love him.

Well, I think I might love him, but my relationship with chocolate is solid.

"Yeah, I guess I am," I say. His thumb rubs circles into my cheek, and his other hand cups the other side of my face. He runs his nose up from my jaw to my temple and breathes me in deep. My breath catches and my eyes flutter closed. Holy shit, this feels amazing.

"Tell me who I belong to, Melinda." His lips ghost over the corner of my mouth, and my heart is beating so fast in response that I'm worried I might pass out.

"You belong to me," I whisper and turn my mouth toward his. Our lips touch, but just lightly. He applies more pressure, and so do I. I get so lost in the feeling that the next thing I know, we're hanging on to each other for dear life and panting as our lips slide over one another. He's relentless and demanding as he holds me in place, right where he wants me. I try to move my head the other way, but he won't be budged, so I submit to him.

And it feels incredible.

And powerful.

And perfect.

Chapter 16

IT'S DAY FIVE of working at the clubhouse to try and keep it clean. I never did find out what that fight was about, but I don't care anymore. I've been a little preoccupied by a certain man who's been at my kitchen table every morning since the day we kissed. He greets me with a kiss on my forehead and says goodbye with one on my lips. I definitely prefer the latter to the former, but I don't complain. The one time I tried to go for a kiss on the lips when he greeted me, he whispered something naughty in my ear that I'm just not ready for.

Don't be greedy. Greedy girls get a spankin', and I don't even know your limits yet.

And the night after he said that was the second time I've used that sex toy. It wasn't as scary as the first time, but I still panicked when I inserted it. Progress is progress, though, so I guess I can't beat myself up too much about it.

I drag the soapy rag over the bar top and scrub at the sticky spots that refuse to get clean. Keeping this place even remotely clean is ridiculously hard. I've worked alongside Chel twice now, and she's even cooler than I thought she was the first time I met her. Every day it's a new damn mess in this place. I asked for this job, so I don't say anything about how messy these guys are.

"You're not coming, Ma. You'll be distracted," Ian says as he enters the room.

I stop what I'm doing and peek over my shoulder to get a look at him. He said he belongs to me, so I'm calling dibs on him as my man. The more kisses I get and the more mornings he drinks his sweet coffee, the more determined I am to make this thing between us grow.

"I will not," Ruby says as she works to catch up to him. Michael and Alex trail behind the pair, engaged in their own conversation. Behind them, Ryan walks in with the biggest sourpuss look on his face that I've ever seen. "I always go with you guys. You know how much smoother these things play out when a lady's present."

"If that's true, then why the hell do you think you'll be any use?" he says with a snicker.

Ruby slaps his arm and grumbles something under her breath then stares up at him expectantly. She seems happier now, lighter and more carefree. I guess finally having all of her kids in one place will do that for a woman.

"Absolutely not," Ian says. His head lifts as his eyes fall on me. He gives me this sexy nod-smirk combination that almost makes me have to clench my legs. If I wasn't so worn down and damaged, I'd probably be a slushy pile of lust right now. "I already told Mindy she could come."

We had no such conversation, and I don't even know where I'm going, nor do I care. But I'm going somewhere with Ian, and that's what matters.

"And there's only room for one extra body?" She's copping an attitude now as she stares down up at her son. His lips form a grim line, and he shakes his head.

"It's business, Ma. You've been an emotional wreck all week."

"She even know what to do?"

"She will," he says confidently.

She levels him with a flat look before shrugging her shoulders and walking away. He waits until she's around the corner and comes up to me, placing a kiss to my forehead. I swear, a thousand butterflies are let loose in my belly at his touch. People always talk about the first time like nothing will ever top it, but they're so wrong. Our first kiss was gentle and then crazy hot, but it doesn't compare to every kiss that's come after it. Even this one, with his lips to my forehead, is more memorable than our first kiss. Every time he touches me, it means more than the last time. Every kiss feels more intimate and more like a promise that we haven't verbalized.

Either that, or I've lost my fucking mind and I'm imagining it. Not that it matters. He's mine now, and I'm not letting go.

"Where are we going?" I ask when he pulls away. His hand is around the back of my neck, and he gives it a small squeeze. His lips are turned down now, and he's looking at me like he's sorry. The smile on my face falls. I didn't even realize I was smiling until I lose it.

"You're not going anywhere. I just needed her off my ass."

"Oh hell no," I say a little louder than intended. "You're not ditching me."

"Club business, Melinda." His voice has taken on a hard edge, but I don't give a damn. He can put me over his knee and spank me for all I care. Actually, I *might* be up for that.

"Not happening, Ian. Apparently you normally bring Ruby, so why can't you bring me?"

"Ruby's the president's old lady," he says in a frustrated tone. I don't miss the quirk of his lips, though.

"Your point?"

"Old ladies are different than—" He cuts himself off.

I place a hand on my hip and raise my brows, waiting for a real explanation. I've been dying to know what we are to each other, in his mind, ever since he kissed me. I can't just ask him, though.

Well, I probably could, but if the answer isn't what I want to hear, I might not recover from it. He told me that I belong to him, and he asked me who he belongs to—that's all well and dandy, but I need to hear the words. I need the reassurance that this is really happening and there's really an us for me to be excited about.

"Nice try." He smiles and slides his hand around to the base of my throat. I suck in a deep breath and stare at him with a look that would embarrass me if I could stop myself, I'm sure.

He's got this look about him, no matter his mood, that draws me in. He's breathtaking, and I don't mean that in some silly, schoolgirl-crush kind of way. He's breathtaking, like he's shrouded in mystery and pain, and I feel a sense of security when I'm with him that I've never known before.

My father calls him a killer, Holly calls him dangerous, and Nic says he's disturbed—but to me he's just Ian. They might all be right. Maybe he is disturbed and dangerous, and maybe he is a killer. Those things might have scared me a year ago, but now I find peace in knowing that about him. I grew up thinking life was really simple. You grow up, try your best at whatever you're doing, and you just be a good person. Nobody ever talked to me about the evil things that can happen in life. Nobody ever told me that good girls with high GPAs can grow up to become junkies. They never talked to me about the dangers of experimenting, and they didn't tell me that former good girls on the road to redemption can be violated and humiliated. My father, the cop, never shared the horrors he'd seen on the job before, and I didn't know to ask.

All of the awful does exist, though, and a significant portion of it has happened to me. Some of it I've even done to myself. I used to long for a time when I didn't know how much pain I could endure or how strong I really am. I used to wish to turn back the clock to the eighteen-year-old girl who had such a bright future. I've given up on that now. That girl is gone, and in her place is someone I'm still getting to know. All I really know about her is that she likes a man who carries the evidence of his scars on his face for the world to see. She yearns for a man who the scariest men she's ever met fear to cross. She's in love with a man who will kill for her, even if he doesn't love her back. That kind of security doesn't come along every day, and not every man can fulfill that dark need—but Ian can.

"You don't know what you're asking for," he says quietly. His hand slips around my neck, gently caressing the front of my throat with his thumb.

"Then explain it to me."

"It's not something you explain. It's just—this life. You don't want to get any more involved in . . . the club." The way he says *the club* sounds like it's forced, like he wanted to say something else but decided not to at the last minute. Why he can't, or won't, just talk to me about whatever's going on here is maddening. "You've been hurt bad enough. This club—what we do—is dangerous. You already know that. Why would you choose this when you have another choice?"

"Do I have another choice?" I ask. "From where I'm standing, this is it for me. I used to be somebody else, and now I'm—I need this, the club. It makes me feel normal. It's like this person I've become can't really exist with the rest of the world. But here, with you guys, I feel like you guys *get it*."

"What do we get? What is it about us that makes you feel normal, Melinda?"

And just like that, we're back to bossy man. He's losing his softness and sharpening those hard edges he almost always has.

"I get so angry, so mean. I look at normal people and I can't help but wonder how fucked up they are. I think about it a lot, about what I want to do . . . to *them*." This is the first time I've said this to someone, what I fantasize about. If anyone will understand this darkness, it's Ian. "Those men . . . I *hate* them. I want them to suffer, but they're dead, and I don't get that. I wanted Leo to suffer because he scared me."

"What you did could have gotten him killed if I didn't like the guy so much," he says.

"You should have killed him. You should have tied him up and set him on that stupid fucking seawall at high tide. You should have let him drown in the Pacific."

"This shit isn't healthy. You're on a path to destruction, and I'm not going to be responsible for it when you wreck."

"No," I say.

He slides his hand behind my neck and tightens his grip. He holds me in place, his eyes searching mine, and his nostrils flaring.

"I'm already destroyed. There's nothing here for you to save."

"The fact that you believe that shows how naïve you really are." His voice rises as he barks out the words, and the grip around the back of my neck gets even tighter. It hurts, but I refuse to tell him that. "You've never stared into a man's eyes as he takes his last breath. Your blade has never pierced a man's flesh and ripped apart his insides. You've never been coated in someone else's blood. So don't tell me there's nothing left of you. There's plenty of good left."

There's an uncomfortable layer of silence that settles between us, and I search for something to say. Anything would be better than this quiet. If he would just maybe scream at me, it might be better than this. That way I won't have to stand here, staring into his eyes, thinking about what he's just said. I'm doing everything in my power to *not* think about it. I'm afraid how I'll feel if I do let it sink in.

"I know you think you want me. You think you like this life because you're hurting, but this isn't for you. Every one of our women is either born into this world or life fucked them into it. You can't stomach hearing about it, you won't be able to stomach living it."

"You can't know that." The words don't come out as easily as I want them to. He doesn't think I can handle his world, and I can't find the words to convince him that I can. I'm not sure I can stomach the things he's mentioned—not that I'll ever admit it.

"You aren't fucking listening. Why aren't you listening?" He's shouting now and stepping away from me. I see his temper rising as his eyes dart around the room, searching for something to take his aggression out on. He stomps over to a wooden chair and places his hands on the back and leans into it. His shoulders are rising and falling with each strained breath and the bulge of his muscles as he fights for control of himself, which he's clearly losing. Somewhere in the back of my head, I'm telling myself to run for it to avoid the blowup, but I can't move. Even if I could get my feet to work, I'd stay. Leaving would only prove him right, that I can't handle his world.

"Well?" he screams. His entire body vibrates with his anger. Even his facial features seem incapable of staying still. I can't decide if it's sexy or intimidating or maybe a mix of both. "Why aren't you fucking listening? You used to listen. You did as you were told."

"Because I'm not that girl anymore!" I shout back on my way to the bar where I sit on one of the stools. If he's trying to run me out with this sudden mood swing, it's not going to work. I make a grand show of sitting on the stool and getting comfortable, ensuring it sends the right message. I'm livid, partially because our moment's been broken by his attitude problem and partially because I'm just a yeller and I hate how quick I am to raise my voice and it bothers me that he's brought this infuriating trait out in me.

"Fuck!" His straightens his back and glares at the chair he was just leaning on. In one swift movement, he lifts the chair over his shoulder and throws it with all his might at the exposed brick wall. The chair sails past me and smashes into the brick. I jump at the loud crashing noise it makes even though I knew it was coming and it wasn't really all that close to me. That stupid worrywart voice is going off in my head again, telling me to leave, but I ignore her. I'm far too angry with him for ruining our moment. I like our moments, and he can't just go around ruining them because he feels a foot stomping session coming on.

Asshole.

"Go ahead and throw another one. See if I care," I say and pivot around on my stool to fill one of the clean glasses that's on the dry rack with water from the tap. I don't really like the water from the tap, but I'm thirsty and it's either this or the

Jägermeister that's just down the bar from me. I've been aching for a *real* drink since I broke my sobriety, and even though I haven't slipped up again, the gnawing desire won't go away. Especially when I'm feeling crazy, like now, I just want to drown out all of the insufferable feelings I'm experiencing. I remind myself, like now, how good the crazy feels one I reach the peak. I'm not there yet, and my fingers itch to reach for the green bottle, but I focus on what's important here—Ian.

When I'm settled back in my seat and taking a sip of my water, he moves on to another chair and lifts it over his shoulder, then waits. I nod and give him a hand wave, inviting him to throw the fucking thing.

"What do I care? This isn't my furniture," I say calmly and take another sip. As far as I'm concerned, they could use an update in décor anyway. Nothing really matches in here, and half of it's so old and beat up that it's probably doing the guys a favor to break it to pieces.

He throws the chair, and just like the last one, it breaks into pieces of all different sizes against the brick wall.

"You like this? You really want to be with this?" he says. His face is red, and there's a line of sweat on his brow. He turns over a retro-styled metal table that looks like it could be out of a 1950s Sears catalog. I give him a bitchy eyebrow, and in response he gives me a snapped pool cue that somebody left lying up against one of the couches. When I don't respond to the pool cue, he kicks over another chair, and he does it so hard that he breaks one of the legs in the process.

I set my glass of water down on the bar and give him a slow clap, like I'm proud of his He-man accomplishments. As expected, it just pisses him off further. He moves quickly toward me, like a lion stalking its prey, knocking over everything in his path. He doesn't bother to simply walk around the furniture. Instead, he insists upon toppling it over, kicking it out of his way, and making a big show out of the whole thing.

"What the fuck is wrong with you?" he yells, so close to my face that a few drops of saliva fly onto my cheeks and nose. I startle slightly—and I'm way too proud of myself for only being slightly startled—by the close proximity of his shouting. "You don't know me or the shit that gets me off. You can't want me, so just fucking let me go."

He wants me to let him go, only I didn't know I had him. He hinted at it, and sometimes it sure seems like I do, but others he's so evasive and steadfast in his refusal to clear up our relationship. Ian has been the only thing that's kept me going since those men tried to break me. In a way, I think they did break me, but I don't want to be put back together. The woman I used to be wouldn't have been able to handle this outburst. She would have run from the scene, safely retreating back to her boring life.

"You don't belong here, so get the fuck out!" He's still shouting, but it's not as unnerving now. My ears have adjusted to his volume pretty quickly. He places his hands on either side of my, cupping the ledge of the bar top, his knuckles turning white from the effort.

The volatility of his words make me feel about two inches tall. I've spent the better part of a year wanting this man. He's the only reason I'm not still freaking out over every sound, every touch, and every single fucking thing in life that normal people manage with ease. He's everything to me, and if I don't have him anymore, what do I have?

I have nothing.

"Fuck you," I scream back at him like my life depends on being heard by a rescue team miles away. I've lifted my butt off the stool and am unsteadily standing on the foot rest, leaning into him with my nose touching his. "I'm not leaving!"

I hear people rushing in but can't see them. I don't care who they are or what they have to say about what's going on between us.

"When are you going to get it through your fucking head, huh? I'm not a good guy. I *like* being Forsaken. I get a fucking hard-on when somebody misses a payment, because it means I get to break their face open. And don't even fucking ask me how many men I've taken out, because I don't count the bodies."

I press my nose into his harder now, my body shaking with anger. How fucking dare he. He keeps talking about how I don't want him or this life, but it's like he's rewritten my history in his head.

"Who the hell do you think you're talking to? I'm the dirty junkie, remember? You don't want to know the shit I've done to score. It would turn your stomach if you knew the disgusting things an addict will do for their next fix. I'm a twenty-four-year-old widowed junkie. And in case you fucking forgot, my pussy is tainted because a couple of fucking animals raped me."

I'm going strong until the very end where my voice breaks. I don't normally use the r-word because it's too on point. I don't feel comfortable with it. Saying you were assaulted is always followed by a victim label. I don't want to feel like a victim anymore. I spent long enough feeling sorry for myself over Heath and then the drugs and drinking that I can't stand the idea of feeling victimized by another awful fucking thing happening in my life, even if this one wasn't my fault.

Ian moves to wrap his arms around me, but it reeks of pity and churns my stomach. I don't feel very good now, but I'm too angry to admit any weakness. I was weak for months after the . . . *after it.*

I'm not going to be weak anymore.

I won't be.

So I shove Ian out of my way as hard as I can and hop down off the bar stool. Ruby and Jim are standing near the hallway that leads down to the private bedrooms and the Chapel. Duke and Jeremy are at the pool table watching us but trying to look like they're not. I see Chel in the distance with a half-naked woman I don't know and Ryan and Diesel by the front door. I lower my head as I run around the corner and into the bathroom just off pool room, slamming the door behind me.

Inside and alone, my hands shake and a lump forms in my throat. Everybody was just standing there as I unleashed my most private shame on everyone. I didn't give details, but it was enough. I said the one thing that I've spent the last six months trying not to think.

Rape.

My arms are wrapped around my torso, like I'm trying to give myself a hug. Tears fall down my face in a blurry rush, and I walk in circles in the sizeable room. With every lap I take, I feel the burn of my nails dragging down the flesh at the back of my arms even harder. I don't know how many laps I've done or how long has passed, but there's what I think are tiny drops of blood on my fingertips. I'm freaking out in an epic way, worse than anything that's come before it. I'm not back in Eileen's office this time, and I'm not remembering every vile way they violated me. No, this time I'm hearing the EMTs talk to one another. They're checking me out before they load me on the stretcher. Ian's nearby and is helping the EMTs give me privacy before they cover my lower half with a sheet to spare me my decency.

While making my circles, I snort at the memory. What fucking decency? I had none left. I had nothing left. Ian's wrong. There's no good left in me and no way for me to make any because they stole that from me, and it's not something I can get back.

Raped.

Excessive force.

Foreign object.

Blood.

So much blood.

The only word that stands out to me, though, is the one that I can barely bring myself to think.

Raped.

It's not like I don't know what happened to me. It's just that putting a label on it makes me feel like a statistic. I grew up hearing grown women talk about things I didn't understand. Women in big cities talked about not going out after dark, living by a "rape clock," carrying pepper spray with them, and how something like one in every six American women will be raped or nearly raped at some point in their life. Being a rape victim is like being a breast cancer patient. Everybody either has suffered from it, knows someone who suffered from it, or they've come close to suffering from it. Worse than being a fucking victim is being a fucking statistic.

A guttural, violent, crazed scream flies out of me. It's not fearful like it always was before I started working through my damage. No, it's angry and hateful and just plain fed up. I scream like it's a battle cry and I'm about to rush into war without an army to back me up. My feet move quicker now, in their infinite, dizzying circles, until I have to stop or fall over with the room spinning.

In my last crazed loop around the bathroom, I stop at the sink and grab hold of the edge of the countertop. On both hands, my fingertips are covered in a mix of fresh and drying blood from my arms, but I can't bring myself to care.

Blood.

So much blood.

Raped.

Everything around me is like a backdrop of a picture perfect landscape that doesn't really exist. Tears still fall down my face, and I'm hiccupping now and even more frustrated because I hate having the hiccups. The woman who stares back at me in the mirror is a pathetic bitch with red, puffy eyes and tear-stained cheeks. She's practically hyperventilating, and there are a few streaks of blood on her collarbone just above where her T-shirt hits. I don't remember touching my collarbone, but it doesn't matter because the evidence is right there.

There's a knock on the door that I ignore. And then another. And another. But I don't give a single fuck.

I can't stand to look at her anymore, so I slap my hand against the mirror right where I see my face reflected back at me. I hit the mirror harder than I intend to, and the impact makes my palm tingle. It's not quiet painful and it's not enough, so I do it again, this time harder. When I remove my hand from the mirror, I realize that I must look almost as bad as I looked when Ian got into the room and tried to block my exposed body from being viewed by the entire club as they barged into the room to rescue us. I haven't been knocked across the face today, nor have I been choked or kicked, but I look pretty bad, and I hate my reflection all the same.

"Go away!" I'm screaming into the mirror as I slam my fists into the reflective glass, wrists side first. For half a second, I'm terrified it'll break under my assault, but then when it doesn't, I'm disappointed. The knocking on the door turns to banging, which turns into something heavy being slammed into it. There's yelling on the other side, but I don't care.

I was raped.

I slam my closed fists into the mirror again and again with all my might until it starts to crack under the pressure. The door behind me is broken open just as the glass shatters against my fists. Ian is yelling behind me and pulling me away from the mirror just in time for me to see my handiwork. My wrists are covered in blood, and they throb from my fingertips straight up my arms. I can feel wedges of glass caught in my skin. It's painful, to say the least, but also kind of exciting. Finally, I have a physical pain that's the closest to what I remember feeling back then. Still, it's nothing compared to detoxing, which I thought was going to kill me.

"What the fuck are you doing?" Ian asks with a strained voice as he pulls me into his body and slides down the wall. I'm tucked into his lap with his face buried in my neck. He's holding one of my arms and inspecting the damage. I don't

177

know how he can see anything through the blood that's streaming down to my elbow and onto our clothes.

"I was raped," I whisper. The tears start again, even more fiercely now. Before they were a steady stream, but now I'm wailing. My grief can't be contained any longer. My entire body shakes in Ian's steady, firm hold as I scream and buck against him, shouting the only thing I can again and again until I'm no longer doing anything, no longer aware of being alive or dead. The world doesn't melt away—it just drifts, and a black void takes its place.

I was raped.

Chapter 17

"IT'S OKAY. YOU'RE okay." My words are meant to reassure her, but I'm doing a shit job of it. It doesn't feel okay, and with the way she's sobbing in my arms right now, she doesn't feel like she's going to be okay either.

I don't know how we got here, but we're here, and there's no going back. I should have left her alone after her attack. I should have respected her father's wishes and not forced myself on her and her family when she was in the hospital. I shouldn't have shown up at her house the day she went home, and I shouldn't have shown up every day afterwards for months on end. I should have left her alone, but I'm a selfish bastard, and I didn't want to be away from her for too long. But then I left her anyway, and by that time, it was too late.

Getting close to people only leads to pain. It starts out innocently enough. You meet someone, you like them, they like you, and next thing you know you're stuck cleaning up their messes and dealing with their crap. I have enough relationships within the club and my own fucked-up makeshift family. It's not like I need a relationship for sex, and even if I did, I wouldn't go after Mindy for that. At least, I've tried to keep the two separate. Mindy would run a mile in the other direction if she knew half the shit I think about doing to her when she's being cute. She'd probably run straight out of the county—and with how fast she can run, it wouldn't take long—if I told her what I want to do to her when she's being ornery. Maybe I should have shown her that instead of forcing myself to be gentle. But now isn't the time to think about

Mindy being ornery, because she's in my lap and hysterically crying. And I fucking refuse to think about whipping her when she's this upset.

"I'm taking you home." My voice is gruff but low. I don't want to upset her any more than she already is. When she nods her head, I rearrange my feet beneath me and stand. It's not easy, but I'm careful not to jostle her too much in the process, keeping one arm under her legs and the other behind her back. Firmly held in place against my chest, she lies motionless, as if unaware of what's going on around her. She's not unaware, though. I can tell by the way her heartbeat speeds up when we rise from the floor and then breaks out into a frantic pounding when we walk out of the bathroom and past the small crowd that's gathered.

My brothers are a bunch of nosy fucks, but the looks on their faces don't display an insatiable curiosity. Instead, I see worry and sorrow marring their features. Even Ryan, who by all accounts is as self-consumed as our grandfather, Rage, stares at the woman in my arms with a sadness in his eyes. It's the same look he gets with my sister. He loves Alex—I have no doubt about it now. I'm just continually being surprised by his growth over the last year. Before Alex stormed into our lives, he would have walked away from Mindy's freak-out, telling everybody, including her, that the "bitch needs to get her shit together." He's fucking lucky he's grown up since those days. Asshole knows how I feel about that shit, and I'd hate to make Ma bury her favorite son. Well, he used to be her favorite, but with Michael in the picture now, he's probably second in line.

Ma nods her head at Chel, who's closest to the bar, and retrieves Mindy's wallet-wrist-strap-thing—what the fuck is that thing even called?—and her keys. I stretch out the index finger of the hand that's holding her back up to make a hook. Chel hangs the wallet and keys on my outstretched finger and gives me a sad smile. Like everybody else, Chel likes Mindy. She's hard not to like.

Rink is at the front door, propping it open for me as I walk us into the parking lot. Mindy's car is a little white Acura that's about as old as she is. It's way too small for me to be able to lower her into it. Damn it. Maybe I should have grabbed Ma's keys and taken the Suburban.

"I'm going to set you down so we can get in the car." I lower my face so I can see her eyes. They're glassy and red, and her mascara is smeared. Black lines trail down her cheeks from the makeup she's cried off.

I did this to her.

But I can't think about that now, so I set her on the ground and don't let go of her torso until she's steady enough on her feet. Once she's in the car, I walk around to the driver's side and eye the seat's position—way too close to the steering wheel. Without even trying to see if I'll fit, I slide the seat back as far as it can go and then get in and adjust what I need to. The drive to my house is quick. I'm pleasantly surprised to find that the little coupe has a good bit of pickup and handles well. If it weren't such a chick car, it might be fun to boost up the engine, slap on some new tires, a few roll bars, and a harness and race this baby down the backroads.

We get to the outskirts of town, heading down Sherwood Road, on the same path I've taken to get home for the past four years. If I pass up the little dirt road that splits Ma and Pop's property from their neighbor's, I'll end up on the wrong side of the woods and at my parents' place. Technically it's not a real road, but it's the only legit means of getting to the cabin from Sherwood. So I'm careful not to pass it up but end up taking the turn a bit fast. The car responds well and purrs like a dream as I pick up speed again and keep a casual eye on my surroundings. Things have been quiet for a while now, and they should remain that way for a bit longer, but that doesn't mean shit. Everything was fucking peachy before Michael and his buddies got to town and kidnapped Alex. Shit can always go wrong, and it can go wrong quick, regardless of what's going on around you.

The cabin's address is technically on Cypress Road, on the opposite side of the Noyo River from Sherwood Road, but the cabin itself sits on the Sherwood side, and the old wooden bridge to get from Cypress to the cabin is a fucking disaster. I've been patching it here and there, but it's not my responsibility, and the city hasn't done shit about it, so instead of wondering when my Harley and I are going to end up under water, I just take the alley road to get home.

Near the back of the property, just a few hundred feet before I reach a smaller wooden bridge that brings me directly to Cypress, I veer off the dirt road and through a break I created years back in the property's fencing. I've driven through here so many times that the dirt and grass is so flattened it almost looks like a sectioned-off path. I haven't brought anything but my Harley through in a while, though, and the grass along the sides of the car is getting pretty high. I can't even see the river over the grass, which is fucking dangerous. I'll have to do something about that if Mindy's going to be here for long.

And she will be here until I know she's safe and being responsible with herself.

By the time I make it through the clearing and into the woods, Mindy's eyes are closed. She's not sleeping, I don't think, but she probably should be. I try to ask her if she still has the sleeping pills they gave her at the hospital, but she doesn't respond, which is fine. The more exhausted she is, the less likely she is to fight me on getting the fucking glass out of her arms. I wish I could say I don't know what she was thinking, hurting herself like that, but unfortunately I have a pretty good fucking idea what's going on in her head. The signs are all there, and I of all people should be able to recognize them. I was too much of a bastard, focusing on the shit I shouldn't have been instead of making sure she's stable. No, I was focused on her smell and the way she smiles. She's gotten this sassy walk in the last several weeks that she didn't have before, not even before her attack.

I park the car in the small clearing in front of the cabin and get out. Mindy's eyes shoot open at the sound of the driver's side door shutting. She looks around for a moment before getting out herself and checking out her surroundings.

"This isn't home," she says quietly. She moves to cross her arms over her chest but stops when her face screws up in pain. Her pale blue shirt is smeared in dried blood, and her arms have small streaks of blood still seeping out. It's not much, so she should be fine, but if any of the slices are too big, she might be better off getting stitches at the hospital. Lowering her face, she lifts her arms and gapes at her arms and shirt. Her face screws up again, and I shake my head and signal for her to come to me with the crook of my finger.

"It is now," I say and hold her eyes. It takes a while, but when we finally get into the cabin, her eyes dart around at everything around her. It's a small place, so there's not a whole ton for her to look at, but she takes the time nonetheless. The cabin really only has four rooms—the living room, which we're standing in now, and the kitchen, just beyond the wall in front of us. Aside from the wide doorway to the kitchen, the only other door in the living area aside from the front door is the one to my bedroom. I point at the open door and wait for her to move. She barely looks at me as she leads me in, her eyes way too distracted by the "dated décor" as Ma calls it. I haven't done anything with the place and never cared to until now.

Having Mindy walk through my space, as fucked-up as she is right now, makes me feel like maybe I should have done something to make the cabin feel like a home. I don't fucking know, but the place hasn't been updated and barely any furniture has been changed out since Sylvia, Pop's mom, decorated the place back when Ryan was born.

"Bed," I say and point at my full-sized bed. It's messy as fuck, and I honestly can't remember the last time I changed the sheets. Couple years back, when Fish hooked up with his chick, Mary, the first thing he said about it was that he always had clean sheets. Sure, he had a woman to bust his balls, but he also had someone making him dinner and keeping his clean bed warm. We laughed at him, fucked with him over giving a fuck about something like clean sheets, and still won't let him live it down. But the truth is, as I watch Mindy sit herself on the edge of my bed, I'm dying to know if she does laundry—and if she does, I might commit a few felonies to keep her around.

In the bathroom, I grab the supplies I need and toss them on the bed next to her. She's silent as I gently take her arm and clean her up, but she watches my every move.

"You shouldn't have to take care of me," she says.

"Don't have to. I choose to."

"I'll pay for the mirror."

"Don't worry about it." Some of her cuts are a little deeper than others, but thankfully there's very little glass in her skin from what I've seen so far, and the pieces have been large. The cuts that need it get super glue on them, and the others are either left open after they're cleaned or they're bandaged up. Once all the blood is cleared away, it doesn't look nearly as bad as it did before.

"Did you mean what you said before?" Her lower lip trembles as she says it, but she sounds determined.

"I always mean what I say—I just don't always mean to say it."

"You said I can't want you. You said I don't know what I'm asking for."

"I did." Fuck. She's going there. I wish she wouldn't, but I guess she wouldn't be Mindy if she didn't. This girl fucking guts me, and she doesn't even know it.

"You only know one side of me. I couldn't have you and then lose you." I finish up her other arm and place a hand on her knee.

"You're not going to lose me," she says. Her full lips form a pout, and she stares at me with a tired expression.

186

My thumb rubs small circles on her knee, comforting us both. She lets out a soft sigh and blows out a breath. With both hands, I cup her face and pull her close to me.

"I want things for you—a good man with a safe job, a couple of kids, and a nice house. I want you to be secure, and taken care of, and for all this sick shit to be a distant memory. You can't want me, because I don't want someone like me for you." It's the realest thing I've ever said, and that scares the shit out of me. I'm not afraid of my feelings, but I'm not usually into sharing them with anyone. With Mindy, though, I want to do more than to share with her. I want to be everything for her. I want her to want me because of who I am and not what I represent.

But no matter how desperate I am to have her, I need her safe and free of my shit even more. I love her too much to not be selfish with her. Seeing her dreams come true, even with another man, is what I need for her. I'll always watch over her, making sure she gets what she needs and deserves. I just won't be the man giving it to her.

She leans in and drags her nose along mine. Tears pool in her eyes and fall down her cheeks when she scrunches them closed.

"Is that what you want?" she asks. "I mean, the kids and house part?"

"Why? You offering?" I try to tease her, but when she opens her eyes, there's an emptiness there that fucks me up, so I go about answering her honestly. "It's expected that brothers will take an old lady eventually. Most of them end up with kids, but it was never my thing." I hate admitting that to her. For some reason, I wish I could tell her that I want the whole normal family bullshit. There's this look in her eyes that I can't exactly make out. It's too sad to be sure, but she's definitely not saying something that she clearly wants to say. And it's too difficult to stay here, holding on to her and knowing that I'm not enough.

Ryan changed when he met Alex, so maybe that's what happens when you find the person that just fits you. If I allowed Mindy in the way I wish I could, I'd do the whole house and kids bullshit. I'd probably fucking love it, if I'm being honest with myself. Ma and I were lost as fuck back before Pop sucked her in, but when he did, we became a family. I liked being part of a family as much as I like being part of the club, more even. But I see the path she's going down, and I don't want to be the thing that destroys her. I don't know how I'm going to keep her close and get her to understand why we can't ever happen, but I have to try.

I place a gentle kiss to her forehead, then stand up, and cross the room where I grab a clean shirt and pair of boxers for her to change into. Her clothes are a disaster, and she's tired.

"Change into these and take a nap," I say and move to head out of the room, but she clears her throat and stands from the bed, so I pause in case she has something to say. She folds her arms over her chest and narrows her eyes. Oh, she has something to say all right, and I'm probably not going to like it.

"You know, if you want me to stop being interested in you, then you really should stop kissing me."

When I leave the room, I mentally kick myself in the ass for kissing her to begin with. I hate when people give bullshit excuses like how they couldn't help themselves, but fuck if I could stop myself from kissing her that night. Everything was so fucked-up and so right at the same time. She was just there, and she's Mindy, and I've never wanted anyone as much as I want her, so I kissed her. I didn't even get to taste her the way I wanted to, but it doesn't matter anymore. I can't subject her to a life with me, not really anyway.

The front door shuts behind me, and it's so quiet yet so loud at the same time. Standing on the front porch, I lower my head and close my eyes. One deep breath and then two and three, and it's not enough to calm my heart from beating out of my chest.

I loved Mindy yesterday and the day before that and the month before that. I even thought I loved her the first time she pressed her cheek into my palm on top of that playground structure. I thought I loved her a thousand times on a hundred days. And I was wrong every single time.

If I thought what I felt then was love, I have no fucking clue what I'm feeling now. Every inch of my body hurts even though I'm not injured. My brain is running a million miles a minute with racing thoughts of how much I love her, of how desperate I am to have her and protect her. Nothing will ever be the same after this moment. I've never been in love, didn't even know I was capable of it. I've liked women before, been amused by them, but never have I wanted them as fiercely as I want Mindy.

Loving Mindy isn't something I'm prepared for. I don't know if you can ever be prepared for this. I love Ma, I love Pop, and I love Ryan. I even love Alex and Michael, but it's different with each of them. I want them in my life, and I want them safe and happy. But I'm selfish with them, and I'm okay with that. I don't really care too much if I'm difficult with them, or if I'm not good enough for them because they're my family.

Everything is different with Mindy.

I'm different with Mindy.

I leave the cabin in her Acura and drive into town. Before I know it, I'm parking the car and getting out. The For Sale sign hangs in the window of the still-empty space that used to be Universal Grounds. I've been by here more times than I can count since it happened, but this is only the second time I've stopped. Mindy might be getting better, but I'm not. The more I feel for her, the harder it is not to torch this fucking building. I'm not one of those people who gets over shit that goes wrong in life. I work it out in my head, make a plan, and then take out the offending party. It's really that simple. The people I can't find or deal with immediately are on a mental list, and I don't fucking give out pardons.

But I can't kill the men who hurt Mindy. I can't kill them because they're already dead. Duke killed the fucker who tried to choke Mindy to death with his dick. Holly took the other one out with a fucking brick to the guy's face. He was so fucked-up by the time we got there, I have no idea what he looked like before she got started on him. The other one, though. I remember his face as he lay dying on the floor, just feet from my girl. I'll always remember the face of that sick fuck.

My mind drifts to what our life could be like together. I'd do everything in my power to make her feel safe to be with me. I wouldn't be able to stand it if she feared my touch in any way. I'd give her everything Pop's given Ma, except I'd probably give her a couple of kids if she wanted that. We'd get married at some point because she deserves the highest level of commitment I can give to her. I'd move her into a real house, where she could bake cookies and shit and make the fucking place a home. I'd take her on my bike as often as I could because I know how much she loved that one ride I took her on. I wouldn't ever be enough for her, but I could spend every day of my miserable fucking life trying to be worthy of her.

I try to keep it at bay, but I can't. There's a darkness in my world that I'm trying to ignore. Mindy would be at home baking cookies, and I'd come home covered in blood. Our kids wouldn't have a normal childhood with visiting their fucked-up dad in prison. I'd tell Mindy not to bring them, but she would. The woman wouldn't listen, I already know that. She would tell me how much she loves me, even if she doesn't mean it, because that's just who she is. She would make sure our kids were fed and clothed and cared for, but what would I do for them? I would do what my dad did for me. I'd give them a man they know loves them, but he'd still be a sadistic killer. I'd try to make it to their baseball games or dance performances, but the cut I'd wear the times I'd be able to show up would tell their friends' parents that we're not the kind of family their kids should hang out with.

Money is flush now, but if the state legalizes bud, we're pretty much fucked. Our business is built on the illegality of it, and while we'd still have a business to pay our bills with, we'd have to pay bullshit taxes and deal with regulatory crap that would severely cut into the profits. That's best case scenario. Bud isn't our only business, and there's no fucking way the other shit we got our hands in will become legit. I've been locked up before, and I'll be locked up again, and what the fuck would Mindy do on her own?

The pain in my chest gets so bad that it feels like my bike got dropped on my fucking ribs. I didn't know it could hurt this bad, had no fucking clue how painful it is to realize how much you love someone, knowing you're not good for them.

Mindy's future is a fuck lot brighter without me in it. She could have that house and those kids and not be with a man who reminds her of when her body was torn apart and her soul was fractured. Mindy deserves peace and happiness, and I may be able to make her happy at times, but I'll never give her peace.

And because of that, I have to let her go once she's stable enough. I'll be a selfish prick for just a little while longer, and I'll guard the time I have with her as ferociously as I can, because when our time is up and she's gone, I'll have nothing left but the memory of the only woman I'll ever love. And then I'll become more of what I hate, because if I can't have the only thing worth breathing for, then I'll become the creature nightmares are made of.

Mindy

Chapter 18

"OH, IAN," **I** moan and shove my face into the pillow beneath my head. My naked body slides against the aged, dark red sheets, my legs twisting the fabric into a tangled mess. I stretch out and arch my back, enjoying the feeling of being naked in his bed. The only thing that would make this moment better would be if Ian were here with me. A sigh escapes me at the thought. Oh, the incredible things he could do to my body if only he were here. Well, you know, here and willing.

"I'm naked and in the man's bed," I tell myself with exasperation. "If he won't touch me like this, then I give the hell up." I'm no slouch, and I know that, but Ian's little temper tantrum today wasn't exactly an expression of love. It was more like a desperate plea from a volatile man. He sees things in me that I don't see in myself, things I can't bring myself to believe—especially when he refuses to let me in. I'm not asking him to be someone different. I've fallen head over running shoes in love with him just as he is—scars and all. I only wish he could see what's in my heart. Then maybe he wouldn't push me away.

If he knew that this isn't a phase and I'm not going to run away when things get dark and scary, then maybe he would allow himself to love me the way I so desperately need him to. No matter what he thinks, he's it for me. He wants me to have this idealistic life that can't exist. The darkness will always be there, in my life, because it's a part of me now. I can't just pretend it's not there like he does. The darkness and pain have shaped me in an irreversible way. I can't even imagine who I would be now without all the fucked-up little bits that brought Ian to me, and I don't want to. I'm not sure that I really like who I am now, but it doesn't matter.

He's what matters.

Sucking in a deep breath, I revel in his scent. It's a strange mix of sweat and mint with another scent that I can't really place. My entire body relaxes as I hug his pillow and try to relax. When I fell asleep earlier, I was wearing Ian's boxers and T-shirt. They were comfortable, and I should be putting them back on now, but I couldn't help myself. I just wanted to know what it would be like to lie naked in his bed just once. So now I'm lying here, obsessively breathing in his scent and wondering exactly when it was that I fell off my rocker and right on my head. But I'm not too concerned, so I suck in another deep breath and inhale his unique scent. If I'm not careful, I could fall asleep just like this.

In the distance, I hear the rumble of a Harley. At least, I think it's a Harley. A yawn escapes me as a light shines in through the front of the cabin. The sound grows louder as it nears. It takes me a moment, as I wiggle in my spot in the bed, to realize that I have company. I try to untangle myself from the sheets and fly off the bed in a frantic search for the boxers and T-shirt in the dark room. It must be the middle of the night because the sky is pitch black outside. There isn't a clock in this room from what I can tell, and I haven't bothered doing anything but stripping naked and rolling around in the bed like a nut case. The noise from the bike stops just as I find the T-shirt and slip it on. Heavy footsteps sound from the front porch, and the front door opens. Just in time, I find the boxers and slink back into bed, pulling them on and lying there awkwardly and try to pretend that I'm asleep.

The front door shuts, and moments later, Ian walks into the bedroom. He stops in the doorway and leans against the frame. With his arms crossed over his chest, he lets out an unamused laugh and says, "I know you're not asleep."

"How?" I ask and sit up immediately. I could have tried to keep up the charade that I was sleeping, but there's little point.

"You snore." Through a sliver of moonlight, I can see the faint smile on his face. If it wasn't such a wonderful and rare sight, I might be annoyed by his observation.

"I do not snore." I do, but no lady wants to admit to such a thing. "And even if I did, you wouldn't know that I do, but for the record, I don't."

"You do."

"No, I don't."

Liar, my brain screams at me.

"But you do," he says. "Starts out with heavy breathing, then this nasally business, and finally a snoring-wheezing thing once you're fully asleep. If you're having a nightmare, you talk in your sleep."

Pushing off the door frame, he walks out of the bedroom and opens the front door. I'm half-stunned by what he's said and half-scared that he's going to leave again. Sometimes it surprises me how well Ian knows me. I guess he picked up on my sleeping habits when I was in the hospital. I can't imagine where else he would have learned all of that.

"Where are you going?"

"Out." The tone of his voice tells me he's tired and maybe even annoyed, but he's trying hard to keep it from showing. I guess I know him pretty well, too. Just like I know that yelling after him won't keep him here with me. He doesn't respond to normal pleas, so I don't even try. Instead, I go straight for what will get his attention.

There's not a whole lot in the bedroom for me to work with, but I find an empty glass on the table beside the bed and grip it in my hand. I don't have much of an arm, so I focus really hard on what I'm doing and take a deep breath before tossing the glass at the closing front door. It shatters against the solid wood, and sure enough, the front door reopens instantly. Ian's standing in the doorway, staring me down. I'll have to remember to clean the glass up the first chance I get. The last thing I want is to step in that mess.

"Was that necessary?" he asks in a bored tone and walks back into the house, shutting the door behind him.

"Yes."

"You gonna clean up your mess?" He's back in the bedroom now, and he's leaning over the bed, his teeth gritted and his voice rough.

"No." I lift my brows and tuck my legs underneath me. I have a brief moment of being shy when my breasts bounce as I reposition myself. I was fully clothed when he left earlier, well before I dozed off for my nap. I notice his eyes fall to my chest momentarily and then dart right back up to my face.

"There a reason you're throwing shit?"

"Yeah."

When I threw the glass, I just knew that I didn't want him to leave, but now that he's standing in front of me, I realize that it's so much more than that. I've been working up to being able to be touched and being ready to be with him, but he keeps pulling away. We get closer and then he pulls back, just like clockwork, and it's sending me over an emotional cliff. He said he wouldn't be the reason I fall apart because of my reckless behavior, but the truth is, there's nothing he can do to not be the reason I break. Everything I've done has been for him, to be with him, and I'm not going to let him take this from me. I've lost too much already. I won't lose him, too.

Be brave.

"You gonna explain?"

"No."

His jaw ticks at my one-word answers, but I don't care. My heart beats frantically in my chest, my palms are sweaty, and I'm damn close to hyperventilating, but I don't let any of that stop me.

"I want you," I say firmly.

"This again?" He barks the words out, now definitely annoyed. "Been over this, babe. I won't subject you to this life."

"No," I say more firmly. He has to take me seriously, or I'll never be able to get over the shame of it. "I *want* you."

My fingers practically strangle the fabric of the T-shirt as I hold the bottom in my grip. They're shaking. I'm fearful that he's going to laugh at me. Or he'll reject me and pity me for even having to beg someone to touch me after how badly I've been damaged. Tears well in my eyes as the panic sets in. Before I can stop myself, I lift the hem of the shirt while studying his face. His expression darkens, his eyes totally fixed on my torso, which at the very least tells me he's physically interested in what I'm offering.

"I want you to fuck me." My voice squeaks at the end like I'm some kind of virginal school girl, which couldn't be further from the truth. He purses his lips and his hands form tight fists at his sides, while his eyes still haven't left my covered breasts.

Be brave.

With one last breath, I squeeze my eyes shut and lift the shirt over my head. A tear escapes, but I try to slyly wipe it away as I discard the shirt on the floor.

"You don't want this. How I fuck—you won't like it," he says. Every word sounds strained, like it's painful for him to say it. Still, he leans in and places his closed fists on the bed to support himself as he bends over. He lifts his eyes to mine, but his head is at the height of my breasts, forcing his attention back on my exposed flesh.

"I don't want it soft. I don't want gentle. I didn't ask you to make love to me. I told you I want you to fuck me, and by that I mean I want to be fucked hard and fast and I don't want you to take it easy on me."

He licks his lips and swallows the saliva pooling in his mouth. It's so obvious now that he desires me physically even if he wishes he didn't intellectually. Hooking my fingers around the sides of the boxers, I slowly slide them down my legs and try not to look too stupid as I struggle to get them off with the position I'm in. I have the offending material still around my calves, tucked under my ass when he surprises me by reaching out and grabbing me behind my knees. I reach out and place my hands on his shoulders to steady myself as he pulls my legs out from underneath me.

"Use your safe word and we stop. You can turn back at any time, but if this is what you want, then I'll give it to you," he says. My legs are stretched out before me now and he easily slides the boxers off and tosses them on the floor. He removes his cut next, but keeps the tee shirt on that's underneath.

"Your safe word is bayonet. Use it if you wish for the scene to stop. You will use colors to communicate how well you're handling what I'm doing to you. Green means you're fine, yellow means you need me to slow down or lighten up, and red means you're close to breaking. Saying red or bayonet will stop the scene immediately."

He unbuckles his belt and tosses it aside, then goes for his jeans and pulls them down his long legs. I study him and the instructions he's given me. He's using terms I'm not really familiar with, like *scene* and *safe word*, but I have an idea what he means.

"What if I want more?" I ask.

"You won't," he says in a harsh tone.

"But what if I do?"

"If you say purple, you won't like the consequences." His voice has taken on a sneer now, like the very idea of me saying purple disgusts him. I don't even know what it means, but it definitely means something. A surge of panic makes me second-guess myself, but I refuse to verbalize my worry. I won't lose this moment for anything. I just can't.

"What are your limits, Melinda?"

"My limits?" Slowly, my mind catches up with the reality of what we're doing here, and I realize what's going on. Ian is clearly into some kink that I don't know much about. I've heard bits here and there but nothing worth noting. He asked for my limits, so I try to think about what I definitely don't want him doing to me.

"My backdoor is a no entry zone," I say.

"What else?"

I fumble over the words but finally get out what I need to say. The anal play thing isn't a firm no, as in never ever, but this next one is something I absolutely can't deal with.

"I can't," I say with a shaky voice and have to pause. "My mouth. I can't . . . put . . ."

He nods his head and narrows his eyes in contemplation.

"You don't have to finish that sentence. I know what you're trying to say."

Of course he would know. He heard everything they did to me, not just from the hospital staff when they pushed me to describe my assault, but firsthand over the phone while it was happening. I hate that he heard that. I hate that he even knows about it much less had to suffer through listening to my cries.

"Restraints?" he asks. He's only wearing his boxers now, and he stands on the side of the bed with his eyes on the floor beside him.

"Restraints are fine."

"If you dislike what I'm doing or you're uncomfortable with the level of play, say *yellow*."

"Okay."

This isn't how I pictured this happening. I kind of thought I would take my shirt off and he would lean over and kiss me and we would get busy the normal way. Even though I'm nervous and out of my element, I can't deny how hot this conversation is. When he asks about restraints and limits, my mind wanders to all the things I'm trying to imagine he could do to me. This is what I want, so it doesn't really matter what he wants to do to me. I just want this experience with him, to be as close as we can be. Maybe afterwards he'll see how good we can be together and he'll let this happen. I know better than to assume that having sex with a man will lead to a commitment, but this is Ian, and I can't imagine sex won't mean anything with us.

"Stand in the corner, facing the wall," he says and walks into the walk-in closet. I do as I'm told and wait for him to come to me. My nerves are shot by the time I feel him behind me, his breath hot on my neck.

"I've never played with a virgin before, so I'm going to go easy on you. As I try things out, I want you to tell me how you feel about what I'm doing to you. What are your colors?"

He must mean a kink virgin, because he knows all too well that I'm not really a virgin. The reminder of my damage almost ruins the moment for me, but I push through, refusing to screw this up for the both of us.

"Red or bayonet means stop, yellow means I'm uncomfortable, green means I like it, and purple means I want more."

He leans in and whispers, "This isn't part of the scene, Melinda. I'm warning you that you do *not* want to say purple. Try to just enjoy the experience."

A shiver runs up my spine at his nearness. I nod my head in understanding, but in true Ian fashion, he demands a verbal acknowledgment. "Your words, Melinda."

"I understand," I say, even though I don't, but am terribly tempted to push the whole purple boundary he's got going on.

"Until the scene is over, you refer to me as Sir, and I'll refer to you as Melinda. Do you understand, Melinda?"

"Yes, Sir," I say and try to fight the smile that's lifting the corners of my mouth. My body hums with excitement, but it's my heart that's really getting the work out. Submitting to Ian is setting something off in me. I've never felt more cherished and cared for. We haven't even done anything yet, but it feels like we've done a whole lot. I want to give this to him—my submission—because I know he's going to value it. I can show him that I belong in his world, not just in the club but here in his bed as well. I can show him that this doesn't scare me and that I'm ready to surrender myself to his demands.

"Good girl. Who do you belong to, Melinda?"

"You," I stutter out. My breath catches, and I mentally kick myself for not answering him correctly. I open my mouth to correct my mistake when he slaps my ass cheek lightly.

"Every time I touch you, I want you to give me your color. Do not call me Sir when you do so."

He slaps my ass again, this time a little harder.

"Green," I say breathily.

His hand at my ass gently rubs my cheek. The soft touch spikes something in the pit of my belly, and my hands shake at my sides. I find myself practically yelling as I say, "Yellow!"

His hand slaps at my ass again, even harder than the last time, sending a thrilling jolt through me.

"Green." The word comes out on a light moan. His harsh slaps do the opposite of what I expect, but I don't know why. The few times I've touched myself since *that* night, I haven't been able to be gentle about it. Something about the soft touches and sweet little bursts of pleasure sends me into a frenzied panic that I can't control. I tried to be slow and easy with myself, but I only ended up in tears. I should have expected that allowing Ian to touch me would be no different than when I touched myself.

Ian drags the back of his hand up my spine from my ass to the middle of my back. His touch is featherlight and once again I'm saying, "Yellow," and fighting back tears. He pauses, turns his hand over, and drags his nails up to the base of my neck. A rush of excitement fills me as I say, "Green."

"My girl doesn't like it gentle, do you, Melinda?"

"No, Sir."

"You're learning. This pleases me."

Gathering my hair in his hands, he places a soft kiss to the crown of my head, and it's the first sweet touch that doesn't make me panic. He always kisses me sweetly, and I never freak out about it, but the sexual stuff is another story entirely.

"Place your hands against the wall in front of you and open your eyes.

I do as I'm told and wait for the next touch. My hair falls against my back, and he steps away from me and lifts something that makes a slight scratching sound against the floor. Hard bristles drag along the back of my slightly spread legs from my ankles up to the backs of my knees where he places more pressure on my skin. A round of gooseflesh breaks out.

"Green."

The bristles disappear before they're back and dragging faster and harder up my legs and to my ass where they disappear only to slap at my sensitive bum with a swiftness that takes my breath from me. My chest is working overtime to keep me breathing, and my legs feel weakened by the excitement of it.

"Green," I say louder than before as a wetness pools in my core. This is happening and I can do this. I can really do this. The bristles slap at me harder now, several times. He drags them to the other cheek, and I hear the whistling of the instrument fly through the air before coming down hard on my ass. I gasp, and my eyes fly closed for a moment before remembering his instructions to keep them open.

"Color, Melinda."

"Green, fucking hell, green!" My nipples are hard and I'm panting heavily now. Without thinking about it, I push my ass at him, desperate for more.

"Spread your legs, greedy girl."

"Yes, Sir," I respond and spread them as far as I can while remaining steadily on my feet. I feel exposed but not in a scary way. It's empowering, accepting what he wants to give me. Willing him to give me more of it, harder and faster. I *need* more. I tip my ass up again, practically begging for his touch.

The bristles roughly drag up in the inside of my leg to my inner thigh and swoop across my open core. And now I know, without a doubt, that the instrument of my pleasure is a broom. I'm never going to be able to use a broom without remembering how exciting it is to be spanked with one.

He drags the bristles of the broom down my other leg and then back up as he slaps it at my core. The surge of pleasure is wonderful, but an underlying fear tickles at the back of my neck. I don't want to say it, but I know I have to.

"Yellow." I scrunch my eyes closed in fear that he'll stop what he's doing entirely.

"What do you fear, Melinda?"

"The handle." Tears well in my eyes. *They* used a prop and it hurt me. It took more than just my blood. It took my future, and it took me a long time to heal from it. A panic attack settles in, and I can't breathe.

"I will *never* put anything inside of you that will hurt you," he says, sets the broom down beside me, and places his hands on top of mine against the wall and presses his chest into my back.

"Listen to me, Mindy," he whispers in my ear. "I remember every single thing those sick fucks forced Holly to tell me. Every word and every terrified cry replays in my head every single night. I lay awake, fantasizing about killing those men and hating myself for not having been the one to do it. They hurt you in a way I can't ever make right, but I will never, not ever insert anything into you that isn't my flesh."

Chapter 19

SOBS RACK MY body and I cry out, frustrated, with the ruined moment. He called me Mindy, and he told me the scene would be over when he did that. And I cry harder, but not for the fear of the broom handle—that's gone now. I'm crying because I don't want this to end. I need to have this with him. For the first time in a damn long time, being touched sexually doesn't just feel good, it feels perfect.

"Please, Sir," I say through my sniffles, trying to convey what I need without sounding too pathetic.

"Mindy," he says. His voice is so quiet and strained. I can't handle losing this with him. He turns me around so I'm facing him and cups my face in his hands. "This is a mistake."

"No," I say loudly and place my hands over his on my cheeks. "I want this. I want you. I *need* this from you. Just . . . let me do this."

His eyes search mine, like he needs further reassurance that I'm okay. I don't know if okay is the right word for it, but it'll have to do for now. I drop my hands to his waist and slip my index fingers into the waistband of his boxers. I take a peek down and try to force back the blush that explodes on my cheeks when I see the tent his erection is creating.

"The only thing that makes me better is you," I say and pull his boxers down and redirect my eyes to his face. His brows are pulled together, his expression severe. I want to see his hardness, uncovered and ready for me, but I need his eyes. I need him to see me, really see me as I offer myself to him.

"You don't have to like it, but you do have to accept it."

"Do I?" He loses the hardness in his features, replacing it with a sadness that breaks me apart in ways the memories of what *they* did to me never could. Looking at him now, there's no doubt in my mind that he doesn't believe he can be good for me.

I might not be able to convince him that he's good for me, but I can show him how well our bodies will fit together. He sighs heartily and lowers his hands to my waist, gripping me firmly and pulling my naked body against his. I gasp at the smooth hardness pressing into my stomach. His hands are all rough and calloused, and his arms and legs are firm with his well-crafted muscles. He's so rough everywhere, except for here. The flesh of his shaft is so soft. I don't remember Heath being this soft, but that was a long time ago.

"I belong to you."

He smashes his lips against mine. We each battle for dominance over the other, like we're trying to prove a point to the other person. He's insisting that he's bad for me with every bossy caress of his tongue, and I'm demanding he see reason as I lovingly nip at his lips. We're not competing for something, just arguing the only way we can now that we've worn out the words and have grown sick of the pain. I'm moaning and rubbing myself against him shamelessly. In response, he wraps his arms around me, holding me so tight against the hardness of his body that the twitch of his cock only encourages me. I slip one of my hands to his ass and give it a hard squeeze. He groans and pulls his lips from mine just an inch.

"I'm not going to be able to be gentle if you do that," he says.

My lips turn up into a sly smile, and I do it again, this time standing on my toes and rubbing on his cock more forcefully than before.

"I'm not asking for gentle."

"Are you ready to be fucked, Melinda?"

He's all business now, the scene back on. Hearing the sharpness of his tone thrills me, and I have to clamp my legs together to calm the thundering in my core. I place my hands back on the wall, where they were before the scene broke.

"Yes, Sir."

He leans to the side and grabs the bandana that's on the dresser nearby. He folds it twice and then reaches around me and ties it over my eyes tightly.

"Green," I say, remembering my color.

Ian moves away from me, though I can't tell what he's doing. The blindfold blacks everything out. I stand in place, waiting for his next move and what it will bring. I hear the scraping of something against the wooden floor beneath my feet. Cold metal slaps against my legs, and then my ass, stinging my skin along the way. It's not one solid piece, which is confusing as hell, but the sensation is incredible, distracting. I moan in response to the metal hitting my side just hard enough for it to sting. I'm going to be covered in scratches and welts when we're done here. I can't wait to see evidence of our fucking on my skin long after we've sated ourselves.

"Mmm, green."

He hits me harder and faster from my calves up to the sides of my breasts. Worn leather casually slaps at my flesh, following the metal and it's only now that I realize he's using his belt. More slaps, one after the other, switching between the metal and the leather. He bends behind me and wraps the belt around my upper thigh, holding the ends and yanks, pulling my ass into his hard cock. He must be bending or something because the tip of him brushes between my ass cheeks, pressing in, lower than he was before, and slides down to my anus. My ass is a limit for me and he knows that, so I'm not even worried that he's going to try something. My body hums in response to the erotic way he's touching me.

He tugs on the belt again, this time pulling my leg and spreading me open. One hand gathers my hair at my neck, twists it around his wrist, and pulls my head back. The other

209

moves the belt from around my leg to my wet pussy. The leather slaps hard and fierce against my aching core, sending electric currents through my body.

"Fuck. Green."

"Do you want more of that, Melinda?"

"Yes, Sir." I so want to say *purple*, but he's in control, artfully so, and I doubt he'll react well.

"I'm going to slap your pussy hard and fast until you can't take anymore, increasing the speed and pain until you use your safe words."

But I'm determined to take everything he's willing to give me, and even more if I can manage it.

The next slap against my clit comes lower than the last and harder, too. My heart jumps, and I arch my back as he does it again and again until my entire body is shaking and I can't make heads or tails of anything apart from the powerful pulsing sensation in my core. He speeds up his ministrations, intensifying my pleasure. The slaps of the leather bite against my swollen, aching flesh. Each touch more incredible than the last. My body heats, a sheen of sweat covering every inch.

"Did you forget your words?" he asks. His voice is strained, like he's on the verge of breaking.

"No."

"You're going to bruise. This is too hard," he says. His attempt at reasoning with me does no good though. I know I'm going to bruise. I'm counting on it.

"I want it hard." I let the words slide out on a moan. He's backtracking, trying to take it easy on me, but I'm much too far gone, well past taking it easy. I want it fierce and intense. I want it to hurt. I don't want to walk normal tomorrow. I want it hard enough that even if he never fucks me again, I'll have this memory.

We're in the corner of the room with my hands on one wall and the other to my left. An idea strikes me that might be a bit crazy or might be pure genius. I turn my body slightly, not enough to be obvious, but just enough to achieve my goal. Ian moves in response, his feet at an angle that suggests his back is practically against the wall to my left. I'm still panting from the crazed slapping of the leather against my pussy. I want more, but he's not going to give it to me, so I have to find a way to take what I really need.

The leather belt wraps around one of my wrists and then the other, binding them together. He pulls on the belt, lifting my arms above my head and propping the outside of my forearms against the wall, then lowering them, with my elbows bent at a ninety-degree angle. He doesn't know it, but he's just given me exactly what I want. Placing his hand on my spine, he forces me to bend at my waist and prop my ass up in the air. I keep my legs spread as I move them backward to accommodate my new position.

"Tell me you're not ready. Say bayonet, or red, or something,"

"Green," I say with a smile.

I feel his wrist leading his cock to my aching entrance. Very slowly, slides in just an inch before stopping. He takes a deep breath and waits a moment before moving in farther. A spike of fear assaults me, reminding me of *that* night. I'm so wet and slick now that he doesn't hurt me like they did—Ian would never hurt me that way—but still. A cold, inhuman vibrator isn't the same as a human being. He's so warm, like they were, but that's where the comparisons end. The farther he slides in, the less I think of *them*. The slower he goes, the more time he takes, the more I'm able to separate what happened then with what's happening now.

I won't let them take this from me.

Nobody is going to take this from me.

He's fully sheathed inside me now, filling me up with his deliciously large cock. I squeeze him and moan because he feels perfect. When he starts to move, the low buzzing intensifies, but it's not enough.

"Green," I say firmly and shove back into him. He stills me at my hips and rocks back and forth with such gentleness that it makes my stomach turn. Fuck this gentle shit. Fuck his attempt to control this. I *need* hard and he's not giving it to me. I try to buck against him again, but again, he stills me.

"I won't hurt you any more than I already have," he says and slaps his hand on my ass in warning.

"I said green. I'm fine."

"The rules, Melinda!" He slaps at my ass again, this time slamming into me harder, forcing a moan from my lips. God. That felt good. I need more of that.

"Fuck me harder, please, *Sir*." I shove back against him and revel in the swelling ache behind my legs. He doesn't listen though, intent on making me suffer. A lump forms in my throat, the slower he goes, the more he makes this something I'm not ready for. Even though we're standing up, with my wrists bound and a blindfold over my eyes, this is starting to feel much more like making love than fucking. Loving Ian and being prepared to make love to him are two different things. I can't . . .

I can't do this.

He's being so careful with me, like he's cherishing my body. This is how a husband makes love to a wife, how a man promises forever with the woman he's committed to. But Ian refuses to give me those things, so I don't want this bullshit attempt at easy, slow sex.

Moving my forearms around the wall in a slow, blind search, I find the edge of the door frame and press my right forearm against it, angle my body farther in toward the wall behind me, and take a deep breath. He's going to be so mad at me in a moment.

Pushing back off the wall, I welcome his cock slamming into me hard and fast. I moan, loudly and unapologetically. He grips my hips, trying to still my movements, but I refuse to let him stop this. I slam back against him again, pressing down so hard that he hits the wall behind him, and I fuck his cock as hard and fast as I can. He groans and sucks in a deep breath, letting himself get into it for just a moment before he comes to his senses.

"God damn it, we're going to have to work on your submission, Melinda!"

"I'll submit when you follow your own rules. I told you I wanted it hard," I shout and keep on with my hard and fast pounding against his smooth, hard cock.

"You want hard? Fine!" He's screaming from behind me, angry now. Good. I want him angry.

He shoves me farther down the wall and back to where he had me before I got the bright idea to force him into giving me what I want. He pounds into me so hard, so fast that I suck in a breath and forget to breathe. My legs shake, my heartbeat is pounding in my ears, and the world around me is disappearing again. He drives into me harder with each thrust, working up to a painful assault on my pussy.

"Use your safe word," he demands and slaps his hand so fucking hard on my outer thigh that I lose the strength in my arms. My nose hits the wall in front of me. It stings, but I fight back the tears. When I don't answer him immediately, he does it again, this time driving into me with even more power than before. Reaching around my torso, he twists one of my nipples. I cry out frantically, but refuse to give him the power of knowing that this is getting to be too much.

"Safe word, now. Say yellow and I'll slow down. Say red or bayonet and I stop."

"No, *Sir*."

"Fuck!" he shouts and slams into me in a frantic rhythm. His breathing picks up, and he's struggling to maintain the rhythm of his insatiable rapid fire thrusts.

I'm dizzy with the need to come already. My arms and legs want to give out, but I can't prove him right, so I keep myself upright despite every instinct to just sink to the floor, panting, struggling to breathe, and desperate to give my body a break. My vision crosses. Even in the darkness under the bandana, I know that I'm reaching my breaking point. Even Ian's struggling to power through his exhaustion. He's grunting, letting out frustrated, hasty breaths.

"Sir?" I keep my voice small, like I'm giving in to his will.

"Yes, Melinda?" The words barely come out audibly.

I'm quiet for another moment as the explosion of pleasure builds in the pit of my belly and spreads swiftly through my legs, arms, and down my spine.

"Purple!" I'm gasping for breath. Unable to prop my head up any longer, I drop my forehead against the wall and scrunch my eyes shut to fight off the impending nausea that's building. This is so intense, too intense. I can't handle it. Fuck. I can't manage this much longer. But somehow, I do. In a show of stubbornness—or strength, I'm not sure which—I keep myself upright and take every painful, angry inch he gives me. My sore pussy swells and locks down around him as he grabs hold of the belt at my wrists and pulls on it. Oh my God. Shit. He's got my body propped up, half-bent into this wall as he fucks me mindlessly. His hips crash into my core so hard that I swear I can feel him hitting the very depths of my pussy.

He comes on a roar, loud and volatile in my ear, as his other hand grips my hair and yanks my face to the side, my neck exposed. His torso covers my back, the hand holding the belt at my wrists wraps around my waist, and he continues his merciless pounding. His tongue drags from my shoulder up my neck, leaving a cool, wet trail to my ear. The new angle forces my orgasm from me so violently that I lose my footing, and the only thing keeping me from falling onto the hardwood is his arm around my waist. I'm screaming my release, darkness closing in around me, and a simultaneously suffocating and freeing breaking of consciousness as the blackness takes over. The last thing I feel is his teeth at my neck biting down and sending one last savage shock to my system. My arms and legs shake uncontrollably as his bite registers and the blissful euphoria consumes me.

Chapter 20

WHEN I CAME to yesterday, I was wrapped in Ian's arms, our naked bodies intertwined in his bed. My body had been rubbed down with lotion, and he had taken great care to ensure my comfort. My wiggling in the bed woke him up, and we had a lengthy discussion about the rules, and why they exist. I pushed not only his limits but mine as well, and even though I don't regret it, I feel a little guilty.

"I won't be touching you again," he had said. Apparently he was much more serious about the purple limit than I thought. I don't believe him when he says he won't touch me again. I can't accept that. But I pushed him enough, so I'm backing off for now and letting him cool off. Maybe, in time, he will see that we can make this work. I want the pain, I want the brutality, but I don't want to risk losing him over it.

"Floor's clean, babe." He comes up behind me, taking the broom from my grasp and propping it up against the wall. I eye the broom curiously, thinking back to how he used the one at the cabin to give me pleasure in ways I couldn't have imagined before.

"Huh?" I'm distracted and can't seem to get my brain in order. I was scatterbrained enough at the cabin, but here in the clubhouse, I'm a hundred times worse. There's so much going on today, with one of the patched members just having gotten out of jail, and the clubhouse is a buzz of activity and excitement. I refuse to go anywhere near the pleasure palace for fear of seeing people I normally like engaged in activities I definitely don't like—together. I'm not a prude, but Bear suggesting that he and the dude who just got out, Torque, should run a train on Chel—a woman I happen to really like—and watching her smile and walk toward the palace is enough for me. The three of them seemed so comfortable with the idea, like it wouldn't be the first time they've done such a thing.

"You've been sweeping the same spot for five minutes," Ian says, pulling me back into the moment. "What's going on in that pretty head of yours?"

"Chel," I admit. Ian heard the exchange. He knows they headed down the hall for the pleasure palace. Surely he can figure out why this bothers me.

"Lost girls are here to keep the brothers happy, but make no mistake about it—they're here because they want to be, and they only do what they want to do. Especially Chel. Torque wouldn't hurt her."

"It's hard to imagine . . . two men . . . that she'd want that." God, I sound like such a freaking baby. This is ridiculous. Chel is a grown-ass woman, and if Ian tells me she's safe and this dude, Torque, won't hurt her, then I need to fucking believe that.

"Hm. Hard to imagine you'd like to have your pussy slapped with a broom, too. But the weirdest shit gets people off." There's a sly smile playing at his lips that sends a blush to my cheeks. Oh Christ, now I'm thinking of everything except for Chel and the two large men who are impaling her as we speak.

"Just tell me that broom wasn't dirty," I say. I hadn't thought of it at the time, but looking at the dirty broom propped against the wall makes me wonder exactly how *dirty* that scene was.

"First time I touched the fucking thing was to tease you with it."

"It was new?"

"Ma dropped it off sometime last year, some kind of hint that I needed to clean the fucking place."

"You mean to tell me that broom was in your house for a year and you hadn't used it once?"

"Got better shit to do than clean, babe," he says and turns his attention to the line of men disappearing down the hallway to my side. They pass up the pleasure palace—thank goodness, too—and head straight into the chapel. "Shit. Church. Hang out here with Baby Boy, 'kay? Don't want you running off anywhere."

Like I'm going anywhere without him. We rode his Harley in today, and I'm damn determined to ride it home, too. I couldn't imagine it possible the first time I got on the back of his bike, but I actually love riding Ian more than his bike, and I can't get enough of either.

"Don't worry," I say and grab the room, giving him a cheeky smile. "I won't get swept away." I wiggle my brows and break out into a full grin, laughing at my own joke. "Get it—swept away?"

"Fuck, you're cute," he says and hooks his hand around the back of my neck, pulling me into his chest and kissing the top of my head. I can feel the smile on his lips with that kiss and the lightness in his tone. For a brief moment, he looks happy and relaxed.

"Think you're going to keep me now?"

"I gotta go." He dodges my question, which is just so typical.

A commotion breaks out at the end of the hall, distracting me from Ian's shady behavior. The man I haven't officially met, Torque, waves a black plastic device in his hand and is individually checking the brothers' out by waving the device over their jeans and boots.

"What the hell is he doing?" I ask. Torque has pitch-black hair and squinty brown eyes. He looks kind of like a real life villain with the way he waves that plastic wand and cackles at the men who stand in line at the door. Ryan stands in front of Torque. He pulls what looks like a mobile phone from his pocket and drops it in the box Jeremy's holding.

"Paranoid fuck. Always been his thing. Asshole doesn't trust anybody, not even us," Ian says. I nod my head in understanding. I already know they don't allow phones or weapons in Church. I've just never seen anybody play security detail before. I fight back a laugh when Ryan disposes of two guns, three knives, and a firework into the box.

"What the hell?" Jeremy asks as he pulls out the firework and eyes it curiously.

"Thought I'd shove it up your ass later."

Jeremy's face pales at Ryan's comment. The foulness of it all doesn't even surprise me anymore. Ryan is always going on about shoving things up people's asses. It's kind of his thing, which makes me wonder if he's ever topped another dude. I wouldn't be shocked if he has, to be honest.

"Here," Ian says. He pulls out his mobile phone and hands it to me. "Waiting on a call from a breeder about a new line of stock. Call comes in, answer it. Tell that lazy fuck I need my product and I need it soon."

"Um. What kind of breeder? What product?" I probably don't want to know, but I can't stop myself from asking anyway.

"Dog breeder. One of his bitches just had a litter, and it's about time we replace Tegan and amp up our detail."

"Oh," I say and laugh to myself. "I so didn't think that's what you were going to say. Um, do you think I can go with you to get the puppy?"

I haven't let myself be upset about it in a long time, but I really hate not having any pets. We used to have a dog, years back, but when Bugsy died, Dad refused to replace him. I loved that dog and really loved having the company. Heath and I never had a dog, and after Heath, I wasn't in a place to take care of anything—not even myself.

"Won't be getting a puppy. Our dogs come fully trained and old enough to stay focused on the job at hand. But yeah, my girl likes dogs, we'll get her a dog."

He's still smiling as he heads down the hall and tosses his knife and gun into the box in Jeremy's arms that's now practically overflowing. I'm smiling so big, being so ridiculously happy, that I can't contain myself. Ian's getting me a dog. Holy fuck, I'm getting a dog! Even though I know this is likely a strategy to distract me from the whole "no sex" thing he's trying to implement, I don't care. I'll let him distract me with pets any day. Maybe if I continue to push the topic of sex, I can get a cat out of him, too.

"This is bullshit and you know it, you stupid fuck!"

My smile falls from my face when I see Ian trying to keep the peace between Fish and Torque. Fish is yelling and trying to dodge Torque's plastic wand. The device makes a loud beeping sound when it slides over Fish's pocket. Something looks off about Fish. His words are slurred, and he's unsteady on his feet. It takes but a moment for me to realize that he's high. It's not like being high is a no-no in the eyes of the club, but it certainly is during Church. Chel once told me that being a little stoned during Church is encouraged because it keeps them from whipping their dicks out, but being full on fucked-up is a pretty big problem since it's technically a business meeting.

"You already got my phone, man," Fish says and scrubs a hand over his face.

"Then you got another one. Get it out, motherfucker," Torque orders. Jim appears in the doorway and demands they get a move on already. Looking defeated, Fish pulls something small and black from his pocket and tosses it in the box, then waits until Torque has scanned him with the wand and lets him into the room. Torque closes the door behind him, shutting me and Jeremy off from the chapel.

"For once, I'd rather be out here than in there," Jeremy says and drops the box on the table beside me.

"I'm guessing those two don't get along."

Jeremy nods in response and sorts the contents of the box. He's concentrating awfully hard on his task. Last fall, right before *that* night, I stayed with Duke and Nic and Jeremy at their house. Jeremy didn't say much at first, but once he opened up to me, I couldn't get him to stop talking. We bonded over our shared prison sentences. He'd been a lifer, looking forward to parole when he turned eighteen, and I was the new arrival he'd schooled on how to get by without too much bitching from Warden Duke. Much to Jeremy's dismay, I never did get have to suffer the warden's wrath.

"How's parole?" I ask.

He snorts and shakes his head. "Wouldn't know."

"Adulthood not what it's cracked up to be?"

"You know prospects don't actually get paid? I put in enough fucking time with this club, and I'm lucky if the warden spots me a fiver for a fucking sandwich every now and then." Jeremy's navy-blue eyes narrow. He's such a handsome kid, so tall, and with a huge heart. He's still just a teenager, though, and has some more maturing to do.

"Worth it," I say casually. He just stares at me like I'm speaking a foreign language. "You can bitch all you want, but we both know this is where you belong. Forsaken's your family, and if Duke is tight about sharing the wealth, then it's for your benefit."

One thing I know for certain about Duke from my short time living with him is this—he's as generous as can be. As long as Duke's around, Nic won't want for anything.

"You sound like somebody's mother," he grumbles, staring at the gun in his hand like he's trying to figure something out. Finally, he places it next to another gun and a phone. I bite back the pang of sorrow his comment creates. "Not that I'd know what that sounds like."

"Of course you know what a mother sounds like. Nic's been trying to mother your stubborn ass for years, not that you've made it easy on her."

"Figured she'd miss a pill and get knocked up at some point. Had to make sure she knew what she was doing—for Robin's sake, ya know."

"Totally," I say and nod my head, smiling. I get to babysit Robin about once a week or so now. Sometimes it's just for an hour, and other times it's longer. Jeremy puts in his fair share of time with her, too, which I know he enjoys, though he'll never admit it.

Ruby walks up and places her hands on her hips and looks at Jeremy's seemingly random arrangement of weapons and mobile phones laid out over three of the smaller tables. She shakes her head and laughs.

"Jim's really putting you through the ringer, huh, kid?"

"Pres thinks this will help me learn to pay better attention," Jeremy says. Ruby places a hand on his shoulder and gives it a squeeze.

"You've done good."

Jeremy's eyes volley between Ruby and his arrangement before his eyes widen and he gapes at her for a long moment. A smirk graces his handsome features. He gathers up the items and places them back in the box, checking the guns to make sure the safety is on each one, and shakes it. Ruby takes it from him, sets it on the table, and quickly takes out and arranges everything very similar to how Jeremy had done just a few minutes ago.

"A good old lady makes her old man's business her business. It's not her place to stick her nose in. It's her job to keep his shit running, and that means knowing his brothers and their club."

"Take notes, Bean." Jeremy whistles and elbows me in my side. I tense up but try to shake it off. Ruby's eyes roll dramatically at his comment, but I ignore it. I don't think she likes me much, but I don't have the energy to deal with that right now and busy myself with wiping down the empty table tops.

One of the mobiles Jeremy arranged on the tables chirps, but I ignore it. Then it rings, and rings again, before Jeremy's bothered with checking out the phone and inspecting it. It chirps in his hands. He shakes his head and sets it back on the table just as it starts ringing again.

"What the hell? Ian's phone never rings," he says and silences it.

"Oh crap. Gimme that!" I drop the rag I'm cleaning with and snatch the phone from his hands. I can't believe I almost forgot the dog breeder was supposed to call. I press the green answer button and hold the phone to my ear. I'm about to say hello when a rough, Italian-accented voice sounds in my ear.

"You ever answer your phone? We got Jennings. Just waiting on your signal to get him out safely." The man on the other end sounds out of breath. His words don't make sense, but they send a chill down my spine anyhow. I lose my breath and pull the phone away from my ear and end the call. That wasn't the dog breeder.

"Bean?" Jeremy sounds worried, but I can't be bothered by it. I stare down at the phone in my hand and try to make sense of what just happened. My hands shake, and I can feel myself paling.

"Um, Jer? Is there a Jennings aside from *the* Jennings?"

I hate that name. So much of the last year has been spent hearing the name Jennings, and it's never good. As far as the town knows, Darren Jennings was a victim of a vicious attack that may or may not have been in response to his father's supposed gambling problem. His parents disappeared some months back, which has only strengthened the gambling rumors. According to the town's rumor mill, on top of everything Darren's suffered, he's also developed a drug problem, even going so far as to having drugs smuggled into the hospital. He overdosed last month and landed himself in the psych ward. Mom says it was such a shame since he'd been about to be released after nearly a year recovering from his injuries and subsequent coma.

The truth about Darren Jennings is far darker and more disturbing than anything the newspaper will ever print. I've known him for years now, though not well. His parents are members of the same church as my parents, but that's not why his name makes my skin crawl. Darren Jennings is the reason Nic has those star tattoos on her body—one for each time he raped and beat her. He's also the reason . . .

"Why are you bringing that fucker up?" Jeremy asks in a gruff tone.

I didn't even realize that Ruby walked away some time ago until her boots clack against the concrete floor and she comes to stand beside me. She places a hand on my back and leans in, speaking quietly. "You okay?"

I try to answer them both. No, I'm not okay. I can't . . .

Panic swells in my chest, unsettling my stomach and forcing the breath from my lungs. There's got to be a good reason for Ian getting a call like this. No way in hell Ian would take part in anything that would keep Darren Jennings safe. Not ever. The phone rings in my hand, startling me. I answer it immediately but don't say anything when I bring it to my ear.

"Banks? We need to move. Are we clear or not?"

I end the call and force myself to work through the panic. Banks? Who the hell is Banks? I use my free hand to pat down my pockets and find what I thought I might—Ian's phone. Pulling it out, I stare at Ian's phone in one hand and its twin in the other. Ruby and Jeremy are practically on top of me now, both staring at me with faces full of worry.

"This isn't Ian's phone." I hand Ian's real mobile over to Ruby and try to poke through the mystery phone that Jeremy mistook for Ian's. It has a password lock on it, so I can't get in, but there are several text message notifications showing on the lock screen. They all come from the same phone number with a four-one-five area code.

"Everybody else's phones are accounted for," Ruby says. Her attention is fixed on the tables full of guns, knives, and cell phones.

"Who is Banks?" I ask.

Ruby's eyes dart to mine, her mouth parts, and she stares at me blankly. The memory comes to me slowly but surely when

I think back to the scene at the end of the hall as Fish and Torque argued about Torque's trying to check Fish for another phone.

"Solomon Banks. That's the only Banks I know," Ruby says and then clarifies. "Fish."

"The second phone," Jeremy says with his eyes narrowed.

"That was a man calling Fish's phone to tell him he's got Jennings but needs Fish to signal him to get him out safely. When he called back, he used the name Banks and said he has to move and needs Fish to give the all clear."

"The rat is Fish," Jeremy says to Ruby. "He's working with some asshole to get Jennings to safety?"

Darren Jennings is the reason I was raped. I put two and two together well before Holly ever told me anything. Darren raped Nic years ago, then tried to do it again when she was pregnant with Robin. The club took care of Darren, and then *randomly*, some months later, I'm raped by two men who keep calling me Nic. I wasn't even out of the hospital yet when Darren's parents disappeared from town. I thought I might be paranoid at first, but the more I thought about it, the more it just fit.

"Looks like it," Ruby says. Her face is hard with anger, but she seems to be keeping herself in check. "After Church, before anybody heads out, I'll talk to Jim."

I don't want to speak up, and especially don't want to argue with her, but that seems like an awful idea. Whoever Fish is working with is waiting on his response. They won't be waiting forever, and if we don't do something now, they might get away. I have to do something.

"What if they get away because we're waiting?"

"Bean's got a point, Aunt Ruby," Jeremy says softly. "I'm sure Pres will understand the interruption."

"Fuck," she says and grabs one of Ryan's guns from the table. I only know it's his because his is the pile with the most weapons and that damn firework he threatened to shove up Jeremy's backside. Ruby shoves the gun into the waistband at the back of her jeans and stomps off down the hallway toward the chapel. I stare after her in panic, terrified of what's about to happen.

Chapter 21

"IT'S BEEN TOO long. Where is he?"

More than half the club returned some time ago. They were escorting two men with dark hair who were wearing suits and disappeared into the chapel immediately after they walked in. Only Jim came out for a minute, completely ignoring Fish, who's gagged and bound to the chair in front of me, as he took a moment to talk with Ruby. I don't know what they said, but she nodded her head solemnly, and that was that. He went back into the chapel, slamming the door behind him, and hasn't come out since. I'm calming down little by little, getting better at keeping the panic at bay than I was when Ian first left with his brothers. Ruby tried to pull me away from my seat, but I need this. I have to keep my eye on the traitorous fuck in front of me, or I'm going to go nuts. I just want to know that Ian's safe, and every passing minute that I don't know how he's doing just makes the knot in my stomach larger.

Jeremy passes by in a rush. He's got an angry scowl on his face and a gas can in one hand with a large canvas tarp in the other. I hop up from my chair quickly and chase after him. It's the first time I've really moved since Jeremy and Rink shoved Fish in that chair and bound him to the damn thing. I kind of appointed myself his babysitter, but if I stare at his disgusting face any longer, I'm going to start kicking him just for the heck of it.

"Have you heard from Ian?"

Jeremy doesn't slow down. He just strides right out of the clubhouse and to an open white van where he drops the gas can and tarp in the back.

"No. He's busy, though. Once he's taken care of shit, he'll be back here and you'll be able to chill out." There's a slight edge to his voice, warning me not to push it too much.

"I just want to know that he's okay. Is that too much to ask?" I throw my arms up in the air, exasperated by the entire situation.

Jeremy ignores my pleas and stomps back into the clubhouse just as Ruby's walking out. She rolls her flannel sleeves up to her elbows and stares at me as she obviously thinks something over.

"I don't know if I like you," she says and places her hands on her hips. A few hours ago and I'd likely shrink in embarrassment and frustration over her comment. But now I'm at the end of my rope.

"Right," I say in frustration and nod my head. There are several things I could say to her, but none of them are helpful. Still, I find it too difficult to keep my thoughts entirely to myself. "You can hate me all you want, but don't expect me to argue. I don't have the energy for it."

"Never said I hated you. Said I don't know if I like you."

"Same difference." I cross my arms over my chest and wait for her to explain herself.

"You're strong, beautiful. You're pretty fucked-up, too."

I throw my head back in laughter, unable to contain the toxicity of her statement from spreading through me.

"Now that's an understatement. Is that your issue? That I'm damaged?"

"God, no. We're all fucked-up," she says and purses her lips. Ruby's an intimidating woman, and it's not her size or the way she carries herself. She's not much taller than me, and even though she walks with an easy confidence, what really intimidates me about her is how much the people around her love and respect her. The kind of respect she has from the club and extended family is a reflection of who she is. It doesn't help my anxiety that she's Ian's mother. I may not get along with my mom, but I know that's not the case with Ruby and her children. I know enough to know that her opinion matters to Ian. I'm up against enough without her hating me to boot.

"I'm his mother. I love him fiercely, and I'm having trouble sharing him."

"There's a lot to love," I say.

She nods her head and walks away. Ruby's a tough nut to crack, that's for sure. Maybe my honesty will win me some points with her. If she loves him as fiercely as she says she does, she has to be able to see my motives for what they are—pure.

Jeremy walks back outside with Grady on his heels. Grady's got a cell phone to his ear. I'm not left to question who he's talking to when he says, "Love you, babe. Keep yourself home. No, I'm headed to—" He cuts himself off when we make eye contact while he closes the back of the van up. Holly must finish his thought, because he agrees into the phone and then shoves the thing in his pocket and climbs into the passenger side of the van. Jeremy starts her up and they peel out. From what I can tell, Ian, Duke, and Ryan are with Darren and his family. And it seems Grady and Jeremy are on their way there, too.

Nobody is being particularly open and helpful with information around me, and they're acting shady as hell, which tells me that something is going down that Ian doesn't want me to know about. He must have given the orders when he was with everybody earlier, because I still have his phone. When the brothers poured out of the chapel after the "come to Jesus" interrogation on Fish, they headed to the tables and grabbed for their weapons and phones before rushing off on their bikes. I didn't even get a good idea of what was going on then. Ian had Jeremy hole me up in Ian's bedroom, so I was forced to wait in there until they'd had Fish bound and gagged. By the time we emerged, Ian was gone.

"Ian?" Holly shouts into her phone as she answers my call. I shake off her confusion and get to explaining myself quickly, hoping she can see reason.

"Nope, it's Minds. I have Ian's phone."

"Oh," she says and waits a beat. "What's up?"

"I know you know where Ian is. I need you to tell me."

"Mindy," she says carefully. Holly has this way about her, where she gives everything away even if she doesn't know it. She always sounds like this when she's trying to hide something from me. She blows out a breath on the other end of the line. "Let him take care of this."

"I don't want to stop him," I say. "I just need to know that he's okay. Sitting here waiting is killing me."

"Honey, you have to let them deal with this stuff in their own way. You don't want to see how they do it." Holly keeps telling me what I don't want to see or remember, like the cross she bears is so much worse than mine.

"Real talk. Do you regret what you did?" We don't talk about this. It's painful enough for both of us to have experienced it once, let alone choosing to relive it together. But I need to get through to her now, even if it means admitting a truth I'd rather deny.

"Not for a single second," she says. Her voice edges on defeat as she comes to realize she won't win this argument. She's going to tell me where they're at—it's only a matter of time now.

"You were protecting the man you love, you were protecting me. I don't know if I ever thanked you for that."

"I don't need to be thanked," she says, taking on one last defense before she cracks. I know her too well to think she won't give in soon.

"I know," I say. My thanking Holly for killing my rapist is uncomfortable for her, like it's a gift she's given me but doesn't like to be reminded of. "Do you wish you hadn't done it?"

"No. Somebody had to."

"Doing it yourself was kind of therapeutic, huh?"

"I really shouldn't tell you where he is, Minds," she says carefully.

"I'd tell you," I say. She knows I would. I'd want to protect her as much as I could, but I'd still respect her need to see the man who hired her rapists pay with her own eyes.

"I wish you didn't need this, but I get it. Grady told me about that stunt with Leo, ya know. He had trouble wrapping his head around why you did it, but I know why. Sometimes violence is the answer, and sometimes the only way to feel in control is to dole out the punishment yourself."

"Remember when we were kids? Dad and Uncle Edgar would tell us that violence doesn't solve anything." Of course Holly remembers—we only heard it every day of our lives. "Dad doesn't really talk like that anymore."

"No, I can't imagine he does."

My dad's changed, in many ways, just like I have. His unshakable faith in right and wrong has been destroyed. He used to hate the club and everything they stand for. It's not like he likes them now or anything, but I think he understands them better. At least, I know he understands Ian. Contrary to everything I thought I knew about my father, there's still so much I don't understand. I tried to and failed, but just like Holly, I couldn't live up to the Mercer family ideal of perfection.

"The last thing I want to do is to help you hurt yourself," Holly says on a sigh.

"You're not." My voice is so quiet, I'm practically whispering. "I'm finally starting to heal. Larry Jennings tried to hurt Nic and kill Robin, but he got me raped instead. I have to do this."

Tears well in my eyes, but I refuse to let them fall down my cheeks. Aside from Holly, the only other person I think might understand my needing this is Ian.

"Maybe you're right, and this will help you. Nic is better after she . . . nevermind. I love you, honey. They're at the Jennings' house."

"Love you, Holls."

I hang up the phone and dart across the lot for my car. The lot is always either locked up or under supervision—usually both, I suspect—so I'm not surprised to find the doors unlocked and the keys in the glove box. Most people aren't stupid enough to mess with the club. Before anyone notices what I'm doing, I start her up and peel out of the lot, heading for the Jennings' house.

Though it's a short drive, I find myself starting to panic on my way there. It's not a fear of what I might walk in on—it's a fear of disappointing my dad. I didn't think of him when I tried to take out Leo, but maybe I should have. The overwhelming need to talk to him hits me like a ton of bricks, and before I can stop myself, I'm dialing his cell phone.

"This better be good news, Mr. Buckley," Dad says.

I laugh, once again having forgotten that I have Ian's phone, not mine.

"Hi, Daddy." I sound like a freaking child. It's so ridiculous how I get around my dad. Before he can even respond, I'm pulling to the side of the road, a few houses down from the Jennings' house.

"Baby girl," he says with a smile in his voice. "Phone must have broke and that's why you haven't called your old dad."

"I miss you."

"What's wrong, baby girl? That man of yours hurt you?"

"No, I just needed to hear your voice."

"Well, something's upset my favorite girl." I try not to but end up crying. My mom and I may not be very close, but Dad and I have always had a bond. I don't know that I realized how important having him in my life is until right now. It's weird, how different my two favorite men are and yet how similar at the same time.

"We need to talk soon. I have some things I have to tell you some things about me that you're not going to like." My voice catches and I sniffle. I'll never tell Dad what I'm doing here, but I need to tell him about who I used to be. I'm tired of hiding things from him, being terrified that he won't love me because of it.

"Are you crying, kiddo?" Dad's at work, I can tell from the background noise. He moves to a quieter place, telling one of his coworkers he needs a few minutes alone. Everything is quiet on the other end for a long moment before he's back to talking. "You say it when you're ready, baby girl. But if this is about what I think it is, I already know. Known for a long time now. I'm just sorry you didn't think you could lean on me for support."

Shame fills me at his comment. How could I ever doubt that my dad would be there for me? Why didn't I think I could trust him?

"I'm sorry," is the only thing I can manage. I'm full on sobbing now, so undeserving of his love. I'm sorry for more than not reaching out to him for support. I'm sorry for being an addict. I'm sorry for destroying my life. I'm sorry for everything except for what I'm about to do.

"Don't be sorry, kiddo. Nothing's ever gonna stop you from being my favorite girl, you got that?"

"Got it." We hang up shortly after that, and with tears still wet on my cheeks, I get out of the car and head for the Jennings' house. I barely make it up the driveway when the front door opens, and Ryan is standing there, with his arms crossed and a grim look on his face.

"Get your ass inside or put a fucking ad in the paper that we're here," he says, barking at me.

"Like anybody reads the paper anymore." I rush into the house. I've never been here before, but I know my mother has a few times. It's hard to imagine her in the space as it is now. Furniture is turned over, months and months of dust has created a thick film on everything, and there's the distinctly potent smell of gasoline that nearly chokes me.

"Shouldn't be here," Ryan says, locking the door behind me. He comes up beside me with a sick grin on his face. "Gonna piss him off. The man's an artist when he's pissed."

"I need to be here, Ryan," I say quietly. He meets my eyes, challenging me the same way he did the last time we had a heart-to-heart. "Ian thinks I won't like his darker side, that seeing him like this will send me running."

"You'll look at him differently," he says. There's a hint of fear in his voice that betrays his hard-ass exterior, and I'm reminded how much Ryan loves his brother.

"I want to know this side of him, and I want him to see the darker side of me."

Chapter 22

WE DON'T SAY anything else as we head up to the second floor and into the master bedroom. Jeremy and Grady stand in the center of the room, their eyes intent on what lies ahead. When they hear us coming up behind them, they both turn around, and I can see all hell is about to break loose. Ryan spares me the trouble of pleading with them for their silence when he shakes his head and whispers, "Don't."

It's a long, tortured moment before Grady and Jeremy turn their attention back to what they were focused on before.

The master bedroom is large and opens up to an equally impressive en suite bathroom that can be closed off by a set of pocket doors. The decor is definitely high end, but that's not where my attention is. There's a light smattering of blood on the floors and walls, mostly pooled at the feet of Larry and Joanne Jennings, who are each tied to a side chair with their backs to me, facing the large, sunken garden tub that overlooks a large window. Duke stands beside Larry with a gun in his hand and a scowl on his face. Ian is crouched in front of Larry, a knife in his hand and a sadistic smile on his face. I take a few steps forward into the room, passing Grady and Jeremy. Ian and Duke stop what they're doing and look at me. The vicious smile that once graced Ian's face falls to a horrified grimace.

"Melinda, help me!" Larry screams from his seat, but Duke silences him by wrapping his hand around Larry's neck.

"Get her out of here. Now." Ian's words are pained. He looks so distraught over my presence that I almost wish I didn't come.

"I know what he did," I say to Ian, ignoring Larry's cries for help. Joanne stares at me in horror as tears fall from her eyes. She's acting like she doesn't know what she and her husband have done to deserve this from Forsaken, but she knows. I've overheard Joanne Jennings often enough to know she's complicit in how her son was raised.

"You need to leave," Ian says. Larry jerks in his chair, kicking Ian in the shins and earning a firm slap from Ian. I step closer, the smell of gasoline gets stronger, and it's only now that I see the crumpled, unconscious body of Darren Jennings in the bath tub. "These memories don't go away, babe. I won't be able to fix this part of you."

"No, but maybe I can fix this for myself." The tears I cried in the car have dried on my cheeks, leaving my skin irritated and red. I wonder what it says about me that I'm not scared of what I see. Two people bound to chairs, one in the bath tub covered in gasoline. Another man tied to a chair at the clubhouse. All deserve their fates. All need to pay for their sins. I don't have an ounce of pity to spare for a single one of them. "I hate what *he* did."

My eyes leave Ian and lock on Larry's fearful face.

"What's wrong, Mr. Jennings? Are you scared?" My voice sounds foreign to my own ears. I can barely believe it's me saying the words. It's like I'm watching a movie with characters I can't connect with. The men ready to kill their enemies, the woman desperate to just *somehow* make everything a little bit better for herself. Who are these people? Who am I? Mentally, I think I'm breaking. It's not the same as before, with the panic and sickness and fear. It's different now. I'm disconnecting from my humanity, and even though I know it should scare me, it doesn't.

"What's wrong with you, Melinda? What have they done to you?" Larry asks with disgust in his voice.

Joanne snarls from her chair, tucking her chin into her neck and twisting her face up. Tears fall from her cheeks, and for some reason, her pain comforts me.

"Who, Larry?" I ask. My voice is breathy, exasperated. I fight to keep control of my burgeoning emotions. I'm feeling everything, every single ounce of pain, every drop of fear—all of it—and it ignites something inside of me, encouraging me to take it a step further. "Forsaken? Or the men you had rape me?"

His face pales like the pathetic fucking coward he is.

"Does that make you uncomfortable? Knowing you had the wrong woman raped?"

"Babe, stop," Ian warns. He comes to stand in front of me, almost completely blocking my view of Larry, who starts screaming about something or other. His voice is muffled almost immediately by Duke's fist smashing into his jaw. "I'm taking care of it. You don't have to talk to him. Don't torture yourself."

"Don't you see? This helps me. You told me once I might benefit from therapy," I say. A soft, amused laugh escapes me.

"I didn't really mean torture porn," he says, fighting off his own smile.

A thrill shoots through me. I place my hands on his chest and lean in, kissing his throat.

"Does this make your dick hard?" I'm whispering, trying to keep this between us. I don't care if Larry or Joanne hear us. They won't be around much longer anyway. It's Ryan who won't ever let us live this down. "Because I'm getting wet at the idea of your blade spilling their blood."

He groans and presses his hard cock into my belly. My face heats and I lick my lips.

"Christ," Ryan says and voluntarily slams his head into a nearby wall. "Quit dry-humping your bitch and get to killing these assholes already. I'm bored!"

"That word," Ian barks out loudly at Ryan. His chest heaves in anger, but there's an excitement in his eyes that I've never seen before.

"Fuck, sorry," Ryan says without even looking our way. He waves us off, still with his forehead against the wall.

I watch the exchange with curiosity. Duke steps away from Larry and goes to talk to Grady for a moment. Grady nods his head and fires off a text message.

"Men degrade women with that word. It's not something I tolerate," Ian explains.

I'm close to spilling my guts right here and now. This man just melts me, always saying the right thing. Ian must have seen a lot before his mom and Jim got together. I've heard enough about their world before Forsaken came along to know it wasn't pretty, so painful in fact that it still haunts them to this day. I wish I could take that away for him, could make it better. I want to silence his demons.

"No wonder you two wound up together. You're both sick," Joanne says, spitting the words out. "Disgusting freaks."

Ian takes a step back and uses the blade of his knife to gently lift Joanne's face to meet his eyes. He stares at her kindly, willing her to calm down.

"You'll be my first. Would you like that? I've never gutted a woman before. You should be honored." His voice sounds so pleasant despite the message he's sending her.

"I should have had *you* raped instead," Larry shouts at Ian, taunting him. Duke moves back toward Larry, but Ian lifts a hand to stop him. When nobody moves to silence Larry, he keeps going. His eyes are wild and wet, and his chest expands and contracts rapidly. "That trashy whore framed my boy, lied about him, got him hurt. But I see how I messed up now."

I turn my body fully toward Larry, staring at him in disgust. Remembering my conversation with Ryan that day at the house, I recall what I told him. Threatening to kill somebody doesn't work if they don't care. Larry already knows he's going to die. He has nothing to lose.

"Melinda doesn't deserve what happened to her." Larry's eyes fall on mine, and he actually looks remorseful. "But you—you *like* hurting people. I guess it's true what they say."

"What do they say?" Ian says, a maniacal smile on his face. He tosses his knife in the air and catches the blade in his hand with the graceful expertise of a man who's spent hours practicing the move.

"Juvenile records are more accessible than you think, Mr. Buckley. It's a shame that man didn't get more than a year for what he did to you."

Ian is frozen in place, a look of horror mars his beautifully scarred features. The other men in the space don't move either. I think I hear a sharp intake of breath coming from Ryan. My mind slowly puts two and two together.

No.

No.

My heart aches as the truth settles into my soul. It's painful, more than I think I can bear. Someone hurt Ian. No wonder Ruby is so protective of him. I can't handle this. I can't stand here and listen to this man torture him like this. How dare he bring up something so clearly painful?

"I suppose it's some consolation knowing his penis and scrotum were severed before the police found him. Did all of mommy's boyfriends like you that much?"

The second the words are out of his mouth, I'm landing on him with a hard thud. The chair topples backward, and my hands are at his throat. I'm screaming at the top of my lungs and slamming his head into the tile flooring beneath us. Joanne screams from across the room, crying frantically and doing her best to free herself from her bindings.

Ian finally moves, like a statue come to life. In a daze, he walks to Joanne and shakes his head before slicing her throat open with his blade. I punch Larry in his jaw and use both hands to shove his face flat into the tile, forcing him to watch his wife bleed out. Blood spurts from her neck, and her body slumps in the chair as her life drains from her. I can't even bring myself to care that I'm watching a woman die. I don't like violence. I hate the pain vengeance causes. Everybody loses, but sometimes violence *is* the answer. Sometimes the only way to make peace with your pain is to share it with someone else.

"My woman shouldn't have seen that," Ian says quietly. "You're going to pay for making me do that in front of her."

Larry bursts into tears, giving up on fighting me now. His body relaxes into his devastation. I'm lifted off him and cradled in Ian's arms. I rest my head against his chest and wrap my arms around his neck. He walks me to Ryan, where he gently places me on my feet. Ryan extends an arm around my waist, holding me in place. His touch doesn't bother me, nobody's does really, not like it used to. I place my head on his chest and cry for a little boy who suffered in ways even I can't imagine. And I want to make it better for him, but I know I can't. Some scars never heal.

Duke walks into the bathroom and gives Larry a sinister smile. He pulls out a pack of matches and lights one, then blows it out. He repeats the action with half the pack before he says a single word. "Been looking forward to this for a damn long time. Two things I've learned in the last year. First is how much I can love somebody. My daughter and her mother are the most important people in my world. You tried to take them from me, which was a huge fucking mistake."

"I'm sorry!" Larry's screaming and crying, nearly on the verge of hyperventilating now. He's not sorry—he's just scared, and he doesn't have the stones to answer for his actions. Instead, he's lying there, still with his back on the floor, bound to the chair, repeating his false apology over and over again.

"Second thing I learned is how much hate I can carry." Duke lights two more matches and blows them both out. The third one he lights, he doesn't blow out. That one he throws in the bath tub right on top of Darren's unconscious body which bursts into flames immediately. Ian is crouched behind Larry now, forcing the man's eyes open.

"You're going to watch the consequences of what you've done," Ian says.

Jeremy and Grady both pass me and Ryan and move to stand on either side of Duke. Jeremy places a hand on Duke's shoulder as the men watch Darren being burned to death. I untangle myself from Ryan despite his protests and stand beside Grady. He spots me out of the corner of his eye but keeps his attention fixed on the fire before us. I place my head on his arm and try to find a way to comfort him. Holly and Nic both told me how scary Grady can be, but I don't see it. At least not anymore.

Ian and Ryan lift Larry's chair from the floor and prop him up so he can better see his son's death. To my surprise, Ian frees Larry from his bindings and orders him to stand. The man can barely get his body to follow orders. His knees buckle under him, and he has to try again, still finding it difficult to get himself upright. He's still crying, clearly devastated by what he's witnessing, and trying to turn away.

"Be a man for the first time in your pathetic fucking life and stop being a coward," Ian says. He shoves Larry toward the tub where the fire's contained. The man stops at the edge, then screams out a painful cry and throws himself into the flames. He chose his own fate, something I can respect.

"Do you still like what you see?" Ian asks. I catch the misery in his eyes and want more than anything to make him feel better. The truth is on the tip of my tongue, but I'm scared to say it. More than ever, I want to just be brave enough to tell him the truth, regardless of how well he takes it.

"Nothing and no one will stop me from loving you. They deserved worse than death, and if you had let me, I would have killed them myself."

"That's what scares me," he says. Our eyes are locked as we stand in the room as it fills with smoke and the bodies of father and son smolder into nothingness.

July 23rd
9 months to Mancuso's downfall

Chapter 23

SO MUCH HAS changed between me and Ian. We're closer now than before, but there's a wall between us that unsettles me. I love him in a way that consumes me so fully I almost can't breathe sometimes. I meant it when I told him that he's the only thing that makes me feel better. It's probably unhealthy, but when I think back to who I was six months ago, my stomach turns. I was so weak and broken back then. I still have my damage—we all do, I think—but at least I don't feel dead now. He makes me see that our scars don't define us.

On good days, I think I'd like to counsel others through their own trauma. On really good days, I realize that no trauma line is going to hire a woman whose idea of therapy is lighting a man on fire in a bath tub. Not that I lit the match, but still. I could have and sometimes I wish it had been me.

Ian likes to ignore the part of me that revels in the darkness. He also hedges around his own darkness. For the last six weeks, we've had nothing but lightness and soft touches and sweet words. If it were real, who he is at heart, I could stomach it. But this isn't my Ian. My Ian is dark. He struggles with his own image, choosing only to see the hate and rage that fills him, paying attention only to the bloodshed. He doesn't see what I see—a beautiful man with such a beautiful light that no amount of sorrow or despair can come close to quashing it. Sometimes he's the only thing that guides me out of the black void. He's my light.

That's why today is so important to me.

Today, Ian turns twenty-seven.

A few days ago, Alex brought up his birthday in front of me, so I had to pretend like I was surprised and nobody had mentioned it to me before. He told me to drop it, and because we're in this weird place that's something more than roommates but something less than what I want, I did as he asked and acted like I was mad at him. For such a perceptive man, he sure does have a blind spot to things he doesn't want to see. He wants to believe that I've dropped the birthday thing, so when he doesn't see or hear of any evidence to the contrary, he accepts that I care about his birthday about as much as he does, which couldn't be further from the truth.

I've been waiting for this day for a month. Ian retreated into himself after the Jenningses died in an unfortunate house fire that left no survivors, no evidence, and no leads—at least according to the investigators who the club paid off. I was at the end of my rope, having no idea what to do with him, when Ruby and Alex came to me, asking for help sorting out a top-secret birthday surprise. Neither of them actually need my help, but it makes me feel good to be included. All I've really done is distract Ian from figuring out what's going on at Ruby and Jim's house today in preparation for the party at the clubhouse tonight, and I'm not even doing a great job at that. We were supposed to head out for the day an hour ago, but Ian had something mysterious come up suddenly, and he headed over there and hasn't been back since. He gave me an extra hour to get ready, so I spent extra time making myself presentable, but I don't like what I see in the mirror. I look like I'm trying way too hard.

I start over by going into our shared underwear drawer and pulling out a dark red bra and panty set I bought a few weeks ago. The sexy black push-up bra and thong set I got specifically for today is just not comfortable for too long. Maybe, if I play my cards right, I'll be able to get him to touch me tonight. He's given in a few times since the first time we had sex, but it always ends the same. He's angry because I've pushed the limits, which just results in it taking even longer for him to give in to me the next time. I hate anything to hurt him, especially if it's me who's hurting him, so I'm working on it. Every day when he leaves to deal with club shit, I work on my "issues" in our bed. He probably knows I'm doing it, at least some of the time, but it's not something we ever talk about. I just want to be better for him. He deserves better than what I'm giving him.

With the more comfortable red set on, I go into our shared sock drawer and grab a pair of his socks. It's passive-aggressive to dirty all his socks, sure, but he's the one who left me here and didn't even ask me to come to the house with him. Not that he cares much. He knows I've been doing it and will just re-wear them the next day no matter how dirty I get them. In the bathroom, my toothbrush rests next to his in the mounted holder, but I use his instead and snicker to myself because it seems so taboo to use someone else's toothbrush. There's probably hygiene warnings against it, but I don't give a shit. The rest of my morning routine flies by pretty quickly.

I dress in a pair of skinny jeans and my black boots. I pull out the white low-cut tank I had Ruby order for me that reads FORSAKEN across the chest and PROPERTY OF IAN on the back, and I slide into it. Then, like the chicken shit I am, I pull a black tank over the top of it. He hasn't seen the tank yet, and I don't know how he's going to feel about it. I don't really want to be stuck in the SUV with him for most of the day if he's going to be in a foul mood. I still can't believe how far Ruby and I have come in the last few weeks. I suspect Ryan's big mouth told her what happened in that bathroom. She looks at me differently now, with respect and kindness in her eyes.

I nearly make it to the front door before realizing how sunny it is outside and deciding to grab my sunglasses. The walk-in closet has two sets of shelves that are shallow and wide, like they're meant for shoes. There's just so much space that my and Ian's shoes combined don't take up much space, so I repurposed the upper-level shelving for my accessories. I'm running out of time to get to Ruby and Jim's in time for

Holly to arrive, so I rush into the closet and grab the glasses, then spin around to head out.

Something on the floor of the closet catches my eye and stops me in my tracks. It's the old red purse I was using to hide the cash Ian has given me that I choose not to spend. There's close to eight grand in there now, but it's off-limits. Or is it?

"You can't spend it," I say aloud, as if verbalizing this conversation will make the wheels stop turning in my head. "It would be wrong.

"Well, maybe it wouldn't be wrong if I use it to spruce up my new house," I argue. With myself. Aloud. I'm going from silly goose to total whackadoodle pretty quickly.

Without any more thought on the subject, I grab the purse, open it, and find the money is still there. It's a big purse and carries well, so I shove my sunglasses, wristlet, and phone inside and stride out of the closet trying not to feel guilty. He's said it a million times—he doesn't care what I do with the cash. I bet he doesn't even realize I still have this much since he refuses to even talk about money. He gets this grouchy voice and says, "I'm taking care of you, babe. I stop giving you what you need, then we talk about money. Until then, shut up about it."

I don't have my keys to lock up the house, so I don't even try. They've been missing for days now. I even asked Ian if he's seen them, but he just brushed me off and said I didn't need keys to the house or my car. For someone so morose all the time, he is so deliciously possessive about certain things. I'd rather he take me on his bike over driving my car any day, but still, I don't like leaving the house unlocked. If I wait for him, I don't want to stress over it, but I've waited long enough. The man is ditching out on birthday time with me, and that's just not cool.

I try to calm myself about leaving the house unlocked. It's not like anybody is going to find themselves out here in the woods and walk right into the cabin at random on the one day it's not locked up. Plus, anybody who knows the cabin is here likely knows who it belongs to, and they can't be stupid enough to steal from Forsaken.

"You used his toothbrush, and now you're going to get his house robbed. Score one point for being awesome, Mindy." As I make my way through the woods and then across the field that separates the cabin from Ruby and Jim's house, I continue to argue with myself about taking the money and then leaving the house unlocked. I've only ever been good at being bad when I was high or drunk. The rest of the time I'm way too neurotic to really pull it off.

Just as I'm passing the barn, almost to the house, I see a petite figure standing on the back deck. It takes me a moment of focusing on the person's frame before I realize it's Alex. She's got a coffee mug in her hands and is taking slow sips from it. I'm surprised that they're letting her stand out here unguarded. Nic's told me how much she misses Alex. The more dangerous things get around here, the less she gets out. Ryan has apparently kept her under lock and key. The more I get to know Ryan, the more I see him as a brother, but that doesn't mean I can't see the man is fine as fuck. If I didn't have Ian, I might be cool with him locking me away.

"Hey!" Alex says with a wave in my direction.

I wave back and give her a smile, hoping she doesn't think it's weird that I'm just kind of appearing out of nowhere. I never come to the house without Ian or without Alex or Ruby coming to get me. I know we're right on the other side of the woods from the house and technically on the same plot of land, but I don't feel comfortable just popping by yet.

I make it within twenty feet or so of the back deck before I realize that she's not alone. Lying in the sun beside her, with its face lying on its paws, is a pit bull. Its eyes are focused on me, and its butt is raised in the air. It emits a low, fierce growl. I pause, afraid that the dog looks like it's about to rush at me. This is the other reason I don't make a habit out of dropping by unannounced. The first time I came by, Ruby told me I was lucky the dog didn't try to tear my leg off. Apparently they keep highly bred guard dogs on site. Or they did. Now they're down to just one.

But not for long. That's the other awesome thing about today—puppies. Well, not puppies, but Ian and I are heading out and picking up the new guard dogs from the breeder. The man promised me a dog, and today he's making good on that promise. Every time I bring up something he doesn't want to talk about, he redirects my attention by talking puppies, which is totally unfair because it works so well.

I tried to tell the support group I drop in on once in a while post-sobriety sabotage about my troubles, and half the group just stared at me like I'm an alien, so I haven't been to a meeting in a while. They're important to go to, and they do help ground me, but it's weird showing up when my life is so good and other people are fighting so hard for their sobriety. I feel a little guilty about that, like I should be suffering more, missing the high more intensely. I still miss it, even on good days, but it's different now. I miss it, but I don't want it. It's kind of like being freed from shackles but remembering how they feel around your ankles.

"She's harmless," Alex says and urges me forward. I nod my head and keep moving, still slightly nervous about the dog at her side. "Well, not harmless, but she listens well." Alex looks down at the dog and smiles fondly, then takes another sip of coffee. She lowers the mug and speaks in a firm voice, saying, "PJ, up."

PJ stands up. I've never really seen her around the house when I've been there, which I never thought was weird until now. She's still focusing on me like I'm a prime rib and she's starving, but she isn't making any attempt to move toward me.

"Not all pits are dangerous," Alex says.

"I know that." I'm defensive and I know it, but she's being defensive, too. I don't want her to think I have a thing against them, because I don't. "It's just . . . I know what she's trained to do."

"Ryan says I've ruined her. She's still a kick-ass guard dog, but she's more lover than fighter. Let me introduce you to her so she knows you're a friend."

I walk up on the deck and stop when Alex signals for me to. I'm about ten feet away from her and PJ now. I expect Alex to bend down and say something sweet and gentle in PJ's ear, but she doesn't.

"Sit." PJ follows Alex's order without fail and sits down. "Gentle greeting," she says, and PJ stands up and walks to me at a slow pace. She stops right in front of me and sits down with her big eyes staring up at me. And I fucking melt. PJ leans in and bumps me with her head, her little butt wiggling like crazy underneath her. I bend down and pet her behind her ears. She barks happily, and I fall totally in love.

"Ryan told me you and Ian are getting a dog today," she says. "How did you talk him into that?"

I shrug my shoulders but smile ruefully. "I just asked to go with him to pick up your dog. The man offered."

"My brother's got a squishy heart," she says and grins at something over my shoulder. PJ abandons me and runs off. I turn around to see Ian standing at the edge of the deck. He bends to pet the dog and shakes his head at me and Alex.

"Hey there, birthday boy," Alex says with a wave.

He just rolls his eyes and ignores her, a move that is so reminiscent of his mother that it's almost eerie.

"Babe, puppies." He turns around and stalks off toward Ruby's Suburban.

I give Alex a wink and chase off after him. Once we're on the highway and officially out of town, I send Alex a text asking her to make sure we have enough dog food for the new family members. It's lame, but that's the code we agreed on so she and Ruby would know when it was safe for them to go all out with decorating.

"You ditched me this morning," I say, searching for something to talk about aside from what I really want to talk about. I've told him I love him a few times, but he's never said it back, and even though he still kisses me all the time, he's so detached it's painful.

"Don't do that thing," he says, his eyes darting between me and the road.

"What thing?"

"That needy girlfriend thing."

"So, I'm your girlfriend?" I'm an idiot. A seriously certifiable idiot. We're adults, living together and getting a dog, and here I am getting caught up on labels. "Are we actually talking about our relationship?"

"Yeah, we got time. While we're at it, let's talk about that surprise birthday party Ma and Alex are getting ready."

"Oh?" I say way too innocently. I mean, the jig is up, so it's not like I'm blowing our cover or something. "Didn't you say you don't want a party? That's what you told me at least."

"Well, you're committed to your story, I'll give you that."

I stay silent for a long time after that, not wanting to argue. The breeder is based on a plot of land in a tiny town a solid two hours away from home. It would ruin our entire day if we started fighting now.

We're about halfway to our destination when Ian pulls the SUV off the highway and parks in the far corner of the parking lot at the quiet rest stop. There's not another vehicle in the lot, and it looks like we're alone. I keep silent and wait for him to say or do something. I'm not a patient woman, but I force myself not to break.

To my surprise, Ian unbuckles his seat belt, then leans over and unbuckles mine. His long arms slips into the space between my seat and the door. I go to ask him what he's doing when the back of my seat falls back and he's half on top of me. If he'd told me my silence would earn me this kind of action, I'd have tried this tactic a damn long time ago.

"I want my girl back," he says, cupping my cheek. I stare at him in confusion, trying to work out the message behind the comment. I don't know what he's talking about, though.

"You're closed off, like you're scared. What are you so scared of?"

"You," I say and instantly regret it. "You keep pulling away from me." I'm careful not to hedge the topic that plagues me the most, at least not until I'm ready.

"You frighten me," he says. "I care about you, a lot. But you scare the shit out of me. Every time I think you're going to get some sense into you and run the other direction, you adapt."

"It's a survival skill," I say. He's so close now, close enough to brush his nose with mine.

"It's more than that."

"You're afraid I'm becoming too much like you, like you're somehow ruining me."

"I am," he says and presses his lips into my cheek. "I'm worried because I like it. What does that make me—that I like how I'm defiling you?"

My heartbeat speeds up, and I can barely breathe. God, he's fucking sexy like this. The way people used to talk about him around me would make me think he's this stone wall of silence. Nic never even hints at Duke talking about his feelings, and Ryan certainly doesn't strike me as the kind of guy who's up for a heart-to-heart. I know Holly and Grady talk about things like this, to an extent, but it's never really all that deep or drawn out. Holly says that she and Grady just get each other, which is lovely in its own right. It's funny to think of my sweet Holly with the sergeant at arms. She's so big on open communication, as long as it suits her, and he seems so closed off. I guess you just never know about people, because they definitely work as a couple even if it is surprising.

"Human," I say. I've been meaning to share this piece of me with him. I just hadn't gotten around to it until now. Oh, now I'm even lying to myself. It's not that I haven't gotten around to it yet—it's more like I've been avoiding it. But I can't avoid it forever.

"I wasn't that girl who partied or experimented. I was actually kind of lame in high school. Other girls thought about college and a career, how they'd live in a big city when they graduated. I never really saw that in my future."

"What did you see?" He drags his lips lightly up my cheek to my temple. It's such an intimate move. I'm having second thoughts about sharing this with him.

"A house with a white minivan. A big family, lots of kids, and my husband, the accountant." I try to hide my face, but he won't let me. Admitting this to him makes me feel so inadequate and silly.

"Don't hide from me. I like knowing you," he whispers. A smile cracks on his face. "An accountant—really?"

"I was a dumb kid," I say in defense. When he doesn't keep on teasing me, I continue what I was trying to say to begin with. "And the kids thing doesn't matter anyway."

"Why not?" His brows pull together.

"There was too much damage," I whisper, feeling shame in my heart. I didn't do anything to deserve this, but it happened anyway and having to admit that my body can't do what it was made to do is upsetting. Ian's face forms a frown and he mouths, "I'm sorry."

"Anyway. I wanted what every other teenage girl wants—I wanted to fall in love. And then, surprisingly, I did. Heath was a few years older, and he was pretty great. We got married right after I graduated high school, and I thought I was living the dream. Heath was not an accountant—he was an undergrad. But campus jobs don't pay the bills.

"Before he asked me to marry him, he joined the army so he could support us while I went to school. His parents were so angry with him—I can still hear their voices in my head. He didn't care, though. Heath was big on making a commitment and sticking to it. We were married less than three months when he deployed. Before we could celebrate our one-year anniversary, I had a couple of men in uniform at my door telling me my husband was dead.

"I didn't deal with it well. I was depressed. I just wanted to feel better, and that led me down the rabbit hole."

Ian places a kiss to my temple and hooks a hand around the back of my neck.

"I did things I wish I could forget. If you knew the things I've done, you wouldn't worry about corrupting me. You'd know I came to you that way. You're so consumed with the idea that I won't be able to handle your darkness, but what about mine?"

Chapter 24

THE REST OF the drive to the breeder is uneventful. Mindy's words play in my head over and over.

What about mine?

The words are on the tip of my tongue as I fight with myself to have the courage to say them.

Nothing and no one will stop me from loving you.

She was so honest and direct. For all her trauma, Mindy loves openly and pursues what she loves without worry. I envy her that—her strength. In comparison, I'm such a fucking pussy. She deserves better, more, but I'm too selfish to let her go. Who can I be for her? How can I really give her safe and happy when I can't even tell her how she fucking owns me?

Unlike Mindy, I don't love openly. I'm not sure that I even know how. Maybe I have more trauma than I thought. In the absence of words, I spend every day trying to show her how I feel. I'm careful with her, always trying to make sure I haven't hurt her feelings. I give her space when I can tell she needs it, and I do everything I can to not suffocate her. Even though I want to. I just get so caught up in my own head that I lose my ability to be there in the moment with her. I don't even know what to do or say about the kids thing. I remember overhearing conversations her doctors had about the damage from the rape, but I never knew how it ended up. I don't care, not really. The main thing that fucks me up is that she can't have something I know she wants.

All this time I was so worried about my own damage, and hating the person I see in the mirror, that I never stopped to wonder what she sees staring back at her. I've only ever looked at her and seen what I want to see. Mindy is beautiful and strong. She amazes me with her ability to grow. It's taking a while, but I'm slowly coming to terms with the idea that maybe her darkness complements mine.

"What about this one?" Mindy asks as Joey, the head breeder, leads us past an older German shepherd who's napping in the hallway.

I walk close behind her, letting her do her thing. I've been on point for Forsaken when it comes to Joey and his business for years now, but the moment we got out of the SUV and she saw a kennel full of puppies, I lost total control of the situation. I don't tell her that, but I realize when I'm fighting a losing battle. If she keeps eyeing every fucking dog we pass the way she has been, we're not going to have room in the SUV for us to make it home. Maybe I can pass dogs out as early Christmas presents or something. I don't know.

"Beau ain't going anywhere. He was one of our studs back when he was younger, but now he's my wife's pride and joy," Joey says, ushering us into a room at the end of the hall. There's a loud noise that stops him in his tracks. He tries to back up, but Mindy is right behind him, and he has to stop himself from running her over. I grab hold of her quickly and pull her behind me. Metal slams against metal, and a hard thump sounds on the floor, followed by the painful cry of a young dog. There's growling and a commotion that sends Joey flying into the room and ordering me to keep Mindy in the hallway. Motherfucker best get to remembering who he's talking to and soon.

"A dog sounds like it's getting hurt," Mindy says and moves to step around me. I turn around and grab her by her upper arms, stopping her from making it past the closed door.

"It's not our business. Joey doesn't step into my club and tell me how to run my shit, so I'm not gonna come here and tell him how to handle his shit." Another horrific yelp comes from inside the room, followed by a deep, angry growl.

"Cesar, put the fucking thing down!" Joey screams.

Mindy's eyes nearly bulge out of her head. She takes a step away from me as she pulls a hair tie out of her pocket and secures her hair back in a loose ponytail. "They're going to kill it," she says with an impressive edge about her. "You can help me stop it or get the fuck out of my way."

My stomach rolls at the noises coming from beyond the closed door. Until Joanne Jennings, I'd never taken a woman out before. I didn't want to do it, but she was complicit in what her sick-fuck husband had done to Mindy, so she had to die. I've never taken down an animal either, and I never plan to. Shit. If Mindy hadn't taken a stance against whatever's going on in there, I would have reached my limit soon.

"Stay behind me," I say and take a deep breath. This is going to fuck with business, I just know it. We don't even know what's going on, but there's no way I can keep my girl in the hallway while all hell is breaking loose on the other side of the door.

I open the door slowly, checking that the room is safe for Mindy to be in, before completely entering with her behind me. There's a large metal table in the center of the room and an industrial looking counter-cabinet combo in the corner. A swinging door bridges this room from the next. Through the small window in the swinging door, I see a row of cages in the adjacent room. I've been in this room before, but it's been a few years.

Joey is in the corner with a grasping pole out in front of him, while another man, who I'm guessing is Cesar, is holding a bleeding arm with one hand and using the hand of his injured arm to point a fucking thirty-eight at a growling blue pitt.

I keep an arm out to my side, to keep Mindy behind me. The pitt has blood around her mouth, and she's in a protective, angry stance. Something caused the dog to flip out. No telling what, but it must have been bad. In all my years working with these dogs, and pitts in particular, I've never seen one lash out without being provoked. There are bad people, but there are no bad dogs.

When I move farther into the space, I have a better picture of what's going on. The angry pitt looks like she gave birth just recently. Her teats are swollen, and her belly hangs low. Fuck. Just seeing her from this angle, I can tell she's been bred too many fucking times.

Cesar raises the gun in his hand and points it at the dog in front of him. His hand shakes, like he can't believe he's about to do this. His eyes dart back and forth to Joey, visually pleading for help.

"Fucking shoot her!" Joey shouts.

Mindy gasps from behind me and moves to her left, heading right for the angry dog. I pull her back behind me and create a wall between her and what's caught her attention. My eyes follow her line of sight to the little ball that's huddled in the corner with half-closed eyes and a bloody ear. There's a needle sticking out of its side and its crying out. Cesar stands between the puppy and the bitch who I assume is its mother. Fuck. No wonder she's flipping out.

"Get out of here, man. Your woman doesn't need to see this," Joey says, half-mad with rage. He moves in closer to the angry mother and hooks her around the neck with the loop of the pole. She fights him vigorously, nearly getting a hold of his shoe in the process. If she'd been successful, his toes would be gone, no doubt.

"What the hell happened?" I ask. I can't leave this room without knowing what the fuck is going on in here, especially with Mindy here with me.

"Pup's defective. The bitch can't birth a good litter anymore," Joey says. I come to the realization that they were trying to destroy both dogs about half a second too late. Mindy darts around my other side and approaches the tiny dog carefully. Its mother is distracted by the harness around her neck and doesn't notice what Mindy's up to until the puppy yelps in Mindy's arms. Immediately, she pulls the needle full of what I'm willing to bet is a serum that will stop its heart, out of its side and tosses it across the room. The mother redirects her anger at Mindy, but Joey controls her, and Mindy makes it back to me safely. It all happens so fast that I could no more stop her than I can stop what's about to happen. I can feel it in my bones, the direction this is headed.

"Put the pup down, lady!"

"No," Mindy says, still cradling the tiny thing in her arms. Her eyes land on me, and there's no mistaking the desperation in her eyes.

Well, it looks like we have a puppy.

"Does she have a history of violence?" Mindy asks.

"Not until asshole tried to destroy her pup in front of her," Joey spits the words in Cesar's direction.

"Then I'm taking them both home with me," she says firmly.

"No, they're being destroyed," Joey shouts at Mindy, raising the hairs on the back of my neck. I used to like this guy. He's never really pissed me off until now. I got no reason to get my nose in his business and he has no reason to put his in mine, and that's how I like it, but fighting with my woman over a pair of dogs he was about to kill is a surefire way to get my attention.

The next few minutes happen so fast that it's hard for me to figure out what's going on around me. Mindy moves to put the puppy in a travel crate that's on the floor behind us, when the mother notices and lunges for her. With the sudden change of direction, Cesar gets slammed into the cabinet behind him, knocking the gun free from his hand and knocking Joey off his feet. The dog runs at Mindy full force, and I dislodge my gun, clicking off the safety and getting in position just in case. Jumping up on one of the counter tops, Mindy lets the mama dog get into the kennel with her pup. With my girl safely away from the angry dog, I place my gun beside Mindy and pick up the pole. It takes some work, but I eventually get the loop out from around her neck and use my steel-toed boot to close the door shut behind the two.

"Guess you got your puppy after all," I say and lock the door to the kennel shut. "Kind of a two-for-one deal." The crazy woman grins at me and bites at her bottom lip.

Cesar and Joey recover from their fall and head toward us. I tense up immediately at the look on Cesar's face. Joey's annoyed, maybe even a little mad, but Cesar looks downright furious. I pick my gun back up and wait. I should move to stand between Cesar and Mindy, but he can't be dumb enough to try anything with me here. I've never met the man before, but there's a hate in his eyes that puts me on edge.

"What the fuck is your problem, you stupid bitch?" Cesar shouts in Mindy's face. He grabs a hold of her arm and shakes her furiously. I don't even think about what I'm doing. I lift the barrel of my gun to his head and pull the trigger.

Cesar's body slumps to the floor. Mindy cringes and gently props her foot out so when his body grazes her boot, he slumps backward and doesn't block her from getting down without stepping on him. She stares at me with wide eyes and fear in her eyes. *This* is what I don't want to see in her eyes when she looks at me. She sees a killer and always will.

"He's dead." Her lips tremble.

"He touched you," I say.

I warned her once, but she didn't take me seriously.

I'll bet now she does.

"Dude was shady anyway," Joey says, backing away from me.

"I still need the Doberman. These two are free, and I'm not fucking paying for the kennel," I say. Joey raises his arms in the air and backs out of the room.

Mindy stares at me with big, sad eyes. She hates what she sees, I can tell.

"You were protecting me. There's no shame in that."

HOURS LATER, AND we're back in town. I know there's a fucking party going on for my birthday at the clubhouse, but I don't give a shit. Instead of heading there, I take us to the cabin after we drop off the dogs, which Mindy has named Missy and Punk, at a local vet. The vet seems to think they're going to be fine, which is a relief. If Mindy were in a bad mood post-vet, I wouldn't get to do what I want. And it is my birthday after all.

"We're supposed to be at the clubhouse for that thing. Aren't we?"

"Don't worry. We'll show up to my birthday party eventually. There's just one thing I want to do first." Dragging her in the house, I bring her to the bedroom and set her on the bed.

"Figured something out today, babe." I take her boots off for her, then slip my socks off her feet. Her socks are in better condition and actually fit her, but the woman insists on wearing mine. She's smiling as she sits here, watching me.

"That I want to make love to you." Pussy alert. Serious pussy alert. If my brothers could hear this bullshit now, they'd never let me live it down. One, because I'm saying shit that makes me question my sanity, and two, because I'm still too big of a chicken to say what I really want to say.

"I keep messing it up," she says. "I'm trying not to push your limits like I have been."

"I know, babe." I've had my hands over every inch of her flesh, but it's not enough. She's given me her body under such strict requirements—and yet none at all—but I need more. I need her. She gives me her whole body to do with almost entirely as I please, as long as I'm not too gentle. It unnerves her, the gentle touches.

When I've tried to go slow, take my time, and savor being with her, she's pulled back from me. In the past, I was gentle, careful to touch her as though she were delicate and not strong and brave like she is. But she didn't want it. She always says she *needs* the pain, but it's just one more way to torture herself, so I'm done.

"I'm done with rough," I say. My voice is heady with the emotion of this moment. "Kink I can do with you, but I won't hurt you anymore. I can't."

"I don't want to hurt you either," she says and brushes my hair from my eyes. A finger trails over the scar Mancuso put there. "I'm hurting you every time I demand more than you can give. It's not fair to you."

As we undress one another, we talk in an honest and open way that I don't think we've ever done before. At least not on this level.

"The knife I carry around was a gift from the man who scarred my face. It's the same blade he used on my flesh, and it'll be the same blade I use on his." I'm quiet, careful not to say the words too loudly, as if by being louder everybody will hear them. I take Mindy's tank top off only to find she's wearing another one under it. A survey of the back reveals it's custom made with PROPERTY OF IAN in bold letters. I smile wide at the silly thing but keep moving and toss it aside anyway.

"I get wanting to remember the pain. Like if you don't let yourself forget it, then it won't take you by surprise if it ever happens again." She stares at me wide-eyed, fearful even. "But asking me to hurt you, wanting me to take you beyond my limit, can't happen."

"I won't ask again. I don't want to live in the pain forever. I don't want *you* living in it forever."

"Good, because I'm all about pleasure now, babe."

"I don't think I quite understand," she says with a smirk and pulls me on top of her.

I make slow, sweet love to her that afternoon. We lie in bed and talk about the day we've had. Never once does she look at me with fear or disgust like I think she should, and never once do I feel like she's pulling away from me.

"I love you," I say into the dark room around us.

She's quiet for so long that I wonder if she even heard me. Eventually, though, she snuggles in and says, "I know. I love you, too."

It's different than I expect it to go down, but it suits us all the same. She already knew, maybe long before even I did. I won't rush us because I'm not stupid, but she's mine and I intend to make it legal one day.

NOVEMBER

5 months to Mancuso's downfall

Epilogue

THERE'S A FAINT murmur of conversation coming from behind me. We don't have a big crowd here, but it feels like there's just too many. Alex promised me this is a small wedding, as far as these things go. My nerves are on edge, and all I can think is how I should have let her talk me into fucking eloping when she mentioned it. I wanted to give her more than some cheesy roadside chapel and an Elvis impersonator. I wanted to give her the wedding she didn't get the first time.

I'm a fucking idiot.

Apparently we're getting married on short notice. At least, those are the kinds of questions I've been fielding since we set the date. Nosy people who have no fucking place keep hinting at bullshit reasons for only having a four-month-long engagement. If I have to watch my girl tell one more person that she's not pregnant, I'm going to fucking lose my shit. It's not like they know—how could they—but it hurts her, so intent doesn't matter. Every time she has to address it, she fights off the impending sorrow that sinks in. We're still coming to terms with it, the fact that we can't have kids. I've looked into shit Mindy doesn't know about, to see if we could go about procuring a kid or two in another way. So far, nobody wants to give a kid to a man with a reputation like mine. I try not to let it bother me, because finally, after spending my entire life thinking otherwise, I know I have a good heart. I might be everything they fear, but because of Mindy, I now know I'm more than that.

"Nervous?" Ryan is standing beside me in the nicest things he owns. Ma made a point to buy us each a new pair of jeans. She said that we had to dress up a little. Not that either of us have minded. I've caught wind of the things Ryan has been saying to Alex. He wants to marry her, but she's not ready yet. It's a damn good thing my brother is as closed off with his emotions as he is. The desperation is all over his face. Sometimes, when I look at him, I have to stop and wonder if this is real. For so long, neither of us knew we could want this kind of commitment. Settling down isn't something we ever talked about. Pop always said it was something we would just do, like it's not that big of a deal. And now, standing here, waiting for my girl to come to me, I know he's right. This whole wedding is all for show, to give Mindy something she doesn't want to admit she needs. And I'll always give her what she needs.

"Only because I have to say a bunch of shit you fuckers will never let me live down in front of all these people." I peek over my shoulder only to realize everybody is still here, much to my dismay. It was Mindy's idea to get married in the field between Ma and Pop's house and ours, but it's just too wet outside, so we opted for doing it inside the house.

"Proud of you, brother. Don't think I ever told you, but your woman and I had words some months back. She's good people. I have no doubt that crazy bitch is gonna protect your six."

BY THE TIME the music starts up, I'm wiping blood from my mouth and glaring at my brother, who's pinching the bridge of his nose to stop the nose bleed. Good thing Ma put us in black jeans and black button-downs. The blood doesn't show as well as it would if we'd been in white. Harry's gonna love this when he sees it. As it is, Mindy's mom, Claire, is in the front row with the most displeased expression on her face. She mumbles something to Holly's mom that earns them both a severe look from Ma.

My palms are sweating and my heart rate has spiked. Fuck, I'm really doing this. I can't believe I'm doing this. I don't have a clue what Mindy's wearing, and the longer the music drags the fuck on, the more nervous I get about it. What if she looks like a doily? Or worse—what if she looks like a marshmallow? I'm a shit liar with her. I can't stand here and tell her I like her dress if she looks like something out of one of those bad TV movies she likes to watch. Fuck. We should have eloped. The next time I decide to be a good guy, I'm going to remind myself of this moment.

Fuck this shit.

I catch Pop's eyes from his seat in the front row. His eyes wrinkle in the corners, a big smile graces his face, and I swear to Christ, the fucker might have a tear or two in his eyes. Ma's scowl has turned weepy as she lays her head on Pop's shoulder and wipes her nose with a tissue. Shit. Now she's crying, and from the looks of it in the small crowd, so are half the women here.

"Look what you did," Michael says and elbows me in my side. Blood or not, maybe I shouldn't have put this asshole in my wedding party. Ma looks at us fondly and blows her nose.

"This shit is getting sappy," Ryan complains.

"It's a wedding. Show some respect," Michael says quietly in warning. These two assholes won't ever get along, I just know it.

"I'll show some respect," Ryan says tauntingly. "I'll show some respect when I'm plowing your sister later."

I rub my hand over my eyes to block them out. One normal day, just one normal fucking day is all I ask for, and my brothers can't shut the fuck up long enough to give me that. They're bickering but trying to keep it quiet. Even Ma's getting pissed about it.

Mindy's bridesmaids walk down the aisle in simple black dresses sans human escorts because these two assholes next to me fought over who'd walk Alex down the aisle and Holly thought she would walk with Grady even though I didn't put him on my list of groomsmen. If I included my patched brothers, every fucker we knew would be in the wedding party, so we went nontraditional in a few ways. Not that anyone should expect any different from us.

Alex has PJ walking beside her with flowers tucked into the poor dog's collar. Holly comes down the aisle next with Moose, the Doberman I got to replace Tegan. He also has flowers in his collar. I knew Mindy was going to work the dogs into the ceremony, but I didn't realize she was going to subject them to looking like walking bouquets. Joey is going to need to get pictures of this so he knows what his highly bred killing machines are up to.

The moment Mindy and Harry come into view from the hallway, the air whooshes from my chest. I don't know if I'm not breathing or what, but I can't get any air. Harry is wearing his dress uniform, which makes people laugh and snicker when they catch sight of him. The outlaw marries the cop's daughter, and of course Daddy has to show up reminding everybody of which side of the law he stays on. Missy and Punk walk beside them, with Missy definitely being better behaved than her son. Punk stops at every person he sees to sniff their shoes and growl at the scents he doesn't care for. As he's grown, the differences in the lengths of his legs has become more pronounced, and he kind of hobbles. He's one of the most pathetic-looking dogs I've ever seen, but he's ours. I can't wait until the fucker grows up a little more though. He chews on everything, but even still, I can't imagine coming home and not having him in our house.

Our guests may be watching Harry, but it's Mindy I can't take my eyes off of. Instead of wearing white, my girl has on a dark red dress that hugs her figure to about mid-thigh, leaving her creamy legs exposed. She joked last night in bed that she was going to be easy today—I just didn't realize she meant easy access. Fuck yes.

It seems we don't have a bit of white in our wedding, which is fitting, I guess. I don't know how I got so fucking lucky to have this woman in my life, let alone to somehow convince her to marry me.

The ceremony is short and goes by in a blur. The dude marrying us is the same guy who delivered the eulogy at Chief's funeral. I don't know whose idea that was, but as long as this marriage is legally binding when we're done, I don't give a single fuck.

"You're fucking beautiful." The words just rush out now that she's in front of me. Harry gives me a sad smile and walks to his seat beside his wife. Mindy has heavy eye makeup and bright red lips. I'd kill for the honor of touching her even just once. Not that I haven't killed for her already, but I would do it again in a heartbeat.

My girl, my strong, beautiful, crazy girl, stares at me with tears in her eyes. She holds them back and smiles ruefully.

"You promised that you wouldn't make me cry," she says and clears her throat.

"I lied," I say and kiss her forehead. There's gorgeous and then there's Mindy Mercer. I don't care how much I sound like a pussy right now. I'm whipped, and I like it this way. I didn't know I could have something like this. I was resigned to being alone. It didn't bother me. I just didn't realize what I was missing out on.

It's time for me to say my vows. Until last night, I was going to go with the standard shit, but it didn't sit right. Fuck. What the hell am I doing here?

"I don't like the traditional shit they wanted us to say, so I'm doing my own thing," I say nervously.

"We didn't talk about this," Mindy says, anxious. "I don't know what to say. I don't have anything prepared."

"Wing it. You'll be fine." She's only partially amused by my response. I do catch her eyes darting to Holly in a panic, though. She could go with the traditional vows if she wants—it doesn't matter.

"Mindy, you told me once that nothing and nobody will stop you from loving me. I don't know that I believed it at the time. I thought you'd come to your senses at some point. Sometimes I still wonder if I'm just too stoned to realize this isn't actually happening."

Mindy's mouth quirks up in a smile. I rarely get high anymore. I still drink occasionally but not too often. I won't be the reason she relapses, and I won't be a reminder of a time she would rather forget.

"I used to worry that I'd never find the words to tell you what your love and loyalty means to me, but then I remembered something my pop said to my ma when I was a kid. He told her he knew she'd never believe a word that came out of his mouth, so instead of trying to convince her that he was serious, he's spent every day of their lives walking through fire for her. I know of no better way to tell you how serious I am about what we got."

I have to clear the knot in my throat to be able to finish. Rage, my grandfather, is in the back row, and even he's looking a little emotional. His wife, Sylvia, died just a few years after I met them. Rage changed then, and I know he won't ever be the same. As hard and ornery as he's gotten, his heart is still as big as ever. He's going to die with a hole in his heart where Sylvia once was. He gives me a nod that makes me feel proud. The man doesn't give his approval very often, but when he does, he's loyal to it as fuck. I'm distracted from Rage by Ma's wailing in the front row. Even Pop's face is a little red, though nobody's going to call him on it. Not until he officially hands the gavel over to Wyatt anyway.

"You're stuck with me babe. I own your ass." Shit. My eyes sting. I hate fall allergies. Ma needs to dust this place more often.

Mindy lunges herself at me, totally ignoring the officiant's comments that we're not legally married yet. When he gets her to pull back, her red lipstick is smudged, and I just know it's all over my face.

"Ian promised me he wouldn't make me cry today, and he didn't tell me he wanted to make up his own vows, so bear with me. As usual, I have no idea what I'm doing." The crowd laughs at her, but I don't see anything humorous in this moment. I just see a tough-as-nails woman who, against all odds, fought to pull herself out of total darkness, and I'm fucking amazed, once again, that she's stupid enough to settle for me.

"I love you, Ian. I love every piece of you, even the ones you hate. I haven't talked about it, but I chose this date because of something you taught me. You taught me that the pain can only win if we let it. You're the only reason I'm here today. I thought my damage would kill me. It was swallowing me whole. Today marks the one-year anniversary of the worst day of my life."

"Babe," I whisper. She doesn't have to do this. Fuck, I don't want her to do this.

"I won't let them take any more from me," she says. Her voice shakes, but her perseverance humbles me. "Baby, you spend every day walking through fire for me, and I'll spend every day showing you the beautiful light spots in your soul that you forget exists."

We're married just moments later, but I'm barely paying attention. The only thing that matters is standing right in front of me, strong as fuck and more determined than ever to live. I didn't know I could love her more than I did the day she agreed to marry me, but I do.

I so fucking do.

The End

Acknowledgements

Thank you first and foremost to my readers. Your excitement and loyalty amazes me. When I started the Bayonet Scars series, I knew where I was going with it, but I didn't know how I would get there. Ian's character was one that I knew was pivotal to the series story arc, but I didn't consider giving him his own book until *you* spoke up and asked for it. On top of everything you've given me, you've now given me this as well. Getting to know Ian was a joy and I'm only sorry that his story can't go on forever.

Thank you to my publicist, Danielle Sanchez, for her never-ending patience. I'm so grateful to you for having my back and becoming such a great friend. To my mother, Cindy Emery, without whom I might not have the courage or endurance to keep going when nothing is working right—thank you for being the bossiest, pushiest bitch I've ever met. Never wonder where I get it from. To my sister, Brittany, for pampering me while I wrote this fucked-up little fairy tale. One day you might need that lecture on human corpse decompensation rates and variants according to climate. Say the word and I'll bring the shovel!

Thank you to a dear friend, Kaz Blonde, for being so generous with your time and thoughts. The Toffee Crisps don't hurt, but what I really love is your snarky attitude. To Dawn Johnson who was unable to help with the execution of this book, but was no less valuable in its inception and development. Your fingerprints are all over this series. To Brenda Gonet for designing a gorgeous cover, once again, but also for so much more. You were the very first person to read my work and believe in my ability to publish it. To Amy Shearer for enduring so much book drama—again. I'd say next time will be different, but it won't be. To Amanda Jones for always being so supportive and willing to pitch in when I need it. Just relax and keep on growing my niece, mmkay?

Thank you to Michele Milburn, my amazing editor, for getting this thing done despite everything that stood in your way. You're boss and I adore you. To my beta readers—thank you for sticking with me. I love you all! You're ready for Crave now, right? To all my writing buddies, you're freaking fantastic.

And last, but not least, thank you to Charlie and Lola, my feline support system. You're my favorite kind of jerks. Your cat tree is on its way. To anyone I forgot, I get my jerkiness from my cats. Blame them.

Thank you.

About the Author

As a child, JC was fascinated by things that went bump in the night. As they say, some things never change. Now, as an adult, she divides her time between the bad-ass bikers, sexy law men, mythical creatures, and kick-ass heroines that live inside her head. A San Francisco Bay Area native, JC has also called both Texas and Louisiana home.

These days she rocks her flip flops year-round in Northern California and can't imagine a climate more beautiful. Her dream is to own her own Harley and she feels compelled to tell you that she is Team Peeta all the way. JC is the author of the Bayonet Scars series, the Ladder Company series, and the Men with Badges line.

Made in the USA
Charleston, SC
25 October 2015